Maggie Gee has an MA in English, an MLitt on English Surrealism from Oxford and a PhD on the 20th-century Novel from Wolverhampton Polytechnic, but much prefers writing novels to writing *about* them. She was the 1982 Creative Writing Fellow at the University of East Anglia where she edited a collection of writings against war, *For Life On Earth*. She now lives and writes in a sunny basement in London's Camden Town.

This novel, written when the author was twenty-five, is her first published book. She was elected as one of the Book Marketing Council's 1983 'Best of Young British Novelists'.

D1392313

MAGGIE GEE

Dying, in Other Words

GRANADA
London Toronto Sydney New York

Published by Granada Publishing Limited in 1983

ISBN 0 586 05658 0

First published in Great Britain by
The Harvester Press Ltd 1981
Copyright © Maggie Gee 1981
All rights reserved

Granada Publishing Limited
Frogmore, St Albans, Herts AL2 2NF
and
36 Golden Square, London W1R 4AH
515 Madison Avenue, New York, NY 10022, USA
117 York Street, Sydney, NSW 2000, Australia
100 Skyway Avenue, Rexdale, Ontario, M9W 3A6, Canada
61 Beach Road, Auckland, New Zealand

Printed and bound in Great Britain by
Cox and Wyman Ltd, Reading
Set in Times

Granada ®
Granada Publishing ®

Author's note

How Not To Read This Novel . . .

(Those who are angered by stage directions needn't read this note till the end of the book, when it will, like everything else, come round again.)

. . . in other words, this is not a realistic novel. In Life, newspaper reporters are not legally permitted to peddle the kind of garbage that Les Hawtrey writes in the immediate aftermath of a suspicious death. In Life, members of the cunning C.I.D. are not permitted to wear serge uniforms and big police boots: men at the top have found that it gives the game away. In Life, sex murderers are rarely permitted to get away with it six times in a row, with a view to spicing up the narrative. In Life, we spend more time living than dying away from our fictions. And in Life, moist Moira was not permitted *entirely unaided* to write this novel.

This is not on the face of things a serious novel. Comic novels are permitted to be a bit playful in depicting the serious thoughts – about Interpersonal Relationships, mostly – which such Interpersons as John X, Jean-Claude, Felicity, and wet silk Moira glean from the pages of much more serious novels.

This is not quite a novel. This novel is written away in only 161 of the book's 215 pages. On a stage thus cleared of conventional fictional props and moribund characters, the ritual death of the whole sad world, including a few familiar faces, takes up a mere 52 pages: for fables and cautionary tales and jokes are so much quicker than fiction, and the end result is the same (dying, in other words, gone.) And then, yet again, at the other end of destruction, the will to stories goes on. It is time for the book to begin. Dying, in other words, dying . . .

The naked body of the girl was found on the pavement by the milkman, reaching the Crescent just after 7 A.M. on a frosty brilliant morning. Her long dark hair was matted with blood and black ice: her face was hopelessly, bloodily confused with the pavement.

The papers were found on her desk in the third-floor attic room which she rented. She had been there seven years, the landlady said. A regular payer and quiet, the landlady said (though the sound of the typewriter echoed through the house even now.)

The men in charge of the police investigation were sturdy men, and their trousers were of strong blue serge. They were sometimes called Brown, and sometimes called Jones. They were not unfeeling, for policemen must not be unfeeling. They were not stupid, they had passed the right exams. And their heads, it was said, were 'screwed on their shoulders.' So that was all right.

Yet it wasn't, exactly, all right. There were so many papers. The heads got scratched too much, and the eyes got half-way down the page and then started to wander. It didn't make sense, and sense was the one thing they knew about. Not a great brain, Brown would say of himself, but he could use his common. And did, but the sense wasn't there to be found, though they tried in the morning after strong black coffee and they tried after lunch on a strong brown cushion of beer. Which at least gave bounce, and as Jones once expressed it at tea-time, some of it seemed a bit -er- psychedelic – or kinky, as Brown with a sensible laugh agreed. She was kinky, that girl, that was clear, that grew clearer and clearer the more that you read.

Psychedelic, as Brown quoted Jones (with approval) as saying. And kinky, he said, I agreed. So it wasn't, exactly, all right: they read on, but they got no further.

For she may have been clever (said Brown.) And had all those degrees, and her nose three floors up in the air (and her nose now quite properly broken, as Brown was too squeamish to say though the thought bubbled up with the beer.) But she didn't know *logic*, that was sure: that grew surer and surer the more that you read. The sentences started all right but then shot off wildly in all directions: there was violence and horror in everything: everything ended in death. It was obvious the way she was going. Obsessed, I'd call it, said Jones. There was nothing but death, and no logic. For all her degrees, she just didn't know Life, that grew more and more obvious the more that you read.

Though the longer Brown or Jones sat there, the less they were able to read. Brown said it was 'too bloody gloomy', and 'Gloomy, all right' was what Jones succinctly agreed. There was not much else to be said. It was open and shut, as they put it, open and shut: Ron Jones, or Alf Brown, or Alf Jones, or Ron Brown, and they both concluded 'From our careful reading' it was suicide, and the case, they both thought, would be closed, and their sensible lives go on. For the fourth pint told them the kinks and the nutters would always be found smashed to bits on the sensible pavement, their brains forthrightly bashed in.

Yet the papers were found on her desk in the third-floor attic. Yawning and scratching, Brown and Jones read on. 'We want facts', they said, but the thing she had left was a fiction, *Dying, in Other Words*. Reader, read on.

(Single-spaced: typed badly, but carefully corrected, each phrase rewritten again and again and again: page-numbered throughout, with each section demurely titled: no passionate last-minute scrawl of ink at the end.)

DYING, IN OTHER WORDS

Prologue

It begins on the balcony, in summer. It has begun.

It begins on the balcony of the Crescent, which is narrow, with a deep balustrade: not deep enough, as they found, to prevent someone falling. The terrace is cut in a long sweeping curve to the sun this morning. The trees inside it reach up to spread in the light. The bricks of the Crescent are yellow, a sour acid yellow which strives to be green in the sunshine.

Light which grows damp and dull on the dull damp reds of the damp dull North Oxford houses, which stretch in their acres of orthodox rows and squares all around the yellow-green Crescent, shutting it further in (yet a torrent of loud steel and glass roars past not far from the Crescent.)

The North Oxford houses are wholly detached (though they mass together) and quirky. Odd windows, black-paned in the shape of the ace of spades, or red for a heart which died. Winged statues marooned ten feet from the ground in shells of crumbling plaster, gargoyles with green ravaged noses whose gutters are choked with starred moss. Wild faded roses which half-a-century ago went rambling away on their own. Fountains with blurred grey fauns whose crumbling thighs are the haunts of black beetles. Huge copper beeches with ivy and rust in their hearts. Remnants of agonized flowerless rock-plants with long silver leaves which a mad botanical aunt had displaced from the high blue Victorian alps in long-ago rotted blue paper, her name and her silvery laugh and her madness also long ago wholly detached and forgotten – except by one. The brightest light cannot ever bounce back from the mouths of the masonry's wide dark pores, which are sombrely, heavily open, sucking it in. Yet the Crescent within these rank enclaves remains unripe and opaque, yellow-green, turned in on its one-room lives, and each keyhole is locked round a mystery.

The Crescent means really two crescents, turned in on themselves and enclosing an oval garden, which is green in summer and brown and fir-green in winter, bearing a public statue but few flowers. The trees are forced by the arcs of stone to be straight and splendid, rising severely up to the level of the slates and then bursting out in a hundred tender parabolas of branch and leaf, bright individual arcs into space and sun whose natural end is far beyond the Crescent. The walls of the Crescent turn inwards, however. Look in.

The balcony curves three floors above ground and four floors above whatever lives in the basement. In all of the houses, little dark scurrying eyes with reflected lamps in them, mice and silverfish, horned and jointed beetles. In most of the houses a guardian, a woman who does out the rooms and spies on the tenants, reading romances between the deepening lines.

In this house set just on the corner a man who 'has millions' lives, and his sun-roof looks over the Crescent, oiled bodies splay at the sun and the hams underground have gold bread-crumbs stuck to their fat and the veins in the Stilton grow richer, darker, and stink. Old wine with good labels and bottles of fierce black pickles are stored. Here a forty-watt light comes on when the larder door furtively opens, shines in the dark on the bellies of bottles and cold pork crackling cut in glutinous strips, the dark having soaked in stripily after the knife blade.

It is the maid called Ulla, who is Swiss, with a homesick headache. Here she sleeps shut in the earth, and her home in the Alps was so high that even in dreams of flying on long silver leaves like wings she cannot now reach it: flying and falling. She takes out the marmalade, very good marmalade stored in a grey stone jar for her master, with whisky in it, very expensive. 'These days, keeping a maid is very expensive', says Pelham, just grazing her thigh. The door is closed and the light goes out and the mice eat on in the dark with the four tall rustling floors above them.

Over the fourth, the balcony opens on brilliant air. The end of the balcony here is so curved that it faces the hills (though the Crescent was made to turn inwards):the sky stretches clear to the hills and the great winds thunder across them.

A woman is looking across to the soft lunar curves of the hills beyond Marston, distant and hopeful, she thinks, as blue moons rising. Something may happen there once in anyone's lifetime, if they keep looking. Yet most of the time she stays in, stares down and stares in. Her name is Moira, your author. How many others, she wonders, are moving slowly about in the house below her like sleepy koalas, rubbing their morning lids pink and forgetting the ominous dreams which woke them, starting again and dreaming the books of their lives?

Her house is part of a terrace: a curious terrace which curves like a faint half-moon of stone, like a crescent moon. And another half-moon just a circular garden away completes it, so the garden three floors below her sits in two facing crescent-shaped brackets of stone. And the brackets are teeming with self-enclosed fictions, the key to each room turning inwards, teeming with 'freaks' and 'characters', solitaries, drifters, armies of dreamers, memories which intertwine, finally, drifting together, chapters of communal poems and pain. But as yet the rooms are distinct and the walls are opaque and each hair of each head (and the head of each chapter) is numbered.

(Frank in the tight locked room underneath her falls from his dreams: wonderful dreams of flying, holding her

11

hand, he is handsome, yes, he is young . . . loses the thread, and he falls, now ageing, now dying.)

The hairs of the rapidly dying are grey: are gone, or are grey. But their hours can be coats of all colours, their threads too rich to be numbered, out in the sun.

Miss Poynes with her grass-green cheerful eyes and her fragile arthritic bones sits out on her step every morning, and smiles her irregular smile as she sews a bright curtain, following scents from the past and losing her thread. Which is cherry-coloured, midsummer-rose-coloured, floating cotton, cherries and roses: losing the thread . . . Life in the sunlight, the air hardly moving, is long (yet the planes come over too often. Can something be wrong?)

But the regular feet of the pilgrims troop meekly and doggedly past to their regular work every morning, not seeing the garden, too early to feel the heat of the sun. The regular soldiers straighten the curve of the Crescent, sober and shaved and discreet. They are earning their living, dying, in other words, dying. Saving it up for the future, for summers to come. Saving up life, which is dying, in other words, dying. Making a short road home.

And Moira stands high above them, watching their stories begin (but the faces elude her, refuse to tell their beginning.) This time she will catch them. The Crescent curves round regardless, the faces inside it will change and fade and be gone . . . this time her memory will hold them. The stories, she thinks, though in some non-narrative world there is somebody splitting and bleeding, storyless, blood-splattered, splayed on the cold stone, dead – the stories, while memory lasts, will always go on (yet the wordless drone of faint planes is threading the sun . . .)

And so, we begin.

1 Splayed on the cold stone, dead

The naked body of the girl was found on the pavement by the milkman, reaching the Crescent just after 7 A.M. on a frosty brilliant morning. Her long dark hair was matted with blood and black ice: her face was hopelessly, bloodily confused with the pavement.

The papers were found on her desk in the third-floor attic room which she rented. She had been there seven years, the landlady said. In a town like Oxford it wouldn't be hard to find a replacement: it was central, the rent was low. However, it looked as if the room would have to be left as it was for some time while the police went through her belongings, there were so many papers.

Endless heavy boots going tramping up the stairs and back down again, up and down. Mrs Evans liked it at first, it made her important. She offered them cups of tea, peering up to catch them as they trudged up the spiral staircase: she tried to get them to 'have a little chat.' When they wouldn't, she grew rather sniffy.

'Any fool can see,' she said to the neighbours, still all agog for an inside story, 'what happened. Yet they go on and on, up and down and in and out, wasting time and wasting money. In their great heavy boots. Put some people in a uniform and they lose their common sense. Well – saying nothing against my Harry, but that was in war time. You can try talking to them, but they're all the same. Won't listen. Have to do everything the hard way. Red tape. Going all through the poor child's things, all her private papers, I bet she'd've *died*. There were piles and piles of them, oceans, I just used to have a look in. And a chat, though she never had much to say for herself. Up there in that attic, scribbling and scribbling away. What a life. I mean we used to have fun, didn't we? It's not

13

healthy, is it? But you can't tell 'em, these days. I say it's no wonder she did it, locked up all day long in that hole.

'Not that it's not a nice room, a lovely room, with that balcony,' she added in a hurry, moved by a dim sense of loyalty to the crumbling house which she kept for a pittance, but still it was hers in a way. 'Only – next tenant, I think I might take the bars out of the window. Make it more airy-looking, you know. Of course, it'll all be forgotten. Mind you, – having *seen* her – it was me got the blanket, you know, to cover her up – having seen her lay there, all bloody and cold-looking, no clothes on, a morning like that – I don't think I'll ever forget it, till my dying day. You knew she was dead, the angle her head was to her body. But you wanted to wrap her up warm. She was only a kid, after all, and pleasant enough to me. And a very nice smile, when she showed it.' (The teeth were all broken. A child found, two days later, a blood-stained stump, and threw it down a grating, watching it plop into the black oily water underneath, sink through the slime of dead leaves.)

'Still,' said Emma Rose, who was caretaker three houses along, and had got up that icy morning after all the fun was over. 'Nice she may have been, and quiet she may have been, you ought to know. But if she was so nice and quiet as all that, how do you account for her squirming out there between the bars at that hour, with no clothes on? She wouldn't have done that, not on a night like that, if she'd been *normal*. So everyone'd see her in her birthday suit, after she was dead!'

Her friend was impatient. 'No-one said *normal*, did they dear. It's hardly *normal*, is it, not by any standards, go jumping off a balcony and killing yourself, not even if you got a mink coat and your ball-gown on. Funny thing is – you saying her birthday suit – as it turned out, that day *was* her birthday. Twenty-five she would have been, though she didn't look it. And when the post came that

14

morning, there were half-a-dozen cards and some parcels. And the next few days there were some more. Awful, isn't it. Like dying at Christmas. It doesn't seem right. That really upset me, those cards and things keep coming and no-one to open them.'

Emma Rose was suspicious. 'Who did have them then? And the parcels? There weren't any relatives to speak of, didn't you say?' 'No, that's right, she was an orphan, poor thing. Well in the end that man had them, blondey from London, her *friend*, he called himself, wouldn't say boyfriend, I'd seen 'im 'ere a lot. Boyfriend he *meant*, of course. I didn't like the look of him, I didn't. There was a regular set-to about the mail, I can tell you. I either like someone or I don't, and this one I didn't. And that other one joined in, her other *friend*, if that's what she called them, nice-looking boy from next door, they bawled each other out in the street, you could hear them at it from inside. I don't really know if I did right, not really. But I don't really see what use it'd be to let those policemen have them – policemen and birthday cards, it seems such a shame.' And Mary Evans squeezed up her purplish-painted lips and her eyes, which had once been her beauty, now gone: but were still bright wedges of green in the sunlight, despite the thick dusting of powder which whitened the lashes and slack wrinkled lids . . . as the next-door lodger observed, who was forced to pass very close by a sudden convulsive gesture of Emma Rose.

It always shocked him, a closeup like that. The deep cracked lines on her lips full of purple wax. Blooming of veins in the nostrils, faintly, the smell of violets which touched him despite himself, surprisingly brilliant irises stranded in loose white flesh. Not paper at all at that distance: shockingly desperate and real and alive. He shuddered slightly, groping for his key on the doorstep a few yards away from them, thinking. His father's mother, now dead, loved violets. She wasn't repulsive. He'd loved her.

'That's 'im,' hissed Emma Rose, who had darted forward to attract her friend's attention. 'Jean-Claude Dupré' (which she pronounced *dupe*, having once misread his name on a letter delivered to her house by mistake.) 'You remember, the one I saw kissing another one down in the garden' (flicking a hooked and bony hand towards the circular tangle of garden between the two facing brackets of stone.) 'Another man. *You* know.' His door closed quietly. The two craned necks relaxed. "E's a pansy. Call a spade a spade.'

'Oh is that who you meant,' said Mary Evans, the tilt of her purple lips upset. 'Well that settles it then.' 'Settles *what*?' 'Well if I'd known it was *him* you meant. I know *him*, course I do. He was the one I was talking about, that poor girl's other boyfriend. Except he couldn't have been, if you seen right. See I always thought *he* was the boyfriend, the real boyfriend. And that other one just came down from London upsetting things. Oh well. It's a shame.'

What she'd have died rather than tell catty old Emma about Jean-Claude Thingy, if that was his name, was that for ages she'd half-thought he had a soft spot for her. Just odd ways she'd caught him looking at her sometimes, passing him unexpectedly on the stairs or in the hall. Like just now on the pavement. She'd been thinking, he needn't have pressed up so close. And his eyes scorching her so she automatically straightened her hair and remembered it needed washing, you noticed dandruff in the sunlight. He was a handsome boy, tall and strong-looking, on the stocky side, dark-haired, kept nice and short, cared about his clothes even if they were a bit fancy. In short, her type. If she'd been a bit younger. Not *un*like her Harry. She shut the silly thoughts away with a little sick ache of finality. So he was a fairy. Well. She must be getting daft.

She walked rather stiffly into the house, being careful not to slip on the vicious black ice. She felt old.

The stories which appeared that weekend in the *News of the Weak* and the *Sunday Purple*, made her click her false teeth with anger and shock. 'Buxom blonde landlady', 'squalor and decay . . .' Made her sound like a Madam, she thought. And she did try to keep the house decent. Not as if they cared, not the tenants, filthy, most of them, no, not the owners, never so much as showing their faces, sucked up the rent each month like a Hoover but never cared who it was that paid: not even if they died.

All the same – even anger and shock had their pleasures, she realized a long while later. Something to think about. A purpose. A reason for people to look at her in the street and want to stop. Because people hurried past you, on the whole, as you got older. In fact, those few days after the first death were one of the happiest periods for years, since being young and Harry, though she couldn't say why. Not that anyone asked her. Yes, really happy, despite the odd times she woke up to find something sticky and wet and as cold as death had fallen on her from a great height. She was asked more questions in those few days than in the next twenty years before her heart lurched one morning, and lurched, and stopped beating.

Mary Evans was also to fall on the pavement, breaking her nose and making the job of the undertaker rather messy. But being already bent double with arthritis and long past leaping, the distance she had to fall was short to the same black lustreless ice which had failed to reflect her brief mosaic of glamour and death and glory two decades ago.

17

2 'A very nice smile, when she showed it'

The *News of the Weak* gave it three columns, a picture of the dead girl – somewhat out of date, as her best friends noticed, but remarkably clear, considering its grotesque enlargement – and a jubilant headline:

TRAGIC BALCONY PLUNGE OF LOVE TANGLE BLUESTOCKING

The photograph showed a pose of painful artificiality. Girl With Her Chest Thrown Out and her spine pushed up in a difficult backward arch from a tree-trunk, the long-dead sunlight still clear on the cracks in the bark. One foolish emphatic hand was cocked to her cheek with a coyness never seen in life but often in look-at-me snapshots. Her hair was identified in the first few lines of the story as red, a colour found often in stories but rarely in life, where her hair was remembered by most to be brown (or a rich chestnut brown) and was not remembered, of course, by the (recently) living sunlight which shot it, as ever, spread out on the stone on that last white clear winter morning, with fugitive hennas and blues. Where the blood and black ice had not trapped it. And the sun on her hair flashed memories at John, reading on, reading on, flashed red and dull pain. It began one summer, her hair in the sun, in a red-and-blue noticing flash had begun: he had seen her out on her balcony one summer morning, a row of bright milk bottles, dazzling, empty, and then her pale legs cocked heavenwards, long pale feet on the deep balustrade.

He stopped the film there on the familiar stretch of balcony and stared back instead at the stylized mask on the paper, so the pain drained slowly into that and he turned away and was suddenly groaning and pressing his forehead on the wood of the sash window, weeping silently out, gazing blind at the far more bearable blind white sky through the meshing of tears and smeared glass.

Yet curiosity drew him back to the dirty grey rectangles of paper on the table. Who was it, yes of course Mo said it was just curiosity kept you going when things were worst. Just wanting to know what would happen next, what would happen to your friends or your prophecies.

And he did feel curious now, burningly curious, pierced by the public resonant awfulness of the disaster. And his own role . . . how much would that ham-faced fool of a journalist have gathered, how much more would he have invented? At least he hadn't found the flat: hadn't come pestering Felicity with questions. But LOVE TANGLE: that looked bad, it looked like him, it looked like scandal and mystery (and one per cent of his long weary twelve stone of misery tingled and thrilled and impelled his feet back towards the table.)

And the face stared back at him, inanely cheerful and alive. The terrible hair which was only shoulder-length then and bouncily bobbed and fringed like a drum-majorette. And the blouse knotted 'casually', anything but casually under the breasts (little mice, soft mice, he loved them, with small adolescent noses, pale pink) – in the picture, those two cups pushing like missiles – she hadn't worn a bra for two years!

But the waist was the same, white and supple and slender, and the bones were the same, if you closed half an eye and peeled off the expression. Her nose, too broad and too strong, here weakened and prettied in profile. Her eyes which were large, heavy-lidded, in life a startlingly bright pale grey unknown to the camera, the iris flecked with particles like snowflakes, slivers of ice (but the ice which matted the blood on her lashes that morning was black). Her cheekbones, Asian in width and elevation, here flattened by the strong dead light. Full lips and big teeth (but the tooth looked small to the child as it slipped through the grating) . . . And her very worst feature, the much too shallow and delicate jawbone beneath. Her chin called the vigour and decision of the rest into question. Made her ugly, perhaps, to an artist, or anyone who didn't respond to her kind of physical charm. 'My awful weak chin', as she called it, lamenting, and trying all kinds of expression and carriage of head in the mirror to hide it. But he didn't mind it. The rest of her face with a confident jaw to match might well have been beautiful, but it would have been coarse. As she was, sometimes, with her squawking jokes and strong silly appetites, for sun or for pancakes or for women's magazines (he remembered, then forgot, that he had been beginning to dislike her, much of the time, towards the end). Be that as it might, her weak chin made the face surprising, appealing, a question, or rather a plea. It began on the balcony, in summer, when he first answered. A sleepy question, that one: sprawled open to the sun, eyes closed, not caring who answered, chance it was him.

Her eyes had been closed, and when she looked up at him, lazily, the early morning sun dazzled into them, so he hadn't seen that first time how strange they were, pale and possessed under the heavy white bell of the lid. The mass at the centre was frozen, however easily, deliriously, coyly, her lips might smile. The messages crossed, as so often with Moira. But the newspaper photograph missed it, the headline expressed no doubts.

TRAGIC BALCONY PLUNGE OF LOVE TANGLE BLUESTOCKING
GIRL 'FALLS TO DEATH' ON TWENTY-FIFTH BIRTHDAY

A question still hangs today over the fate of 25-year-old Moira Penny, the attractive redhead who apparently fell to her death last Tuesday night from the third-floor balcony of one of Oxford's most elegant terraces. Preliminary investigations suggest the cause of death was a fractured skull and multiple internal injuries. Her naked body was found early the next morning on the pavement below by a milkman, 59-year-old Bill Dutton, peacefully going about his rounds.

'It was a horrible sight,' he told me. 'At first I couldn't believe my eyes. She was naked as the day God made her, and covered in blood. You just don't expect to see that kind of thing at that hour in the morning.'

Mr Dutton, a familiar and well-loved figure in the pretty Crescent, reported his discovery to the police. He was later himself given hospital treatment for shock. His first terrible thought, he told me, was that a murder had been committed.

3 A familiar and well-loved figure in the pretty Crescent

What Bill Dutton actually said was more vivid.

'Seeing her lying there starkers with all that blood on her, first thing I thought of was it must've been one of those rapists. I just didn't think of 'er falling. Course it makes it less horrifying, her falling, not that it does *her* much good of course, because otherwise ooever did it, if 'e'd done it to 'er on the pavement, must have laid about her something terrific, the way 'er poor skull was bashed in. That's what rushed through my mind, standing there staring at 'er. Quick as a flash. Imagining 'im. Must've done it with a brick or something, I thought. Or else held her down and crashed her head down hard on the pavement, over and over' (Bill Dutton's little blue blood-shot eyes were twinkling with excitement, twinkling and

21

watering, sporadically doing a special voice for the reporter's benefit, with what he intended to be reverent intonations and educated vowels) 'well, to do that you'd have to be a real sex maniac, was what struck me.

'There was a case a few years ago, just at the top there at the end of the road leads down to the Crescent, just fifty yards from where I found her. At the back of the Public Toilets. A woman about forty, Betty Tatlock, married woman, I delivered to her every day. She didn't look the type, you know what I mean. Though looking back she was maybe a bit too friendly. Three kids. They reckon he raped her and did all sorts of other peculiar things to her before he killed'er. Evidence of torture was what the police called it. They like that, some of 'em, you know. Like the Nazis in the war. It gets 'em excited. *You* know.

'She had a lovely house. I mean you don't get rubbish, not in that particular area. I've seen to the Crescent for over thirty years, you know. Everybody knows me round there. I'm what you'd call a character, a well-known character, know what I mean.' (He drew himself up to his full height of around five feet seven and a half, found he was still a good two inches short of this scruffy reporter fellow, and suggested they both go and sit down. They were standing in Bill Dutton's little kitchen, where he had just made a cup of tea. Brown lino, a faint smell of something unpleasant, a strong smell of disinfectant, and plastic curtains with a pattern of crude yellow flowers.)

'Then afterwards hubby, Mr Tatlock that is, went and married some young bit half his age and they moved away from the district. Well you can understand that, not wanting it stuck right under your nose. All the same, it makes you think, when something like that happens. I mean, he didn't let the grass grow under his feet, it wasn't much more than a year after the first Mrs Tatlock snuffed it. We mustn't speak ill of the dead, they say . . .' (here his voice broke slightly, choking with piety and hesitation, and he eagerly accepted Les Hawtrey's offer of a cigarette, taking three, which he thought was an understandable confusion in the circumstances, sticking one between his rather wet lips and putting two carefully away in the three-quarters-full box in his pocket) '. . . thankyou, thankyou, much obliged. Well, no offence to Betty Tatlock, but what I'm getting at is, there's no fire without smoke, if I may ring the changes on an old expression.'

4 All sorts of other peculiar things

Pompous old devil, thought Les. This witty, and to Les totally puzzling, inversion was the milkman's party piece, and he delivered it with droll spittle-punctuated emphasis and an outsize flourish of his strong bushy eyebrows, still disconcertingly bright and gingery long after the rest of his head had adopted a neutral covering of innocent white wire. The *fire* in question, as a matter of fact, was the bloody death of Betty Tatlock, and the *smoke* was the sloping road through miasmas of sophisticated vice which Bill hoped she must have taken to get there. And the saying was originally the coinage of Bill's mother, three cold counties away in a terminal hospital, too far away to claim credit. A gentle and over-imaginative woman, she had coined it to attest to her unflinching belief in the complexity and consistency of human wickedness, more especially that of her detested younger son.

Now paralysed and speechless from a stroke, in a long bright puzzling room with even more puzzling smells of rubber and oranges and urine, she could not pursue him for plagiary as she had pursued him all his adolescent life with suspicions of evils more infinite than those she had found out.

Her whole world had become grey and blurry with poisonous fumes of sin after finding the corpse of a starved cat on the bonfire at the bottom of the garden, its ears and its tail cut off and its front legs horribly twisted about with barbed wire. On its coat were burned the initials B.D. The letters were firm and professional, suggesting regular practice. For the next ten years there were no actual discoveries but any dark corner was inhabited for her by unthinkable spectres: headless chickens dangling safety pins, half-skinned puppies, a tortoise prised out of its shell and dragged softly, frequently through her dreams. Though Bill wept and swore on the dreadful day of the cat that he'd only sinned once, egged on by an older and wickeder friend, he could never call off the legions of hideously suffering monsters limping towards her, squirming towards her, crawling towards her wide-eyed pity and rage. No fire without smoke, she said, and refused ever after to kiss him. Whenever his face came close, the foul poisonous smoke from burned grease swam greyly up between. She would kiss him now, very wetly and out of control, when he went on his twice-a-year visits, saw nothing, knew no-one, was 'yellow and puzzled and shrivelled by long strips of whiteness, dreamed dumbly of flying and home.

'Of course,' said Les Hawtrey with the kind of admiring double-nod and mechanical dimpling he habitually used to encourage confession, accompanying the motions with a fixed eager stare. His interest, however, was more personal than professional. The old boy was mad as a hatter, that was plain. Les was a disappointed humanist-turned-professional misanthropist, as he told all his friends. Well-publicized professional misanthropy seemed the only possible way round the fact that he devoted four-

and-a-half days a week to an end which he privately thought soppy, never having achieved the sophistication of some of his colleagues, who thought it camp. As a professional misanthropist, he had in his early days on the paper tried to spread the rumour that he was popularly known as 'Hawkeye Hawtrey.' He failed. But he spent most of his working hours looking for evidence to consolidate his misanthropic and humorous pretensions. In ten years he had never been known to run dry, as long as there were friendly red ears like his own around him, and a pint at his elbow. 'Human peeings – I love 'em,' as his luridly furnished anecdotes tended to end. This was one of Les Hawtrey's better puns. He was not quick, and it took him some time to figure out the meaning of the milkman's wisdom. Fire without smoke? Bill Dutton enlightened him.

'By which I'm meaning, that things might have been far from what you might call rosy, *chez* Tatlocks' (Bill emphasized his one foreign phrase with a long rolling wink, after which his eyeball seemed reluctant to return to its regular red orbit) 'for some time, if you see what I'm driving at. Now what if Betty Tatlock, say, had happened to go out that night, the night of the tragedy, looking for a bit of – consolation. A friendly arm, or more. What if – I'm only saying *if*, mind you, just *if* – what if she'd happened to meet up, just as her bad luck happened to have it – with what looked like a *Lonely Wanderer*' (Bill raised his voice here and slowed down, for chilling emphasis) 'but – which – was – the – MURDERER?' After the piercing hiss of his climax a dramatic pause fell, in which Les tried to look grave and shaken.

'I can see what you're thinking,' said Bill, untruthfully enough. 'All right, she was forty, she was a wife and mother, she was so-called respectable, she wasn't just some tart. But women – I've known enough of 'em, and in my opinion – randy little beggars underneath, and that goes for all of 'em. Can't get enough of us, if truth be told. Rapists? Nah, nah. It just don't *exist*, not if you ask me.'

And they did ask him, seven years later, in detail, the prosecuting counsel in the notorious Nancy Boston case. Bill Dutton was a sex murderer. The court room saw his finest hour. In the dock he confessed or rather laid claim to five other offences, all of them committed in the area where for over thirty years he had been 'a familiar and well-loved figure.'

'Rape 'em? They couldn't get enough of me,' he roared in the dock. Defence attempted to establish insanity, but all medical advice suggested the defendant was completely sane. 'Just has slightly exaggerated views about women,' Dr Willis Frobisher drawled at his single-sex club, cradling brandy and warmth and a brave male truth in his elegant glass balloon.

Clarrie Dutton, by then eighty-seven, very yellow, very faint and completely bald, the mere lopped-off shrunken-up featureless root of a plant which had once had a head and beauty and meaning, became suddenly interesting to the staff of the Home when the papers made mention of the Monster's one surviving relative: printing a picture of Clarrie in her hopeful youth before marriage, with thick curled hair and a smile to make the sun come out (but now there was only a puzzling fluorescent, someone had blocked out the sky), a picture which had been used inside the cover of *Sisters' Weekly*, the periodical she founded and edited for the last golden months before she had to leave teachers' training college for lack of funds, and accidentally forgot how to be happy again, for ever. Not that these facts were either known or of interest to the nursing staff, who preferred to look down at the yellow pleats and wrinkles of the Mad Monster's Mother and shiver. Then thoughtful Pearl Buckle started pinching her when she changed the sheets. Just to show her that she hadn't got away with anything by going so yellow and so very very far away. And she still felt pain, like a plant which shrinks from the fire.

5 'I can see what you're thinking'

This goes beyond your wildest dreams, mused Les (it did, but he had no idea in what direction), trying to impress upon his mind the exact intonation of 'Can't get enough of us, if truth be told' for future impersonation. It was a lost attempt. Les's powers of observation were spirited but imprecise. Only his ambitions as a moralist and attraction to unhappiness equipped him to despise what he did. They didn't equip him to do any better.

Les saw himself as an ironist in a trench-coat with a turned-up collar, a keen-eyed taciturn stranger who rode into town after sundown and left before dawn with a coded notebook full of priceless human foibles and folly, too rare to deploy in his short official reports. All Les really did was to trudge after obvious monsters, the kind with heads cut out of papier mâché three feet high and enormous illuminated noses. They made an amiable show over the rim of the last few beer glasses. Les knew that Bill was a monster, but couldn't see the real and painful Mad Monster of years to come which lurked just to the rear of this stagey St Nicholas figure, with his thick white hair and his tubby, aggressively erect short body, and those round bright lollipops of red on either cheek.

When Bill pressed closer for emphasis or intimacy, the false glow of sugar and paintbox dissolved (but for Les it could not dissolve, was an integral part of the joke.) The red rims of the milkman's eyes had been pressed open on too many icy mornings, were resentful and raw as strips of anchovy. Seen from close up, the ferocity was frightening. Thirty years, and never once in his life a willing woman or a really good pay packet, was too long.

And Les felt this dimly, groped towards it, missed it every time. The most popular lines in papier mâché were comic blimps, prostitutes, vicars and mongoloid idiots, swarming all over the film sets where Les found his weekly drinking stories. The puppets spoke their parts in funny voices: the neighbouring bar-stools, briefly and predictably, shook.

Though Bill was a well-above-average comic milkman and blimp, such details as 'snowy hair' and 'brick-red cheeks' could only dimly be glimpsed down among the dismembered jumble of dusty grotesques in the vague brown beer-soused prop-room of Les's memory some seven years later, when the name barked from hoardings all over the land.

DUTTON CLAIMS FIVE MORE DEATHS:
'MAD MONSTER' RAVES FROM DOCK

And the newspaper photographs were little help, more distant and grey and impressionistic even than the regular reassuring glimpses of Bill which customers caught through a veil of sleep and sunlight and frost-flowered windows in the early morning, a picture-book milkman, familiar, yes, and well-loved.

Yet Moira had grown to dislike him well in advance of that fatal confrontation. His was a face which she carried with others (one other more horrible, young, with a botched putty joke of a nose) engraved on the screen where bad dreams were projected nightly, the wet gleaming rims of the milkman's eyes in intimate close-up, sticking like blood-sucking slugs to the opening edge of her clean fresh morning, snatching the milk from the step and closing the door. When she closed her eyes after dark the face would have pushed in under, the nets of red veins on the cheeks growing into her dreams and his bright blue riveted eyes (on her legs, on her nipples) pursuing her here where her clothes could not be done up and her will to escape turned to mud and the pink swimming slug could enter.

'Oh God,' John had sighed when she told him. 'You *exaggerate*. Mo, he's a *nice* old man. I've *seen* him. You *want* to be frightened. You're impossible.'

Bill Dutton had seen John, too, in the street with Mo or leaving the house in the early morning, still heavy-eyed with sleep, his short blonde hair sticking out in all directions: and had drawn his own sweaty and sperm-soaked conclusions, lonely old man in a locked lavatory. After the regular act he ached, staring down at the regular mean brown flowers on the lino as he buttoned his trousers with military precision, ached at the bleak cold floors of the rest of the afternoon stretching bleakly before him, re-reading the local paper again and again. Every twenty minutes or so he spluttered with irritation as one of his treacle toffees stuck to his grinders, watching the mean squares of light in the small high featureless window grow hopefully darker, watching for six o'clock, aching and shifting his trousers and dozing and staring and growing mercifully dark.

In the pub he would be announcing 'I *like* living alone. Keep everything regular and tidy. Couldn't stand having a woman under my feet all the time, fussing and squawking and not letting you get anything done. If you ask me, all that side of things has got very overrated. I learned not to miss'em in the army. You had good mates in the army, and I've still got a few good mates' (Bill drank with three or four regulars, Bill was 'well-loved' and 'familiar' to his customers) 'and I've got my family of course, and I do set a store by family. My mother's the only woman I ever had much time for, as a matter of fact! Not that I haven't touched a few feminine hearts in my time – touched a few other places too . . .'

(this always brought a laugh from Edgar, the tiny arthritic Social Security Officer, a virgin with one wall eye who suffered elephantine horrors in the presence of big robust claimants, hairy and handsome and disrespectful and strong, with their neckerchiefs and curling chests and their girlfriends laughing in the queue in thin flowered dresses. He admired Bill for his forthrightness and bright red cheeks and vigorous sexual successes, of which, it must be admitted, Edgar had gained a slightly false idea. Bill was a man, and his pal. 'They've framed him,' he flatly declared when he first read that Bill was the Monster. All his life, They had taken from Edgar everything worth having: naturally now They would take his hero as well. At least this time, he mused, They had shown some imagination. In the end, Edgar settled down to enjoy the trial, his tiny form bent into a small gloating question mark, sat in the Snug by the fire each day with his beer and a pipe too big for his face which he sucked luxuriously, thin knees buried in papers)

'. . . but when you really get down to it, I never met a woman the equal of my mum. I go and visit her as often as

I can even now, although it's a good long way if you haven't got a car. When I was in the army I used to write to her every day, long letters they were, she loved 'em.' (As a matter of fact she tore them up into small pieces as soon as she read them, which she did eagerly, ever hopeful of hearing that some painful and punitive disaster had come upon her beastly boy.) 'Course you wouldn't think so *now*, to look at her, well she's just getting into her eighties after all – but she was a real looker once, she was a looker when I was a boy, all right.'

And now every evening when the puzzling lights dazzled down she was a looker again, yellow flesh closed up in a meaningless series of knots round a wild occasional will to look for an explanation, something wet and alive which flashed for a moment, surely, there at the eyes, something desperate which signalled to no-one, trapped in the dry yellow pleats of the lid. As an iris grew restless and fluttered and flew round the long white room like a dazzled grey insect, a mayfly, uncomprehending, flying and falling, bruising itself to sleep on the dazzling walls and then fluttering, waking, looking and looking again for the lost way back, for the thin deep crack into peace and darkness which would explain and release everything. And when her son came, the black beast who had dearly and hopelessly loved her, Clarrie Dutton saw nothing but foul dark smoke and behind it the black and dazzling wall of her tears, as ever.

'It upsets me, see her the way she is now and remember the way she was once. She was hard as nails, you know. A terror. I was scared stiff of her, even when I was a big lad twice her size.' (Edgar, who had never been twice the size of anything human, rolled his beer round his small wistful palate, reminding himself there were pleasures he wasn't denied. He was not to know that Bill exaggerated wildly, never having grown above five foot eight and a half even measured with a crooked knife against the kitchen door,

31

stretching upwards, with thick winter socks on, red wool-
len, while his mother was a straight-backed and forceful
five foot seven, standing by the window with her black
hair loose and summer sandals, knitting red wool with her
quick brown fingers and staring, staring out of the window
as the faces passed by up the street in the gathering
evening, knitting and staring straight-backed at the sky
and away from the boy and her red winter knitting:
watching the small pool of street light outside their front
window grow brighter and briefly imprison and free each
one of the passing faces, some laughing, some tired, some
strangers (some part of her still in her thirties hoped for a
stranger, a man with a big silver car which would shine
like the sun at the window), though no-one had seen her
there in the lightless parlour, all quickly gone to their
separate summer decisions, a lover who stood at the
corner, a cool beer stood by the grate: and Clarrie stared
out through the edge of the glass at the indigo sky above
and behind the live lamplight, stared out as Bill switched
on the light in the room and the blue grew dark in a flash
and made half of the window a mirror where her own set
strange features swam, staring back at her, stupidly asking
the glassed-in figure which knitted dumbly for winter
and her hated son Am I losing my looks, am I losing my
looks, are they going, going, gone?) 'Twice her size,' Bill
repeated weightily, catching the tremor of feeling (respect, as he took it, and not bitter envy) which puckered
Edgar's face the first time he heard the phrase.

7 'Touched a few other places, too.'

Les Hawtrey looked him up and down, wondering what women might possibly see in him. All he saw was a shortish, tubby, aggressive little man, with corns and blood pressure, probably. Still, Les wasn't altogether unbelieving. One of his own great puzzles was working out what women saw in other people. None of the really nice ones had ever seen very much in him. There was Juliet, who was pretty enough if affected. But she left him just like that when the job came up in suburban rep. And now there was only his secretary, Jean, not even his own but shared with Maurice. She was passionate and stubbly and became suddenly blind and alarming without her glasses.

So Les gave Bill Dutton a very careful look. Couldn't get enough of him? Well, it was possible. 'Which brings me on to my main point,' hissed the old man. 'About the girl. All right, so she jumped from the window. Or else she fell. Or else someone pushed her, right? Well – so we don't know. But we do know she hadn't got a stitch on her body. And of course I bore personal witness to *that*.' Bill invented a tragic leer on the spur of the moment, and used it. 'So – as I see it – we've got more than one alternative, but they all leads in the same direction. Either she took 'em off 'erself in the knowledge she was just about to do 'erself in. Which would be pretty peculiar, however you looked at it: wanting to be gawped at by everybody. Though I s'pose that's what they're all after these days, miniskirts and peep-toe blouses and God knows what.' (Les didn't notice the slip of the tongue, not being familiar with the catalogues Bill regularly ordered of *Delilah Rubber and At Home Ware*, his favourite page in last month's issue showing a black girl in a straight glossy wig

33

waving a coca-cola bottle around at groin level, wearing nothing but high red peep-toe shoes and a hip-length fitted tunic in white sheer shiny material, tied with red ribbons at the front and – ultimate excitement – ribbon-slotted peepholes at the nipples, and hers were bulging and enormous, it was probably normal in Africa. He kept it under the bed where he could reach it, open at that page, and he talked to her, quietly and filthily, before he went to sleep, calling her 'Coon-Cunt', making her undo her ribbons for him, strict little milkman, Boss of Coca-Cola for the evening, girls of all colours abusing themselves with empty bottles all over his high-speed executive float, and he never got up until tea-time: contented, falling asleep.)

'Or: she just *happens* to be on her balcony naked in the middle of one of the coldest bloody nights of the year, and all of a sudden she just happens to fall off it. Well. You tell me, isn't there something a bit queer about parading yourself around on your roof in the buff in the early hours of the morning? Or – here's the dodgiest one of all – don't quote me on this, but there's a third possibility. What if someone was to 'ave *pushed* her?' The violence impelling Bill Dutton's *pushed* was so startling that Les swayed forward slightly in spite of himself, and the hairs on his arms stood on end. 'Was it *'im*, ooever it may have been, pulled her clothes off her then pushed her? Or was it *her* took her clothes off of her own free will, on account of him being a *friend* of hers – some *friend*. Mind you, from a thing or two I just caught a glimpse of in the mornings, I'd say she was the type who *made friends easy*, know what I mean?'

Les did. The little eyes were a red-and-blue blaze of excitement under their wild ginger eyebrows, army issue, special for the jungle, guaranteed to catch rain or snakes or loose women plummeting from balconies in miniskirts, red lips screaming (Les began to feel sorry and ashamed

he had let the disgraceful old man rant on so: remembering her pretty young face in the sun of the photo,
innocently coy, now bruised, smashed, dead.) Spittle
formed in a triumphant chain of bubbles between Bill's
two front teeth, bursting and reforming with the individual vigour of his consonants. If Les Hawtrey had
succeeded in noticing and filing away these details, instead
of forming one clear word, LOONY, a sign in capital
letters at the back of his head, he would have felt very
pleased with himself. In fact, he was grindingly concen-
trated on Bill's cigarette, which had gone out half-way
down, and which instead of relighting or throwing away
Bill had blown clear of ash, in mid-sentence and without
even looking at it, and replaced with neat mechanical
movements in his cigarette box. Les was riveted because
he had only just noticed that the box, in which
two-and-a-half of his cigarettes were now safely depo-
sited, was seven-eighths full. Loony, and tight as a screw.
What *he* doesn't know is that I've noticed, thought Les,
trying to turn it into a victory for Hawkeye. Failing. He
wondered about the wages of milkmen, with reluctant
professional interest. Look about you, as old Don Plum-
mer used to bellow, look about you. Les did.

The flat was an old council flat, the furniture sombre
wartime austerity issue, the floorings brownish lavatory
lino with shabby mats. Everything brown and solid and
fixed, with no hint of movable luxury or decoration, unless
you counted the large television in the corner of the room
and *The Radio Times* in an embossed fake leather binder
on the table. And an ashtray from Margate which Margate
frankly wouldn't miss. No books but *The Radio Times*, no
ornaments, no pictures. The only soft things in the room
were the mean lace curtains, which didn't quite hide the
thick frames of the heavy sash windows, the sky growing
darker behind. Nothing, thought Les on an intoxicating
wave of insight. Not a single vestige of imaginative life.

Poor old bugger. Unless you counted the bathing beauty on the ashtray from Margate, which both men were having to share for their smoke. Poor old bugger. What life must be like.

8   What he doesn't know

But then Les had no idea, of course, of the imaginative life piled up under the creaking bedsprings a few yards away in the bedroom. And Les didn't know how much the bathing beauty set square on the rudimentary wiggles of the blue presumed waves of Margate counted. A buxom girl in a swimsuit of old-fashioned cut, waving impishly out from her golden earthenware glaze at Bill's bleak brown afternoon enclosures, which were still so far inland and away in the future when he bought it, just out of the army, a plump and hopeful young man on a fortnight's holiday in boxer shorts on the pier, where a pretty blonde trollop from Brixton made him buy her two candy-flosses, innumerable pink icecreams, and the ashtray, which he sensibly took back when she turned his proposals down flat that night on the sands.

Her name was Rose, and what Bill didn't know was that she was only fifteen, and very frightened by him and his big hard thing and the wild lost noise of the sea and the menacing patterns of the moon on the struts of the pier above them. What Rose didn't know was how pretty she was, with her dark blonde hair in ringlets and big brown kohl-circled eyes, with her upturned nose and red glossy lips and pert toe-nails, and everything smelling of sugar and lemons: how pretty her slim inner thighs, slightly concave, in white cotton knickers which he made her show him. And afterwards cried, though he said he was sure she had showed it to others, which made her cry more. What Rose didn't know was how often he afterwards parted her thighs in fantasy and went inside. What Rose couldn't know was how her lust-hazy image had slowly got confused with the image of the waving belle on the ashtray, how Bill had developed the ritual of stabbing the cigarettes hard on her breast or her thigh. And what Rose couldn't know was that he five times murdered and raped her, reached back and clasped her and had her, still thin and gilded and youthful, through the years and through other women's bruised and battered flesh.

What Bill didn't know was that the girl he evoked, with her long brown limbs and her full yellow rose-bud skirt and her underwear smelling of cheap lemon perfume and seaweed, had died six months later in a car-crash, still smelling of lemons, her yellow-flowered frock, walking bouncily home, glowing bright in the headlights of a man who declared in his club that 'The shop-girl type drives me wild, old boy, I'm afraid,' and he stopped at the cheap yellow roses and gave them a lift. Lucky Rose, on the day before starting, *intending* to start, an exciting career in a luxury clothes-store, selling nylon lingerie and peach silk stockings to ladies, they were *very* particular, said she must never arrive at work without 'proper attention to face and hair': she was going to wash it that night, and give it a lift with peroxide, but never arrived: died without warning, shrieking with terror and biting her lips as the car with its blazer-clad blood at the wheel, nicely-spoken she thought and I love straight noses (she blushed in the dark) but he does smell rather of whisky as well as of *eau-de-cologne*, if he asks for my number I'll have to admit that we don't have a telephone yet, at home – as the car slewed wildly three times across the road and back again, finally back into the dazzling path of an oncoming lorry, which couldn't quite stop coming on in a blaze of white headlights, then glass, blood, bone. And the dark blonde corpse had lipstick on its teeth, and her job was put back in *Sits Vacant*, and the same day's *Times* bore a notice three times as long of the death of Alexander Vere-White, at his family's request No Flowers. So Bill killed her five times for nothing.

And all that was what Les couldn't know, of course, as he sagely considered his host's lack of visible wealth and imagination. Probably the mean type, he thought, not half so poor as he looks. Probably so unimaginative he wouldn't even trust something as abstract as a bank. Got thousands under the bed, I expect. Probably doesn't trust paper money, either, got it in silver in jars. (In the anecdote he was framing he actually caught a glimpse of the jars under the sofa, exploring with one astute foot when Bill wasn't looking.) In point of fact, Bill kept his savings in the bank, and under the bed were his riches, magazines and photographs, best of all his own pornographic accounts of slow murders, all written by hand . . . before sleeping and after drinking, one bold and childish and horribly excited hand, which would suddenly have to stop writing.

9   Exploring with one astute foot

'Know what I mean?' Bill repeated, more insistently. 'Oh yes,' said Les hastily, employing his double nod and dimple. 'Though of course I couldn't really pass comment on the girl without having known her.'

38

'You don't have to *know* a girl,' rasped the slow harsh voice, more relaxed now, losing its peculiar religious intonations, 'you don't have to *know* 'er to smell a rat when she starts being found dead with no clothes on, do you? You take my point. Now I know I'm no oil painting, I'm not trying to say I am. But I don't think I'm being *over-fanciful* in saying that Miss Moira Penny wasn't above having a little bit of a flirt with Yours Truly, once in a while . . .'

Les wanted to get out very badly indeed. The poor smiling sophomore's picture burnt a guilty hole in his pocket. 'Oh yes. Oh yes. Now I don't go along with that nonsense about every woman having a bit of a carry-on with the milkman, if she gets the chance. Some of 'em don't and some of 'em do. But this one – she was an early riser, even when she'd got company, as you might say: and she was always very *perky* with me when she took the milk in, all nods and smiles and *Hallo Mr Dutton, How are you?*' Bill affected a grotesque mincing voice at this point to indicate the upper class, which actually Mo wasn't, particularly, but then neither had she ever in her life said 'Hallo Mr Dutton.'

'Oh yes, it was all Hallo and How are you, and she wasn't a bit particular either about what she wore, and if she wore it whether she buttoned it up or not.' Les was rewarded with a brief vision of a redhead ogling and giggling on the doorstep in the morning in a shocking pink transparent shorty nighty which coloured but did not conceal the flesh, until the inexorable voice started up again and chased her away, kicking over the erect milk bottle. 'So there you are. If you ask me, whatever she got she probably went out looking for. I'm old enough to be her father, but I'm sure if things had gone on the way they were going it would have been "Come inside for a minute Mr Dutton" before too long, and then – Bob's your uncle.'

Walking away, very fast for Les, from the dull brick

houses and bricked-in gardens of Bill's estate, walking for choice which he rarely did with his recently swelling stomach and shortening breath, walking to draw in the fresh blue air of the rainy afternoon which had beckoned him from behind Bill's battened-down heavy sash windows, Les felt marvellous. Marvellous, he instructed himself, pulling his trenchcoat irritably back over his stomach and striding out towards town. Two buses passed him but he strode on. Not much liking what he saw of himself in a few shop windows, ballooning and retracting in the wind, rather pink-faced and anxious, he stared resolutely ahead of him. It was further to the graceful bridge than he remembered.

Swallowed into the glowing inside of the third bus to come alongside him, Les Hawtrey paid his fare with decision and panache. He was glad, he had never been gladder, to be a free agent in a trench-coat, a man who rode in, cast a cool quick eye, and rode out. After a bit he let his mind return to the giggling sprite on the doorstep, shivering away in her shocking pink nylon. Les was a milkman. 'Hallo Mr Hawtrey, how *are* you?' She bent very slowly and picked up the toppled bottle.

10 'Without having known her' I

TRAGIC BALCONY PLUNGE OF LOVE TANGLE BLUESTOCKING

Girl 'falls to death' on twenty-fifth birthday

A question still hangs today over the fate of 25-year-old Moira Penny, the attractive redhead who apparently fell to her death last Tuesday night from the third-floor balcony of one of Oxford's most elegant terraces. Preliminary investigations suggest the cause of her death was a fractured skull and multiple internal injuries. Her naked body was found early the next morning on the pavement below by a milkman, 59-year-old Bill Dutton, peacefully going about his rounds.

'It was a horrible sight,' he told me. 'At first I couldn't believe my eyes. She was naked as the day God made her, and covered in blood. You just don't expect to see that kind of thing at that hour of the morning.'

Mr Dutton, a familiar and well-loved figure in the pretty Crescent, reported his discovery to the police. He was later himself given hospital treatment for shock. His first terrible thought, he told me, was that a murder had been committed. Police now think that the severity of her injuries was consistent with a fall from the narrow balcony of her third-floor attic window.

Moira Penny, 'Mo' to her friends, would have been twenty-five on the day of her death. Cards and presents arrived in plenty later that morning for the slim, attractive redhead with the winning smile, but she was no longer there to receive them.

Moira Penny was an orphan. Her parents both died of cholera in Naples only last year. Their beloved only daughter had tragically swiftly followed them. I talked to several of the dead girl's friends in Oxford, all grief-stricken by Tuesday night's tragic events. I uncovered a story of academic brilliance and success marred only by a private life which did not bring happiness. The pretty bluestocking, I was told, was at bottom a lonely person who often came 'close to despair'. Did she finally come too close, we may wonder, that icy and moonlit night when she made her tragic plunge?

I penetrated within the elegant neo-Georgian facade of the four-storey Crescent to find that Number Fourteen was a rabbit-warren of rooms rented out to tenants of diverse nationality and dubious occupation, to find blocked baths, lightless landings, a general atmosphere of squalor and decay and a landlady who just didn't care.

(Watch out for libel, boy, thought Les. Still, that bit was fun. And true enough, too, if it came to that. Though anything you said about nationality could turn out tricky. But it wasn't as if they were blacks. Well, one of them was, but he didn't appear in the piece. There was that unbelievable old stick of a Frenchwoman, grotesque, appearing at her door on Moira's landing in a nimbus of garlic and paraffin fumes, he didn't know how the girl had borne it, living so near. And stick was the word, her legs and her arms were so thin they were twig-like, he shuddered to think of her risking herself every day on those three flights of stairs, and the stair-rods were some of them missing. Yet she had survived, he reflected, her neighbour of twenty-five. Clothilde was the name on her door, Clothilde Duras, and she opened the door to his knock with a hand to her grey fluffy hair and a smile (brilliant lips, but the teeth were broken and black) and a singsong sweet 'Bonjour?' Les had tried, with a swallow and whirring of wheels had begun 'Je crois. Que vous connaissez . . . vous connaiss*iez* . . . cette fille,' indicating with something like Gallic bravura the other cream door, now so finally locked, and with last-minute inspiration added 'cette fille . . . -là.' But the door was closing already, the split of the smile in the small yellow face and the door were abruptly closed.

Which was queer enough, but the old *were* queer. She was probably scared of strangers, stuck all on her own at the top of those derelict stairs. She had more to fear from the other tenants than strangers, Les thought. Those boys who shared on the first floor, living like animals, the floor of the room a mosaic of bottles and coke-cans and girly magazines. To be truthful (on this point, Les wasn't) they'd scared him, especially the big one, Italian he looked, except for those mad pale eyes, with the glittering teeth and the ear-ring, refusing to answer his questions, dancing about the room so the muscles showed on his black-cased thighs and his buttocks, so Les felt pink and old and obscenely unfit. And his final violent statement scared him worse (pushing his face with its white pointed teeth right up to poor sweet-tempered soft-gummed Les, pushing his face so close that the strange light eyes burned through him, and delicately smiling, delicately baring the fine white points of clean bone: 'She was *trash* – got it? *Trash*, I'm tellin' you, *trash*.' And as Les bulged back through the door he thrust something folded and white into his hand. 'Li'l souvenir. You'll see.'

Les did. The three boys were his last port of call before leaving Oxford, and he sat in the train with his whisky digesting it, feeling rather odd. It didn't add up, not to him, not this last queer violent detail. The boy and his trophy did not fit in with the rest of the things he'd been told. Fitted Dutton's fantasy, yes, but that he had not believed.)

11 'Without having known her' II

From talking to Jean-Claude Dupré, a tall, dark, handsome University teacher in his late twenties who described himself as 'an intimate friend' of Moira Penny's and who lived in the next-door house of the Crescent, I built up a picture of a girl who see-sawed between a life of wild gaiety and one of total seclusion. 'She didn't seem to know what she wanted,' he told me (or words to that effect, thought Les, pressing hastily on before he could diminish the whisky bottle any further.) Now alas, she will never find it.

Or words to that effect, thought Les. He was really rather drunk and a large fatty curry was pressing up uncomfortably from where his ribs must be, though he rarely saw them these days. There was under half-a-bottle left, he noted grimly, and he had no more in the house. He had a headache, and two of his typewriter keys were sticking. The story rang hollow, the photographic record of the girl was too real. He belched, flamboyantly, stretching it out, but gained no relief.

The trouble was, there were two photographs. One was the simpering portrait that the paper would be using, entrusted to him, pressed on him in fact, the first time he went to the house by the poor slob who was living on the floor below Moira, Frank Something-or-other, in a room full of packing cases, with piles of old newspaper for company and evidently also sweet dreams of Moira Penny, now shattered, thought Les. He had brought out the photograph furtively and proudly from behind a dusty old china pitcher with unconvincing blue roses on it. 'Things of beauty should be kept together,' he had joked, gallantly but tentatively, though Les hadn't noticed the humour. It was wrapped in tissue paper and then in a pink envelope inscribed in capitals MOIRA IN THE GARDEN, 1973. Frank rambled, in a well-bred voice which got lost in the greasy collar of his raincoat: Frank smelled. Les wouldn't have liked to have seen what was under the raincoat (it was flesh. It was larderous flesh in sweating pink slabs and bundles, fed from the glistening morsels Frank found at the back of bins.) Les's curiosity was limited, strictly limited. He did vaguely wonder where the picture came from. Quite obviously no girl in her right mind would have looked twice at this shambling canvas of food stains (tomato sauce, that one? chocolate, that one, and that might be egg – but the smells were most definitely rancid butter, with an after-tow of onions, and sweat) with his absurdly public-school voice emerging in timid contralto bursts from the deep pink folds of his chins, protected by the raincoat.

In fact, it was Moira's mother who had written the careful capitals on the envelope: her daughter had let it fall in the bathroom, the prim smile flying and falling, carelessly tucked in a book of poems she was going to read while she soaked, never missed it. She didn't like photos where she smiled. Frank found it that evening, snuffling in after her as soon as her bare feet had pounded back upstairs, hoping for brief sneaked bliss in the hot steamy air full of perfume . . . but *this* bliss would last him for ever, most blessed surprise by the black clawed foot of the bath-tub, and he found a bit of tissue-paper, almost clean tissue-paper, yellow, next day round the bins, and he wrapped the snap tenderly inside it and put it away by his blue china flowers.

It was the second photograph which was disturbing Les, however. Yet it was only a small snap, black-and-white, over-exposed, too contrasty. It had a crease down the middle, an ugly crack where the finish was gone. Had been folded in two, a small white folded thing in the hand of the boy with the ear-ring. Every time Les looked at it, dark pattern of smudges on the corner of his shining desk-top, he felt a slight sick thrill, a mixture of excitement and sorrow and distress. For in this picture Moira was curiously beautiful. She was sitting on a bare wood floor with her feet towards the camera and her thin thighs spread wide, leaning back on her hands with her hair streaming over her shoulders. She was smiling, an utterly relaxed, contented, slightly mischievous smile. Her dark hair was untidy, the picture made it look almost black, with strands curling damply at the forehead. Her pupils were big and even blacker, and the skin of her forehead gleamed. Even to Les, it was quite apparent what she had just been doing. She was stark naked. The ugly crack at the picture's centre sliced her lovely live body completely in two. By a pious irony, it also prevented the picture being obscene in the obvious sense. Neither the picture nor the source of the picture would be mentioned in his article. (Les liked to make stories add up.)

She had many friends (Les paused and corrected that to *boy*-friends), the young Frenchman told me, and enjoyed dancing the night away at wild clubs or parties. But there was another Moira who was studious and dedicated, who was happy to see no-one for weeks on end while she stayed in her tiny dark roof-top bedsitting room lined with books, poring over some particularly well-loved author, scribbling in one of an endless series of notebooks or bent over her second-hand typewriter. For Moira Penny had one burning ambition, an ambition beside which her personal life paled into insignificance, an ambition which indeed the dead girl may have been using to compensate for the emotional satisfactions which always seemed to elude her.

(Les enjoyed himself on that bit. It flowed. He glowed and passed on and was only much later especially cynical about it.)

12 'Without having known her' III

The roof-top scribbler dreamed in secret of one thing and one thing only: to have her name up in lights one day as a famous writer. After completing two degrees at the ancient University, her thoughts had turned away from the narrow confines of the august libraries full of other men's dusty dreams, as reliable sources informed me. She had dreams of her own. She intended to make her own contribution to the literature which she had been studying as a humble scholar for seven years.

Police apparently removed several boxes of papers and notebooks on which she was currently working, hoping that these might throw some light on Moira Penny's state of mind on that fatal night when all her dreams came to a premature and bloody end. I asked Mr Dupré what Moira had written about. 'Novels', he answered. When pressed for a fuller answer he reluctantly admitted they were based on Moira's own life.

('All writers must to some extent use material which they have lived,' was what he had actually said, drunk and grandiose, but at any rate not quite so asinine as Les's transcript.)

He described them variously as 'tragic', 'black' ('black humour', he actually said) and 'full of despair.' (True: by that time Jean-Claude was too drunk to prevaricate.) Yet he insisted that anything which she had written had no possible bearing on the final tragic act of her life. ('The police are clowns,' said Jean-Claude, very slurred and arrogant. 'They'll try and turn art into a suicide note. Great *clowns*.')

I then questioned him about reports close to the dead girl which suggested that her private life was far from happy: reports of hysterical weeping at the top of the rickety stairs, reports of unsatisfactory involvements with married men. (It was the one thing which Frank had managed to articulate clearly, as Les was going, articulated with a stunning simplicity, his innocent blue eyes suddenly shining with tears and his silly contralto dignified by a half-sob. 'She wasn't happy, you know. I used to hear

47

her crying, sometimes. And the scenes – they weren't *good* to her, you know. She *should* have been happy.' And he stopped, and stared down shamefaced at his old gym-shoes. What Frank was thinking, which Les didn't know, as the tears confused the number of knots in the laces he usually liked to count in the afternoons, was that *he* could have made her happy: alone with his papers, laughed at by people, who should have been loving, and good.)

'Of course she was unhappy,' the smooth-speeched foreigner was finally brought to admit. 'Isn't everyone?' he added, evidently very much on the defensive, as he sat apparently at ease on the cream silk settee in his lavishly-decorated flat drinking whisky. (That was a bit mean, Les realized, but it went with a swing. In fact as the afternoon progressed into a maudlin drinking session the two men had become more and more friendly, but Les's dramatic reconstruction was starting to make him feel genuinely aggressive towards this privileged blackguard who had tried in vain to evade his, Hawkeye-the-People's-Champion's, searching questions. The bottle was only a third full now.) Asked if he could comment on allegations of violent rows heard by other tenants, rows which had apparently grown more noisy and frequent in recent months, Mr Dupré declined to give any information. 'You're asking the wrong person,' he said, instantly tight-lipped. Yet friends of the dead girl later affirmed that he had been the dead girl's 'constant companion.'

New light was thrown upon the situation which may have resulted in the frail redhead's fatal plunge (there weren't any synonyms for *plunge*, Les thought, diving fatally, tumbling fatally, plummeting wordless and fatally on) when I made the acquaintance of a mystery visitor from London identified by the buxom blonde landlady (nice contrast, that, with the frail redhead, thought Les) as one of Moira Penny's regular visitors and by her

48

account a rival candidate for her pretty tenant's affections. I first met John X, a tall lean figure with fair hair cut very short, a scar on his left cheek and dark glasses, standing in the dusty hallway of Number Fourteen engaged in lively debate with the landlady Mrs Evans. She addressed him as 'John' but later disclaimed knowledge of his surname. My inquiries quickly revealed that he was attempting to remove the birthday cards and presents which had arrived after Moira Penny's death and which Mrs Evans had taken temporarily under her care. Questioned on what authority he was doing this, he became aggressive and shouted 'I loved Moira Penny and she loved me. I am the proper person to look after these things.' I was later informed by reliable sources that John X is a married man living with his wife in a luxurious town house far removed from the almost derelict interior which I found lurking behind the Crescent's elegant facade. When I suggested to Mrs Evans that the police should be consulted before she engaged in any such transaction with John X, she became upset and referred to the press and the police in terms of violent abuse. ('I don't want any more blinking policemen sticking their feet into my affairs, and that goes for you lot too, for that matter!' was what she had actually shouted, emboldened by her sense of guilt about the cards and by a nice long drink of ginger wine.) The pathetic collection of tributes was accordingly handed over, despite my strong objections, to John X, and we left together.

Jean-Claude Dupré was waiting for us in the street, pale-faced and evidently emotionally disturbed. The debonair Frenchman accused John X of having been the cause of Moira Penny's death, and John X replied with assertions that Moira Penny had despised her next-door neighbour, facetiously suggesting that I should lend his rival my handkerchief. Mr Dupré was indeed too distressed to make any coherent response to my questions, and disappeared at once into his own house a few feet away.

(Which just shows you how much a lot of money and a so-called sophisticated philosophy does for you, Les mused. With his wall full of books and his tie with a Dior label thrown so-called casually over the armchair, pretending the day before he was too damned smart for plain questions. As Les grew drunker he grew tougher and plainer, and he remembered the babyish tears with a contemptuous thrill.)

13 'Without having known her' IV

In the light of the surprising events I had just witnessed, I then rang the door of Number Fourteen to summon the blonde landlady once again. When she opened the door she was on the verge of hysteria and begged me to leave her alone. (This could have had something to do with the fact that her hair was streaming wet and smelled strongly of peroxide. She had thought that doing her hair, as the row raged on in the street above her little sink, would calm her down. Les was too caught up in the tide-race of real life drama to notice, except that she looked a fright.)

I first asked her frankly whether she did not think the dank, dark and ill-cared-for interior of the house might be considered depressing by sensitive tenants. I then asked her to comment on stories that Moira Penny had entertained a variety of male friends in her small room. 'What, all at the same time?' queried Mrs Evans, becoming more and more agitated. 'I've always tried to keep a decent house, and now you people have to come here making trouble!'

(In fact she had said a bit more than that, ending up shrieking 'I don't care! I don't *care* about all her bloody men! No-one around here seems to realize I'm also a human being!')

With this she terminated the interview by slamming the door in my face. (Mary Evans, a mild and kindly woman when sober, had already forgotten the grandeur of her tantrum, which had done her a lot of good and was quickly dissolved with her feet in hot water and a mug of sweet cocoa. Les Hawtrey had already forgotten the precise form it took: he was a mild and kindly man when not too stupid to exercise these qualities, and a cry of such despair from those thin purple lips made him uncomfortable, like Frank's last tearful words. When people said, very suddenly and desperately, that they were also human beings, his favourite pun about peeings didn't seem to work.)

The story was too long as it was, and Les couldn't mention either that she caught the flap of his trenchcoat inside the door as she slammed it, so that after five minutes of Houdini Hawkeye schemes and small shivering rage at the absurdity of his predicament, he rang the bell again, very hard and very hopelessly, his eyes closed tight against the shrieking reappearance of Medusa, with her hair in rats'tails and her eye makeup streaking down her cheeks through the tears (did women always look so awful at that age, he wondered?) But she didn't come back. Someone, two hands coming first, someone shuffled up the steps behind him, in a pin-striped suit, big pink hands with perfectly manicured nails and a signet ring, with a key. It must be an incoming tenant: Les turned his head with an apologetic laugh all ready at the folly of his situation, but the laugh stuck rather as he got a good look at the face of the man who without a word or a smile turned the key and released him. He was thirty-ish, any age, bright blue eyes behind thin wire spectacles, his face pink and creaseless and regular-featured, indeterminate.

51

Except for one thing. It was hard to describe it, but he quite simply *didn't have a nose*: something pink and bland in the middle, some vague simulation the wire cut into –but he actually *didn't have a nose*. Les did up his buttons and went, feeling sick.

Many questions remain to be answered. Nothing, of course, will bring Moira Penny back. The lovely redhead with the charming smile is gone for good from the elegant terrace where she used to cycle happily about in the sunlight. (Nice touch, that, thought Les. There was about an inch of light left in the whisky bottle.) Her dear-held dream, to be a world-famous novelist, lies in unfinished fragments beneath the dispassionate eye of the police. (Their heads, it was said, were 'screwed on their shoulders.') The boyfriends who flocked to her blue front door look back on her fate with passionate regret and mutual accusation. Yet Moira Penny will never rest in peace until the true facts behind the bluestocking's tragic plunge are revealed. In her fate we may find a warning about the hectic pace and almost unbearable pressure in the lives of many of our brightest and often most vulnerable young people, maturing in the hothouse atmosphere of University towns. Squeezed into cramped and often squalid living conditions, their budgets even more restricted than their accommodation (Les was beginning to feel really good again), they react to the strains of too-long hours of study with private lives of hectic and diverse activity but little real contentment. No police inquiry can give the whole answer to the tragic and paradoxical problems of Moira Penny, the girl who had struggled for seven long years to study the books she would rather have written herself (does that make sense? worried Les, but not much: his throat was warm, and the prose felt good, good, good!), the girl with countless boyfriends who nevertheless lived – and finally died – alone.

When he woke with his thumb caught uncomfortably under his cheek his watch stared back at him, without sympathy. 4.15, and the hands from two inches were green wings flying, fluorescent and dangerous, the sign of a plane: flying, and fell. His mouth was foul. The metal of the typewriter had gouged a deep ridge in his forehead. He was cold, very cold, and his body, stiff slabs of cold flesh, hung down sadly around him, wingless and heavy as death, a mass of unexplored aches which would cry out if he moved them. Hell. He shook his head and an iron ball placed inside rolled painfully over and back. He felt a hundred years old (but he would not live to be a hundred: had dreamed of his death with the dead keys pressing his forehead, each symbol ordered and numbered, the green wings flying and falling: dreamed it, but did not remember.)

Les looked blankly at the dead girl's picture, the second picture, the picture with the long live legs slewing open and the gleaming face miraculously preserved from the crease by its position, hanging back and slightly to one side. It was the faint tilt of the head and the narrowing of the eyes with their big black pupils which added an accent of mischief or challenge or question to the revealed contentment of the smile and cat-like plundered body. With a start he realized what the figure in the photo was saying, absurdly, inappropriately, hopelessly to him now in the shared intimacy of the pool of light, to a cold half-drunk reporter she had never met, in the bleakest hours of the night: saying what no woman had actually said to him, let alone a woman looking like this one, though Jean sometimes whined oblique complaints when he got up and went after only doing it once, and that not well enough for her liking – she was saying, somehow slipping it around the cold parameters of night and the fact that she didn't know him, slipping it around his mournful lack of sexual attraction, and around her own access of it, somehow slipping it around the ugly white crack which had slashed her in two, even somehow, by some final gallant artifice, slipping past her own death – her live mouth was saying 'Come on, let's do it again, why don't you?' And laughing.

It was probably the whisky, Les thought next day in the grumpy three minutes on the tube when he let himself think at all, three minutes in a twenty-minute journey which rattled and bored through the bones of his headache, deep underground. They sat in the cold pool of light, the bottle of whisky, empty, the slumped painful figure of the man with a red livid mark on his forehead where the typewriter had scarred it, and the beautiful girl, scarred whitely, open and smiling: they sat in the fierce core of light in the utterly dead and hopeless early morning, and the whisky and the girl were both gone, and the man was suddenly, hopelessly, childishly crying. It was almost certainly the whisky.

He repeated it, walking on flat weary feet along the platform into a gale of rubbery warm dry air, which always made him think fearfully of the dentist. The whisky. And before he could change his mind he reached for the vulnerable thing in his inner jacket-pocket and tore it in two: parting easily down the white wound: and dropped the two pieces in an empty litter basket.

Nothing, of course, will bring Moira Penny back. The lovely redhead with the charming smile is gone for good from the elegant terrace where she used to cycle happily about in the sunlight . . . rather good that, thought Les, relaxing in his office after lunch that day, spinning gracefully round on the ('Sexy, isn't it?' said Jean) black artificial leather. The back of the work was broken. Gracefully flying. Yes, really rather good. But on the rest

54

he had spread himself disgracefully. He settled down to cutting the wordage in half.

(And his body was found almost cut in half in the burnt-out wreckage of his first big assignment, a festive jet to the States and maybe a willing black girl, their arses and long curved spines and their eagerness, do it again, why don't you? . . . the body was black, the back broken, his dying, with so many dying, was managed quite simply, in very few words.

TRAGIC PLUNGE OF HOLIDAY BOEING:

HUNDREDS FALL TO DEATH

15 A mystery visitor from London

John X, not a spy or a crook but a poorly-paid politics lecturer, was not wearing his dark glasses (that day he had a terrible hangover, his eyes were swollen from weeping and the sun was too damned bright) when he read the final version of Les's tragic soap opera. Nor was he sitting in his 'luxurious town house' so movingly contrasted with the derelict squalor of the Crescent by Les. Both the scar and the short blonde hair, however, which had caused Haw-keye's patent computerized screen to flash up in capitals TOUGH, were present. But he wasn't, physically, tough, had a heart complaint 'in theory', as he always added, for he refused to take notice, had carefully avoided doctors after a cosseted childhood, raged against Mo when she made oblique references to it, trying to drag him down into drama and her own obsession with death. The scar was the result of being slashed with a knife at the age of eight, when there were long blonde curls, 'the original angelic Angle', he had told Mo, describing how long it had taken a bright but affectionate child to realize the kindest master at prep school wasn't entirely fatherly. He wanted a father, of course. John's father had often gone away on long holidays in long white last resorts where the lights went out early and the long white windows were barred. He had done it by accident, with the carving knife, allowed to be Daddy again for a treat, in a tall paper hat, with a knife: on the wall a wonderful snowy-white angel, his curls of white paper streaming behind him, flew with a blessing, and the huge pale bird in its jacket of fat was presented. Not flying, but falling, John never forgot the yellowish curved bone handle of the carving knife seen through blood and the awful sounds of his father, just home, half-crying (for men didn't cry) and saying again and again It was an accident. It was an accident, Leave me alone. And the child, not knowing any better, knowing only, now, that his mother couldn't protect him, said Mummy please don't let Daddy ever come back home.

The blonde stubble was also an accident, so John's wife insisted, who had cut it excessively short so he looked like a sinister priest or a convict. She'd never cut it so short before. They had argued, stupidly, afterwards. He said she was jealous, Felicity who was never jealous. She said he was ridiculously vain, and he almost hit her – saying *that* when Felicity knew he loathed vanity, deliberately wore old clothes and got his wife to cut his hair. Later he got to quite like it. It made him look tough. Felicity said that was right, he was ridiculously vain. He was in a good temper that time, so he kissed her.

They really got on very well, far better than he and Moira. Fee worked in a way he could admire. She wasn't an intellectual, respected his theoretical grasp too much to argue: but had done long hours for low pay in a wide range of radical fieldwork, everything from race to political prisoners, took her clear head and her patience and energy anywhere she thought they were needed, typed or made coffee or picketed, good old Fee. Whereas Moira had sat in her attic playing at culture: not knowing, he sometimes said angrily, that the world rolled round at fixed times and did *not* roll round her. It wasn't, he thought, quite fair.

Tough-talking, fair-thinking John X was slumped at the table in the kitchen of his slightly seedy London flat, somewhat larger than Moira's attic it must be admitted, but *'luxurious'* – that was the only part which managed to raise an authentic flicker of amusement. The bath disgorged yellow fluid full of tiny gall-stones when it felt bad. The furniture was theirs, and quite nice, but the kitchen, as his mother complained, was *neolithic*. 'Silly bitch,' as Felicity said, very firmly but kindly, afterwards. 'We're really very lucky.' He loved her so much, he announced in a brief surge of warmth to himself and his grief and the table: not to Felicity, for she was away for the night, at a party he felt too gloomy to attend. 'You might be better on your own, but I'll stay if you want me to,' she said: and he had quashed the small boy deep inside him with long blonde curls who wanted his grief to have an audience, and told her to go.

He had woken this morning alone with a slight anticipatory thrill of excitement: when he pinned it down he felt briefly ashamed. It was Sunday. The *Sunday Horror*, the *Purple*, the *News of the Weak*. He had ordered all three, not sure which the blundering fool he had met represented. Mo starring, but maybe a walk-on role for villainous him, if he read the reporter correctly. And it had seemed easy to read those cross little points of pink light glaring out among the pimples.

16   Villainous him

Washing himself in cold water (the heater had broken again) he found himself hoping they'd got hold of some photos. Moira was certainly vain enough to have enjoyed that. Yes, and he would enjoy it. As Felicity never failed to point out, he enjoyed Mo's prettiness. But prettiness was the wrong word, she was anything but pretty. Her looks. That was all you could say, she had looks. And wherever she went people looked at her, most of them looking for beauty, which just wasn't there in the end, by some trick which came very near it. The odd thing was that she was very photogenic, had learned to pose like a model: he had drawersful. Suddenly the flat became full of dead photographs, fluttering with next year's dust. He turned from the basin in disgust, leaving a new ring of grime, and he towelled very hard, with his eyes squeezed shut so firmly that he saw squibs of yellowish-white through the kind matte redness, squeezing out recognizable images, squeezing out thought.

If only Felicity were here. Since Mo's death he had been aware of a fresh surge of love for Felicity. In a sense, he realized, a stupidly approving love, a love which was rewarding her for behaving better than Mo, for not dying, for still being there and being his. His Fee, who of course had been terrifically good about Mo dying, who was always good (he had teased her about it, viciously, Aunty Felicity, Fee who got high on virtue like other people on pills.) Now he needed goodness, a little boy scarred by accident needing an Aunty. The angel had flown, however, and Fee wasn't here.

It was Clara who rang him, Mo's friend, the very first morning, and told him the news, half-gasping with hysteria at the sheer absurdity of finding formulae to deal

58

with death: of his love, and her best friend. He and Clara had always fallen about together with laughter (though lately she was more guarded, making him guess at Moira's betrayals. Two girls shut up in her attic together, Mo's clear voice saying that he made her unhappy, he attacked her, she thought he was cruel when bored. And Clara all warm clucking comfort, condemning him, thinking him cold.) She was pale, plump and kooky, he liked her, her dry bright sensible mind underneath the zany facade, her shiny white skin which she hopelessly smothered with powder so only the sweet brown eyes shone through, like brown sugar, he thought, living sugar in dead white dust. Her voice was husky and harsh at the edges, sometimes, soft at the centre, slow, and would have been very attractive if she hadn't always sounded on the edge of a cough or a choke or a splutter, a thing he put down to her penchant for unscheduled gales of laughter or else her extravagant penchant for powder, perhaps a small snow-drift of powder set up in her throat so the husky-voiced vamp in the lift always tumbled, tearing her dress with a small harsh sound. Applying it freely, dear Clara, wherever she was, with a huge white satin-backed puff, 'No, it's swansdown, my darling,' not caring, and clouds billowed out through the pub or the train or the bus, with the smell that he loved of dried flowers, very sweet, slightly musty, the matron at school, and like all courageous attempts of the unbeautiful at beauty, sad.

Only this time the break and the roughness were horror and tears. 'Yes, dead. No, I don't. No, I didn't. Yes, yes. Oh JOHN . . .' His mechanical barking questions, his nails tapping pain on the phone. (Feed death into this curious machine. It will retain its upright position and automatically articulate the right questions in the right order. Only the tone of voice will sound a little strange. And yet there, he considered, looking back on it, trying to be clear, there whirring berserkly away underneath the barked correct recording was another tape running amok in the wrong direction, at the wrong speed, a gibbering chipmunk voice saying no no no I can't bear it . . .)

Four days had gone by and still the state of loss had not become real, not settled, not made its shape clear. Only, in desolating waves and flashes he felt it, he touched it, was gulped by the great red throat of the fact, by its ravenous appetite for pain and for weeping. His thoughts about the facts of the death were quite simple: she evidently fell. Had the roles been reversed, she would of course have suspected murder. With multiple suspects, freaks and maniacs, closed doors and mirror-writing, clues only Mo could understand. He had always laughed at her melodrama. Now she was (melodramatically) dead.

From his point of view, from a sane point of view, she fell. That she had no clothes on did not surprise him. She was utterly normal in being, in some senses, 'odd'. Abnormal in also being open and spontaneous, some-times, in actually carrying out her own 'odd' whims. She was an ecstatic, she once told him (he hated her grave egocentric formulations, explaining herself like a child in a maze of exotic delight) – an ecstatic in the same way as others were paralytics. Ugh, he said. He actually turned with a grimace and said it aloud, with a voice that was hard and hate-filled, looking straight back at her pale excited face and the life in the mouth slowly drooping, now battered and dead. But everything made him angry that last six months, her obsession with writing, obsession with dying, with communal death coming suddenly loud from the skies, there were too many planes, too many – on the ground, her growing obsessive fear of the freaks she invented to people the house, of the dwarf in the street with the big cigar and the dogs who would eat him, making her weep – he had *seen* them, all of them, odd-looking, most of them, but not important, not *socially* important as the real working class were important, not fearsome and significant, as Mo chose to make them, a symbol, a threatening symbol, and even a physical threat. They were freaks, and pathetic, just that. Yes, she made him angry. They rowed whenever they met. Now whatever was growing between them could not be pulled out and put right.

18   Grave egocentric formulations   I

And he still felt, he knew, he had loved her. Most blindly and deeply and childishly, sprawled in her shorts in the sun or describing herself with excited gestures, a biro between her white teeth. Too blindly and deeply, too deep to have taken a proper look at the cancer which came at the root. And that image was hers and he hated it, that was the time they had quarrelled more vilely than ever last summer, after they went to St Giles' Fair. At *her* suggestion, of course. The *idea* of that gaudy annual flotilla which bloomed overnight on the quiet grey seas of the city centre appalled him: candy-floss, bric-a-brac, chemical sweetmeats and tinsel and cheap tinny music and all the synthetic scum of a culture in late decline. But Mo didn't see it, or rather saw other things, wilfully, whimsically, just to annoy him (or so he had thought at the time) instead: and her face as it floated beside him was bright with delight (and now dead, now dead) in the furious glare of the stalls, as she shrieked and laughed and pointed with child-like (or childish, he thought at the time) ecstatic surprise at each new horror. On top of a tower of prizes, a purple polka-dot seahorse four feet tall, its plasticky face curling up in an awful subhuman smile, please win me, please love me. Mo read it: THE SMALLEST MAN AND WOMAN ALIVE WILL PERFORM INCREDABLE FEETS OF STRENTH (sic), and the thought amused him, but dwarves upset her, she wouldn't go in. SERENA OF THE SERPENTS, a bewigged and spider-lashed blonde who lay sprawled in bikini in a long glass box full of sand, with a back-cloth of bright blue squiggles of notional ocean, and lustreless shells and crabs, long dead: so serene and so far from the sea she was visibly chewing gum, and the SERPENTS were small grey streaks of terrified snake who wriggled away from her threatening dry pink flesh. And Mo was in noisy raptures. But he was revulsed and bored or he mimed it, spitefully (so he thought now), staring back spitefully, wordlessly, lifeless and cold, at her live transported face, now dead (and he sighed.) Lastly, RED RAWDON, who charged high prices for THROWING SHARP KNIVES AT TWO INTERNATIONAL BEAUTIES AND SWALLOWING FLAME. Mo wanted to see the International Beauties, so in they went. They were early, and Rawdon himself was there by the entrance, a hulk of a man with tall boots and a waxed moustache, bull-necked, with red eyes and rambling angry tattoos in a forest of reddish hair, the massive top of his body bare. John passed very close, and the strong smell of brandy appalled him. Then a Beauty arrived, looking very provincial. Fortyish, plump and sad, with her water-logged breasts hanging down, the brave scarlet tassels and spangles adorning a white beached corpse. Some dispute ensued: Rawdon roared, and the half-dozen people in the audience turned half-heartedly: she wheeled with a shrug and her dead tits quivering, the knives came out and the show went on.

When he looked half-way through to smile at her, Moira was gone. 'I couldn't bear it,' she told him, afterwards, shame-faced, waiting outside. 'But it's *you* who're supposed to adore all that,' he exploded, 'all raw material, *Raw*don material, dear!' 'Yes,' she said, very serious, 'I do though, I love it, I love it, it's what life's like. But then I can't bear it either . . .' (long pause for thought, and he felt hate coming for her grave rapt face, exploring.) 'I want to just swim in it, take it as dream-life. But you *can't*. The facts of it all are too real.' That was her exactly: and it made him want to crush her, stamp on the shell of her, squash the inside which was hopeless, quivering terror. And yet, he had loved her. His worst anger cut at the knot between her and Jean-Claude, with its endless hot-house discussions of outsize tropical egos (or so he imagined, and polished the phrase on the train, and later wished he had used it), its specious tender concern for personal pleasure and pain. He wasn't jealous, of course he wasn't jealous. He just disapproved. Jean-Claude was corrupt, and effete. Mo of course was hopeless, politically, hopeless, too emotional, too pessimistic, too gripped by a sense of metaphysical and individual doom.

But Jean-Claude was quite a different matter. He was actually on the right: he didn't *vote*, of course, that would be *boring* (and Moira had shuddered inside with each word Jean-Claude seemed compelled to drawl, the few times that the two men had met) – he thought that a world without privilege would be *terribly dull* (he was *kind*, she later insisted to John, and *clever* – and John had said crudely, yes, and if the great day comes I shall not be too kind to put clever Jean-Claude and his privileges up against a communal wall.) And he'd done just that, in a way, when he made him weep in the street, John the *macho*, the big bad hero (despising himself, as Mo would have done, as he hacked at the bread and remembered) – enjoying the obvious triumph in front of that pig-faced reporter, enjoying his cheap last line.

It was corny and cheap and despicable. Yet it had helped. And the thing, in the end, was survival (splayed on the cold stone, dead.) And the little boy caught himself playing at cowboys and cheating, and laughed at himself, and felt good. Put the bread in the toaster, my brekker, enjoyed the first smell of its warmth. What was warm was living: and living was (suddenly) good.

19   Grave egocentric formulations   II

And it seemed so natural to him that she should have climbed through the bars with no clothes on to stand on the icy roof-tops. She kept odd hours, didn't need much sleep, and she loved 'all extreme sensation – water and heights and black ice.' From a letter she wrote him two years ago, in a high Swiss glacial valley, the kind of bubbling letter, she said at the end, which would make you shudder, re-reading at thirty, and make you happy at fifty. She was right, except she was dead. And he shuddered, drawersful of letters, drawersful of photographs, gathering dust and guilt. But she fell, that was the main thing, she fell, he must keep hold of that. People fell even when they were happy, by chance, under lorries, down manholes, happy grandmas fell in the street with heavy bags: bombs fell on new lovers, their limbs splayed peacefully, laughing: mountaineers, who had just climbed a mountain, surprised, with the low red sun in their eyes, very happy, surprised by that final dazzle of crimson, surprised by their fear and their sense of unfairness, toppling . . . It was chance. She had talked enough about chance, these were all Mo's images, or ones very like them. She saw people falling all round her, not crying out much as blind fate pulled them finally under, no time to be more than surprised. She saw death, undeserved and unchosen, might fall on them all from the skies. And so Mo did their crying out for them, she said that the artist should – what was it? – said in a letter only two weeks ago, stuck behind the egg-timer, parody, yes, or half-parody, *wholly* meant: the subjunctive still made him angry: '. . . let the artist make sorrow speak for all those too timid to speak . . . and let anger cry out on behalf of all those who bowed down, went without, and accepted . . .'

Re-reading, the fine blonde hairs on his arms stood on end. The blind hands pushed it away with a sudden hot mixture of feelings, amusement and anger and guilt.

For he never answered the letter, deliberately, yes, out of spite. And he knew she had written to clear herself, claiming her real commitment and innocent heart, though the form of the thing was a joke. He had thought he would force her to mention it first, when they met. But that day they had not, in fact, met . . .

There was a creak and a clash and a thump in the hall and it must be the papers, he hurried to get them, grown suddenly large and alarming, impelled to half-run by the shock of the noise to the powerful nerves of his stomach, constricting. And once he had got there, he just wished that Mo was there with him. For there, in the first one he opened, the right one, the utterly, vulgarly, goofily wrong one, the *News of the Weak* with its poor posed pic (bringing tears) and Les Hawtrey, there it all was: TRAGIC BALCONY PLUNGE OF LOVE TANGLE BLUESTOCKING: a farrago of madness and morals and murder of the language which only she, only she would appreciate . . . only she was dead. He felt weak, let the grey sheets plunge to the floor so their linear story-line shattered. His heart was drumming, his breath too fast. He stepped over the crackling paper and groped for the cupboard, pulled out a half-full bottle of Rémy Martin and took a deep swig from the bottle, then another, feeling the fire burn down. Felt stronger, so he could read it (in fact he was weaker.) Started to read. Felt warmer (in fact he was colder: the brandy expanded the surface capillaries, each tiny channel briefly aflame: but the heat bled away on the air and he reached for another, stared at the cold grey paper. Her murdered name.) And he started his own mad mixture of laughing and crying when he finished it, unable to catch his breath, unable to believe it, unable to bear it alone, only she, only she, and never Felicity, no, only she . . . until the steam-engine sound of his own gasped breaths began to frighten him, behind it some rhythmic hysterical muscle that wasn't his own, and he stood up desperately and walked about the room until he found himself walking quite steadily out of his own front door and along the street, quite fast and quite straight, without any idea of where he was going or why, except that if he sat on there at the table and sipped at the treacherous brandy and stared at the paper he would stop, stick, stick – die.

20   The thing, in the end, was survival

Not remembering quite how he got there he found himself
sitting in the thin grey sun on a bench in the park, it was
cold, very cold, removing the frost, though it seemed too
thick to be frost, from the grey wooden slats with his
hands, which of course would go sullen and yellow, how
stupid they were, and he found it so tempting to laugh.
Keep busy, keep busy, said someone presumptuous inside
him who thought it was snowing, and Shut up and sleep,
said another, you might find it softer to rest on the grass,
and he favoured the latter: he favoured the letter, he
wished he had written, he thought, lying down, very
gracious, that letter *deserved* an answer, and now he
would write just as soon as his hands were rested and
warmer. How nice to be numb, how he envied his clumsy
cold hands with their delicate yellow, how nice to have
stilled his wild heart in them, held it and squeezed, to have
stopped it from stupidly shouting and gasping: how nice to
have stopped it, when all his life he had had to be careful,
how nice to have showed all the doctors he wasn't a cissy,
at school they had called him a cissy, weak heart and gold
curls . . .

But his body began to take over, began to feel cold as a
pain: it began to give simple instructions, get warm, oh
please, let's go in. He stood up and blew on his hands,
then licked them, finding the feel and the salt of the flesh
underneath his large curious tongue some comfort, and
then no comfort, because they felt cold as – what was it,
yes it was death, and he knew he must run. Very quietly
said I cannot go back to the flat and was running,
awkward at first for his toes in their light summer track-
shoes were already wooden, then faster, ran faster by far
than the thoughts which were cunningly after him, thus

number one: that she jumped, someone jumped, she was very unhappy, he knew her, but now thank God she was gone: *number two*, that his tongue on those cold stiff fingers, he licked them, was licking at something extremely like, yes he was very perceptive and strong . . . (*like death*, said someone, *someone* survived, in a sane closed register, typing) and yes you can run forever in snow in spite of the doctors, forever, run on: *number three* was a man with a knife but the cold pale turkey would eat him, would swallow him safely away in its long barred passage of bone and the little boy said please never let Daddy come home, but the child was now guiltless and Daddy and Moira were gone . . .

He was running incredibly fast now, his body was light as the cold perfect feathers of snow drifting past him, but *he* wasn't cold. He was fluid and brilliant and warm and he flew like a boy in a dream with his curls, which the wind had turned white, flying gaily behind him and somebody said he was beautiful, darling, and flying he knew it was true. And he flew like a boy in a dream who had never been guilty, on through the whiteness, the blankness, the softness, the dream of fair women, the dream on her high attic shelves of the snow and he knew as he ran with a desperate perfection of bodily motion, the perfect emotion, was it, he laughed, rather pleased as he flew that here you pronounced it Mo, and he did, quite relieved that he shouted but nobody heard him except the soft limitless snow and the Queen said Hurry now little one, hold my Hans Andersen, beautiful snow-white Mo on her shelves and her innocent selves who was leaping, leaping before him and falling as cold sparrows fall and of course their white wings will save them, their wings of immaculate snow and he wept with relief as he flew because no-one had told him, no-one had told him how easy and white to pursue her and falling had been no pain, she had felt no pain and in falling he felt no pain and no pain now to fall in the snow, now tired from his long gallant running, to plunge like a girl or a lost white sparrow, a white sparrow flying and falling and lying now still in the snow with no pain and quite still and could still be with, still be with, still here with Mo, and the blind white snow to enclose them, stilling them, blinding them, binding them, holding them close and still not minding that Moira was . . . Mo . . .

(Not minding that Moira was dead, which his heart prevented him ever quite thinking. For he was in shock, and the snow and the sky were intent on their own freak blizzard and did not protect him. John X was quite dead and a wonderful snowy-white angel by early next morning, the thin clear sun skating redly up into the sky and along the smooth lines of each outflung limb, was far gone, without angles, those flaxen children long gone and the morning displaying the limbs of a wonderful snow-child, a scarless and innocent angel, far gone on a long cold silver-edged flight for forgiveness and home, with his curls of white paper streaming behind him.

(Not minding that Moira was gone: but the piles of white paper streamed on in the attic, the metal feet flying, the white sheets falling, and someone was gaily and acidly typing, quite happy at least that those dull marbled lips had stopped talking.)

21 Life went on as normal, somewhere, and cheerful people were working I

Miss Penny took three Sunday papers, so the list at the newsagents' said. Pet Lockwood was still pretty new to the work, doing Sundays to save up some money for boots and the makeup her Mum wouldn't buy her. Not that they couldn't afford it, not that Mum really objected, but just because of her Dad. She confided these truths to Kitty, who went on chewing, with a small grim twist of her mouth which implied Well that may be so. And the shop was a rest after home. At least nobody moaned. Not at her directly, anyway, they did come in in a rage when they had the wrong papers delivered but Pet had found out that if she looked very hard at people with her eyes which were big and blue, if she smiled her most ravishing smile (Pelham called it 'angelic': she knew that was corny, now) and spoke very very softly, they never stayed angry. It was nice in the shop. No one said that she slouched (which she didn't, except to avoid conversation at meal-times, leaning right over her plate and eating too quickly), nobody said that her hair was in her eyes *again*, nobody said *Don't sniff* as if they meant to cut her nose off, and *Don't sulk* later as if she usually talked non-stop. And he wouldn't really have liked it if she had talked more, because the things she spent most of her time thinking about would have turned them green with rage, even Mum. And the things he talked about were stupid, not real, they were boring. It was blissful just for a few hours not to be got-at, just to be left alone. There was Kitty, of course, but at least she wasn't family, and her bad temper was funny, it didn't really count. And she brought a transistor to the shop every Sunday, which meant there was cheerful music and Children's Favourites later. And there was a ring for coffee (or chocolate: Pet brought her own chocolate, unlike poor Kitty she never got spots) at the back of the shop. It was true Kitty wasn't exactly good company but nobody said, as her father did, 'Well what do you mean by *that*, exactly?' And he wanted her to talk like a university student, like one of his dull beastly students, which she wasn't and never would be, not here and not anywhere

70

(she gritted her small even teeth as she ticked off the names), if it meant growing up like him in the end, sarcastic, dried-up and exact. Or extinct, more like it, she thought. His world wasn't *real*: he just wasn't in touch, couldn't talk to real people. And it made her suffer and blush when he said '*exactly*?', his eyebrow cocked up and laughing at her, and then 'Pet darling, why can't you say what you mean? Do you *know* what you mean? Because *I* don't.' And she suffered and said very crossly and childishly, *knowing* he made her sound childish, it was always the same, 'I'm not *called* Pet any more, as a matter of fact, it's too childish,' and slammed from the room. It was him stopped her having a new pair of boots, though her white ones were now out of fashion and her nice black thigh boots, bought with her Christmas money, were much too tight at the knee for dancing. It was him who refused to double her allowance (he still called it *pocket money*, just to insult her) so she couldn't afford to buy decent make-up and when she *did* try something new he was beastly and rude. Had she been in a *fight*, he had asked, when she drew blue shadows on her lids . . .

There was a crashing and jingling noise at the front of the shop, making her jump. It was only a quarter past seven, and still quite dark: but when the shop door opened she saw it was the milkman, the nice old cheery-faced milkman who they said had been round here for years. Pet was sure that he liked her, if they met in the street he would always have a good look at her and call out 'Ha-llo' in a loud cheery voice or 'How are you this morning?' and smile. Which was nice, and made her feel happy, and she instantly smoothed her long hair and got her smile ready. But he didn't even look at her, today, just bustled in in his flapping white coat with his little woolly hat on, picked up a *News of the Weak*, folded it over with a slap, cleared his throat very loudly to wake Kitty up, and gave her the money, which he had in his hand all ready.

71

Then just as grimly and briskly was gone, like a little fat
soldier thought Pet. How odd. He was always so jolly.
Perhaps it was the weather, which as Kitty had ominously
told her, explaining the two extra woollies stuffed under
her tight blue overall, bulging it out, was 'going to turn.'

'He wasn't very cheerful, was he?' she complained to
Kitty, who was already deep in her *True Love Stories*
again, the same back number she'd been reading ever
since Pet started, at least the two faces on the front looked
the same. Kitty's head never stirred for at least thirty
seconds, then she looked up very quickly (one eye never
moved quite as quickly as the other, Pet noticed, though
you couldn't exactly call Kitty cross-eyed) and said shortly
'Got things on 'is mind: and got *work* to do probably,'
grimly implying that everyone round here had work to do,
probably, but Pet. It was really too silly to answer, and
any way Kitty had turned her eyes (one slightly after the
other) firmly downwards again to *True Love*.

22 Life went on as normal, somewhere, and cheerful people were working   II

It was funny, the way she read that. And was
obviously lost in it, reaching out every ten seconds or so
for a toffee, unwrapping it without looking and popping it
in, and her eyes never stirred from the pictures. Perhaps
she was really very romantic. You wouldn't ever guess.
She was probably getting on for forty, thought Pet, or at
any rate thirty, say twenty-eight at least. And she wore
thick stockings and terrible pleated skirts. And the pleats

were pushed out at the back, from too much sitting. You couldn't imagine Kitty, not possibly, doing – *that*. But then it probably didn't come into *True Love Stories*, either. The girl in *True Love*, Pet considered, with a feeling of vast superiority, was probably a *virgin* (the word had acquired a new ring of derision, since the thing with Macbeth), despite all the legs and the breasts which showed in the pictures: that didn't mean anything. Pet had found out that much, at any rate, from looking at the other girls at the club. It was often the ones who had sexy faces and see-through blouses who *didn't*, it was often girls who looked quite respectable (me, for instance, she thought proudly, but not quite sure of her status) who *did*. Not entirely sure, because she had only just started to do it, but then, she was only fifteen: and she wasn't entirely sure, though she jolly well meant to, when she'd get a chance to do it again. Poor Kitty. Pet looked at her greasy hair kindly, the square red hand under her chin. Poor Kitty was almost certainly, certainly in fact still a virgin. Poor Kitty: because if you didn't know about that, you couldn't really understand *anything*. And since it happened, Pet was beginning to understand it all. It was hard to think about anything else, just lately. But it made her feel guilty, to be thinking about it at home with her mother and father in the same room. And yet they did it too (and she didn't like to think about *that*) at one time, evidently.

It was only really since Macbeth had done it to her that Pet had understood about Pelham. Poor Kitty would have died of envy, probably, if she knew. Because everybody round here knew Pelham, at any rate to look at. Pelham was very very rich, he was said to be a millionaire (but her mother got cross and said it didn't really make any difference, did it, when Pet asked her) and yet he was so polite, with the most perfectly ordinary people, in shops or something, that everyone liked him, she thought, and even her father would say with that little bit of spite in his voice that Pelham could charm the birds off the trees, and her father was usually especially nasty about his friends. And yet, he would probably kill Pelham, if only he knew.

And the charm didn't really mean much, like him saying her smile was *angelic*, she thought, and he really just wanted to touch her, under her skirt, and to make her touch him and to watch as it grew and rub harder and harder until all the white stuff, the sperm, in a queer-smelling salty flood came. And then he would kiss her and call her his *darling*, which made her embarrassed, because she had never felt *romantic* with Pelham, just guilty and hot and excited, all hot and hard and tingling between her thighs. But he just called her darling and kissed her and pulled up her blue lacy knickers himself and smoothed down her skirt. He was just like her father, in some ways: told her she shouldn't wear makeup, it spoiled her, told her to watch out for boys. Which was a laugh, when you thought about what he was doing to her, when you thought about what her father would have done if he knew. But Pelham had been tender and called her his *darling*, it probably wasn't his *fault* that he was a mean old man (and keeping a maid is expensive, said Pelham, expelling chaste Ulla, finally, after the break with Pet: and guilt made him pay her whole passage back to the mountains, her long slender thighs which he'd so much desired pressed tight to her seat as she flew and together, like long silver leaves: and he soon found a new one, a cool bouncy redhead, paid double for access and had it whenever he wanted, the thick fiery curls looking fine on the white of the tablecloth, drinking his coffee with one hand, parting her well-paid thighs with the other, but slept every night without her, weeping for cruel little girls and flying cold seas after Ulla, No *please* sir, wiping the silver, and now in his dreams she would wipe at the long silver sperm-splattered blades of her thighs.)

Pet talked to her friend at the disco, her new friend Elsie, an Irish girl with big breasts who started when she was thirteen. Elsie laughed when she told about Pelham and called her a sucker, and said that she ought to ask him for money, men often liked giving you money, it was part of the game. So the next day she made her voice very very soft, even softer than usual, and looked at him very very hard with her big blue eyes. And her smile, she was sure, was *angelic* as she asked him for money, asked very softly, while he was still moist-eyed and sweating and doing the awful old ritual of pulling her tight little knickers up over her trembling thighs (and she wished, she had wished for ages, he would do more things to her, play with her, give her more hot waves of feeling just *there*, even *sexual intercourse*, maybe, which was still a vague phrase then and frightening, at any rate not just tuck her away again and call her his darling and stroke her hair.) What had happened was awful, humiliating, like being five years old again and told off for stealing a rubber at school and she knew at the time she would never forget it, one little mistake and life suddenly, horribly changed. He had gone quiet and solemn and told her to put on her clothes. Then he talked like a priest or a teacher, pompous and horrible, making her blush and suffer and cringe, with his face gone funny and puffy and somehow the face of an actor, the false funny voice of an actor playing a priest. And he said it was all his fault and he said that he must be corrupting, he talked about honour and honest feelings and how in the oddest circumstances you could feel love. And a whole lot of complicated things to which she wasn't really listening, knowing the whole thing was utterly finished and spoiled. But she quarrelled with Elsie that weekend when Elsie said he was phoney, good riddance, and not to blame *her*. Well he might have been *mean* and *pathetic* and *phoney*, in some ways, and thinking that made her feel hard and superior: but she thought Pelham really had loved her in others, and that made her feel sad and mature. After all, there weren't many teenage girls who were loved by a real millionaire (if he was one), and sometimes he said it had been so lovely he wanted to burst into tears (but now she knew that was corny.' She seemed to know everything, now.)

23 Life went on as normal, somewhere, and cheerful people were working   III

Rich man's girl. It was what Macbeth called her, he was sneering but she knew that it made her exciting, he lived in the Crescent which was almost next door and he must have seen them together. He called her a rich man's girl, and her thighs just started to tingle. Come and have a look at my own pigging palace then darling, he said, or something like that, he was dreadfully common. But gorgeous and brutal and sexy, they all agreed when he went there (not often), discussing Macbeth in the ladies' loo at the club, with his gipsyish face and his strong lean body in leather, a wonderful dancer, his teeth flashing mauve in the strobe. Pigging palace, a phrase she'd remember for ever, they said that you always remembered your first. In her mind it was pigging penis, repeating it softly, when her mother was pouring more tea and watching her worriedly, saying she looked a bit peaky, do have some more to eat. He wouldn't say penis, she knew that, he thought she was posh and he used bad language on purpose, she thought, just to shock, and not knowing she found it so exciting she thought she must be having an orgasm, though she'd never had one, and especially with his two friends watching her, and one of them a negro, you weren't supposed to say negro, just sitting on the filthy floor of his room that evening, and imagining what it was going to be like, her eyes glued to the bulge (it would be so different from Pelham's) at the front of his tight black trousers, his figure was incredible, beautiful, although what happened wasn't quite like she imagined beforehand, her hot thin thighs rubbing scratchily on the rough floor and all sticky and melting between them . . . imagining it . . . so limp and drunk with excitement she just couldn't manage to talk . . . It's no bleedin' fun fuckin' virgins, he said when she told him, but Yes he would do it if she asked him very nicely, you're everso polite you rich men's girls. And it hurt rather like it must hurt you having a baby, but he just went on and said *Fuck* you, *Fuck* you and went on for ever, although she'd got cramp in her thigh and cried out and the floor dug into her shoulder-blades, and below was the real pain tearing and tearing . . . and half-way through he stopped moving and she thought it was finished, but he just turned his head and yelled out Grab and Lou and they came back in from the landing, they'd only gone out on the landing, and watched while he finished it, the negro kneeling beside him and saying crude things to him, by that time she was just too tired . . . and the stuff must have come out inside her, though she didn't feel it splashing, because he made a great roar like an animal and heaved like an animal and then very quickly pulled out, and it was suddenly small. He had told her to leave at once, and she'd put on her tights but forgotten her blue lace knickers – how Pelham would die if he knew where the knickers he gave her and pulled on the first time himself, very trembly and tender and slow, were now.

(What Pet didn't know was that the pretty blue knickers had been dropped in the dustbin by Macbeth, more

77

derisive than tidy, that a spray of old ash had joined her fresh young juices at the crotch, at the melting together of smoke-blue roses: that Frank had found them next evening, poking and sniffing about in the bin as the kind blue darkness blossomed all round him: suddenly, lacy and perfect, they must be Moira's, Flowers and Bliss and a Poem. And carried them off upstairs with a half-tin of rice, Mary Evans', and folded them up and concealed them reverently in his flowered china pitcher, the perfect match . . . so that what had been merely a shrine became actual heaven, which Pet didn't know any more than Pelham, and Pelham at any rate knew an identical pair was now worn by his new young redhead and playmate, the same kind of secretive hairy blossom nestled inside.)

When she was safe back home in bed and had washed away the little bit of blood between her legs, she just felt gloriously *used* and brave and exhausted, a *little* bit painful, only a *little*. She repeated the story to herself that night and again and again through the weeks that followed, so she twitched with excitement at the table and her voice came out guilty and odd, and yet she felt nothing inside her but happy and proud and glad. Which was not what Macbeth had envisaged, exactly, in picking her up, which was not what her parents envisaged, exactly, in bringing her up to be clean and careful and good (there was a small wad of chewing-gum stuck to her buttock when she got home, which she took to be the dried glory of Macbeth's sperm. It was natural that his should be so much more solid than Pelham's, poor Pelham whose pleasures now seemed so pink and tame.)

She wrote PENNY in capitals on a *Purple*, a *News of
the Weak* and a *Horror*, and 14 THE CRESCENT she
wrote and the pen ran out, and she said very loudly
though not bad-temperedly 'Bugger', a word she could
never have used at home but which seemed OK to pop
music and Kitty: who looked across with a fag hanging out
and actually grinned, poor Kitty whose teeth were so bad
or perhaps they were false teeth by now, perhaps they just
made them yellow because yellow plastic was cheaper.
She took out her compact to admire her own. To her
dismay, she saw her own pretty pink-and-white face, but
disastrously smudged with black newsprint, a long black
smudge on her chin and some more on her nose and her
forehead.

'Kitty!' she shrieked, snapping the compact shut, and
Kitty looked up, first one eye then the other, and more
unwilling than ever. 'Why didn't you tell me I looked like
this?' 'Like *what*?' squawked Kitty, at equal volume. Her
thoughts on Pet's looks extended only to the point where
she knew she was another one of those beastly pretty
ones, some people just didn't know how lucky they were.
To which premise her mother, the ancient spit image of
Kitty but lacking her teeth or a husband to make little
Kitty, all toothache and howling with greed, any easier,
assented, when the two women talked it over, bitterly and
often, high up in her dark damp flat. 'All *dirty*! Look at
me, honestly! What will that milkman have thought of
me!'

Little Madam, thought Kitty. 'Well, for a start, it don't
notice, for a second thing 'e didn't look at you, for a third
thing why should 'e care, and for a fourth it's got nothing

to do with me what you look like, I assure you I've got better things to hoccupy my mind.' And she brought *True Love Stories*, which she had brandished with vague menace during this speech, down sharply on the counter with a sound like a cheek being slapped, and turned her back in blue nylon so hard that Pet was quite cowed, and watched her in silence as her red hands fumbled for the page. The radio was playing a rather dismal collection of favourite tunes at the moment, your favourites if you were forty, probably. Well at least she wasn't old. And she finished the list she was checking in silence, reflecting that since she had to come back here every Sunday it wasn't very clever to upset Kitty, who was probably fortyish, ancient, anyway, and had worked here since the ark. She took out her hanky and wiped the marks off, very carefully, then patted her puff with its nice smell over the top. And restoring her looks restored her temper, almost. On the radio, the weak light orchestras died and that big jolly voice came and made her feel quite cheered up: it was Children's Favourites now and the first was something she loved, 'Simon Smith and his Amazing Dancing Bear', and she thought about black furry wrestlers dancing as the honky-tonk piano went tumbling beautifully, endlessly on round her head.

(Back at 14 THE CRESCENT, the newsboy was heaving three papers marked PENNY through the blue front door of the house where he vaguely knew something funny had happened last week because his mother was talking about it, but now he couldn't, and she soon wouldn't, remember, the papers went jack-knifing heavily through and PENNY fell brutally hard on the threadbare carpet.)

In the little shop the music assured Pet firmly that someone bear-like and handsome and tall (but not brutal, not crude like Macbeth and not feeble and old like Pelham) would love her too and would do things to her

80

every day in the way that she liked them. As soon as she knew how she liked them. And the thoughts made her gaze back at Kitty with eyes which were luminous with tenderness and pity, as blue as the ocean, the blue sexual ocean which comprehended the globe. Poor Kitty. For love moved the globe, but no-one will ever love you.

(What Pet didn't know and what Kitty didn't know, sitting in the warm shop safely and sullenly working, as normal, was that Kitty wasn't doomed to die a virgin. That Kitty would be loved in her way, or a bare-legged girl with white teeth and a perfume of lemons loved through her. That Kitty would die in the dark at the back of the Public Lavatories, her little loved dog which she was taking for a walk having silently run off and left her, too dark for her soft yellow teeth or her thick pink stockings to protect her. What Pet didn't know was that doing it, sobbing with fear and having it done to her then after all those years, didn't teach her a thing about life, didn't tell her any more than *True Love Stories* about why she had to be ugly and poor and stuck with her mother, and finally forced to her knees in the mud in the dark.)

25 In the mud, in the dark

And two hands on the dark other side of the blue front door with its scabs of old labels, ESSALAT, PENNY, are swooping over the papers marked PENNY, are picking them up from the threadbare carpet in the quiet dark well of the house and bearing them away off upwards, two pink hands, large regular hands with well-manicured nails and a signet ring, surely not PENNY's (for PENNY, like ESSALAT, bloody good riddance, these arabs, has now gone away) and are bearing them off, not right up to the dark top floor and the locked cream door of the small dark attic marked PENNY, where they should go, surely, though no human feet in the attic are moving, no fresh smell of coffee on the landing, no loud Sunday radio. Is she gone, or is she just sleeping? (But hard metal feet are still tapping, the typing goes doggedly on.) A cream door identical to PENNY's, with a keyhole identical to PEN-NY's, is opening now on the landing below, a cream door marked clearly HANS, C., and the hands go pinkly inside it, it is shut again, locked again, now.

Down below, the white labels, now grey, still hang on the blue front door like shabby old sticking plaster, telling the world and the paper boy 'OMAR AL ESSALAT; Please Ring Three' and other instructions for surnames you didn't believe in, some of them now long gone or perhaps had never existed, you never quite knew, Moira had never quite dared to remove them. Remove the plaster too soon, and some gangrenous old blue blister might be revealed, a wound through which a real tenant had long ago slipped at an early hour of the morning, his coat collar up to conceal his guilty eyes and his inexplicable cardboard boxes, the long frayed flex of a kettle dangling like violence and three months' rent unpaid, slipped away to a friendly Arabia under the paint and his mail would pile in the hall until someone with vengeful and miserly hands, big pink hands, beautifully kept, C. Hans, removed it, and marked it in mean black biro GONE AWAY, By Order of God, then *Bugger those foreigners*, then a wild scrawl of indecencies, Wops and Dagos, crumpled it, letter by letter, smeared it with blood from the cheap pig's liver bought for the dog (not telling the butcher the dog was away, and an Arab), then weeping with anger burnt it, the careful symbols of love on thin airmail paper, bought by Al Essalat's mother instead of her weekly sweets. You couldn't risk sentiment, not with foreigners: couldn't be trusted, not one of them. Though as a rational man I admit that there's always a bit of good and a bit of bad on both sides and there's certainly good in some of them –

(In one of those letters was a folded set of purple International Reply Coupons, for which the old mother with her three brown teeth had foregone two days' busfare to the local bazaar and had walked with her veined brown legs on fire, horribly swelled by the sun, but with love in her faulty old heart for her darling, Omar would pay it all back when he got his English studies done) – (He was gone, he was gone for ever like Moira, died in a stupor of failure and drugs on a cold drenched doorstep in Soho four years later, his forehead split open, *yes it is my son has the brains*, – and she happily never knew they were battered with failure and spilt in the icy black English rain, and the blood dried black on the doorstep.)

– as a rational man (which C. Hans certainly was, with the match in his big pink hand and the pig's black blood still dripping) I know we'd do better to stick with our own kith and kind (although most of his kind had got noses, unlike C. Hans) for blood is thicker than water, you can't deny it (dripping and dripping). *Oh Omar, where are you, where are you, so many letters I sent you, my own one, have you grown unkind?* – never voiced, but she sat through the long light evenings slowly darkening, her cracked lips moving, blackening, blackening, never a sound, GONE AWAY was C. Hans' answer, never to reach her.

Fire air and water, she cried, it flew, and it burned, she cried as she wrote the letter, it flew through the air and then fell and then burned in a splutter of pig's blood dripping black rain on the garden earth, and she cried again in the thick of the night creeping round to the other side of the world that he never answered her letter, and

yet when he left he said *Don't* cry, mother, there's really
no need, I should always come back though I had to go to
the ends of the earth to succeed. GONE AWAY, GONE
AWAY.

And C. Hans, if the hands are C. Hans', walks across to
the window, looks down on the cold grey sweep of the
Crescent curving below, the immaculate roof of his Volvo,
yesterday polished, the luminous gun-metal blue of his
love, looks down on the smudge of a dark head walking,
the lithe dark figure of Jean-Claude Dupré. Coming back
from the shop with his papers, C. Hans, if the lips are C.
Hans' which are just for a moment half-open, is spitting at
Jean-Claude Dupré with his face (which is any way
noseless) contorted, hits only the dirty grey glass of the
window and then with a clean folded hankerchief franti-
cally wipes the long trail of white spittle away.

26 'Got things on 'is mind'

Bill Dutton came jangling and quaking round the Crescent at his usual hour for Sunday, but this morning he
hadn't had his little lie-in. He felt sour, he felt worse than
sour. Only three tokens now, at Fourteen: the old lady,
the Duchess, for Gold Top, naturally, and 'ave you got
thees and that and the other, and wat, I can't 'eer you, all
screeched in her 'orrible foreign voice if she caught him,
you silly old faggot, he thought as he crashed the thick
creamy pints down. Ma Evans, the ordinary two (and used
one for her cocoa, she told him, jaw jaw, it's the one little
way I indulge, she told him. Bill Dutton had seen the

green bottles, however, ginger wine at the basement door.) Crash crash, that was her two, good riddance. No token for Moira this morning, no Moira who hearing the sound of the bottles had run three floors down to the door, with her face all flushed and her blouse or whatever pulled round her. Fresh from it, the randy cow. And he revved up his milk float loudly, and wished it was a tank.

Bill was sourer than usual because he had hoped for some fun. He had got up that little bit early, and broken his usual serene electric journey to pick up the *News of the Weak*: he felt good, and he paid with an air which he felt must be brisk and lordly. Bill Dutton was eager for glory. How big would the photograph be (he had given it Les, he had charged him to guard it religiously) of himself in his heyday, bare-legged and smiling, a (borrowed) blue beach ball held up to the sky, the photo which Rose had taken at Margate, using his camera and laughing so much there was a bright sunny blur round the edges, which didn't really spoil it a bit, he explained to Les, who was escaping, it was really a bit like a halo, it was what modern photos were like, kind of misty – it was *hatmosphere*, and he was sure that the papers liked that.

And he took out the half-cigarette he had saved from Les Hawtrey and sat and relaxed in a safe quiet spot at the back of the Public Lavatories, sat and relaxed in his favourite spot with his smoke as he opened the paper, a copy of course would be sent to his mother, no everyday milkman he. He was there for a quarter of an hour, while a watery sun came up and grew steady: his jaws were aching from grinding. Reduced, cut down and betrayed! His picture not printed, his opinions not quoted, or else not under his name. And the blighter had put in the bit about Bill being treated for shock at the hospital, making him sound like a milksop. Treatment for shock! All they'd done was to give him some chat and a cup of sweet tea and some pills they were sure would help him, not knowing he never took pills and tipped those down the drain in the long afternoon, watched each one plop and go down in the black oily water below, just a' suck and goodbye, that'd show them (another child found, two days later, a pale blood-stained stump, somewhere else, and threw it down a grating, watched it plop into the black oily water, sink through the slime of dead leaves. That'd show them.) In this life, however, you just couldn't win. Bloody rubbish: the world in the hands of the doctors, reporters, and women, he thought, revving up, sitting back, driving on with the paper violently folded under his feet and his blood pressure violently rising. Blow them all up.

But you never could catch them, after: the others, the doctors, reporters, the teachers, the priests. Or the students, the girls like Moira, they all moved on. You tried to get back at them, later, explain what you meant and show them what you were made of, but they would have gone. Drop a bomb on them. He would have liked to have caught Les Hawtrey, to have pinned him to a wall with his tank and then shook him till he said what he was up to, leaving all the important things out, putting gibberish in just to make him look silly. But you never could catch them, after. They stuck together, they made rules to prevent you, they moved on. You could never catch up with them, never get through to them, whatever chance you once thought you had had was gone for ever. If you chased them, they made you look stupid, the buggers. They sneered and talked posh when you questioned them. Just like Rose, with her bloody silly laughing, her silly sheer voice like Betty's and Moira's: those posh women's voices which made him think somehow of stockings, those very fine nylons, sort of sheer and hazy and at first you thought you saw through it but all they were saying was distant and blurred and you couldn't say this was a leg and that was an arm, before you could catch them they'd gone. And reporters and doctors and all clever buggers, the same. Yet this time he'd thought he had won, having got this one in his own home and kept him there, really talked to him, kept him there all afternoon, man to man. Though he didn't look much of a man, all flabby and greasy at his age and his shirt collar dirty. But Bill had felt perfectly satisfied this time after he'd gone, he had said his say, he thought nothing, this time, could go wrong: he had won. And expected it there in the papers on Sunday, the proof of the things he had soundly and staunchly and properly, man of the people, ex-army, said and done. And instead, this rubbish: himself dismissed in three lines, and the nylon stocking was there, the blurred misty nonsense, the clever voice talking *ambitions* and *emotions* and things about *pressures* and *books*. Oh no: no place for Bill Dutton, as always, as ever, not there. Common sense is too common for most of 'em, he bitterly incanted, under his thick white hair, too common by half for Mr Les Hawtrey and the likes of *him*. Yet one day, they'd see, he would show them.

He had, and he did it again, and for two their own stockings would show them, the madman half-laughing and tightening them, tightening them, into the flesh and his weak red rage and the bone. And he made them look silly. Dead, they looked silly, their lips and their eyelids pressed this way and that way and noses, they hardly had noses, just squashy pale lumps on the fronts of their faces, all sloppy and squashy and silly now under the nylon, doing it back for a lifetime, doing it back to them now after all this long time, simply doing it back to *them*, what they'd done to *him*.

27 'And got work to do, probably'

He had got past the end of the Crescent and on to the
strait when they caught up with him, three of them, always
the same three faces, the tallest one always in the middle
with his long hair greased like an Eyetie, but he didn't
have Italian eyes – Boys, Yobs, Yobbos, the yobs in black
jackets who lived on the first floor at Number Fourteen.
One of them with a black face and a mouth like two
beefsteaks hanging permanently open, a wop, a woppo, a
dirty little nigger, a spade (Bill was desperately angry. He
felt his whole body go stiff with desire to fight.) 'Three
pints,' said the tall one, coming too close to him, smiling a
big yob's smile with his teeth like a dog's teeth showing,
pressing up close so the crude painted skulls on the front
of the black leather jacket almost touched him, '*Please*,'
which meant every obscenity under the sun, the way he
said it, that big cheese smile on his lips and the smell of
smoke and stale beer. The other two came round behind
him. Bill jumped, despite himself, slightly, thinking that
one of them had actually touched him, a whisper of wind
on his red woolly hat which he desperately wished he
weren't wearing, suddenly. 'I haven't – we haven't – we
don't carry extra, on Sundays. I told you before.' His
voice didn't sound right: not rough enough, even to him.

'I aven' '*eard* you,' said the big one. 'Don't tell me
things I don' 'ear. Three pints, Dad. I'm tellin' you nicely,
come on.' One of them definitely touched him, a tweak to
his hat and a touch on the back of his calf, a very slight
kick, it felt like a foot. He swung round, and they stood
there smiling, the wet-mouthed wop and the other with his
great stiff quiff. 'Sorl right Dad,' said the white one, and
his quiff shook slightly as he put his head on one side and
smiled and smiled. 'Sorl right. You don't have to serve us

firs'. We're with 'im. Jus' you listen to 'im.' He stood hopelessly fuming, his heart pounding redly with rage, the vein on his forehead in rhythm, and no words came: and absurdly, he felt his red bobble hat was slipping. There was a chinking of glass and he swung round again, and the tall one had three of his bottles erect in his arms, the insistent whites of the milk and the skull and his grin, and Bill knew he would have to do violence, instantly, smash it all up there and then. But '*Want* some, do you,' the big boy said, and the violence began as he held out the bottle to Bill, very slowly, very white, very cool, and then suddenly dropped it, the crash and the tinkle of glass and a fountain of milk subsiding, running everywhere into the gutters, and going dark. '*Oopsy*!' the boy said into Bill's face, right into it, and the other two behind him were pushing each other and laughing. 'I must 'ave been tryin' to do too much, don't you reckon? It's a dyin' *art*, tha', you know, carryin' milk bottles. P'raps you should 'ave '*elped* me. And then p'raps your milk bottles wouldn' all be gettin' *broken*.' The foot was touching again, this time at the back of his heel where he'd damaged the Achilles tendon, once in the army, once in an assualt course, running and climbing and fighting and strong, and then later a hare for the hounds, a decoy, running hard for the dark horizon, leading them all in the wrong direction, somebody typed a report of how well he had done, long ago, long gone. He was old. He was frightened. The tall one was holding out another of the bottles, was going to let it go.

'Don't – oh don't,' said Bill Dutton, 'please don't. You'll be needing another to make up the three,' hardly hearing the weary incredible words he was speaking, just wanting to faint or to sleep or to tuck up his white skirts and run: but for thirty-odd years, since his ankle, he hadn't been able to run (yet he had a strong chest and strong arms which kept many a good woman down.) 'I'm *hearin'* you now,' said the big one. 'Thass right, we'll be needin' another one.' And he pulled off the top of one of his bottles, letting it fall in the grey tide of milk and glass ice at his feet, and tipped it up for a great long swig, pointing it up up up at the small and helpless sun. Bill handed another bottle to one of the others, at least not the wop. But the boy wouldn't take it, he stuck his ringed hands in his pockets and indicated the black with a jerk of his head which brought the vile lacquered quiff in the middle of his forehead startlingly forward. Instead of just taking the bottle, the wop whipped out his left hand with a quick snakey motion and seized Bill's left, which jerked backwards, but not in time. There was something fright-ening and cold in the palm of the wop's curled hand. 'Whassermatter ven, eh Mr Milkman?' said the wop, nearly whispering, holding him. 'You very nervous. Is it somefin' we done?' Bill was speechless, goggle-eyed, staring. 'Wotch out, you gonna drop my milk if you ent jus' *careful*, 'the smiling boy gently and frighteningly said, with his great fat blackish lips smiling, and his free hand took the bottle from Bill's limp fingers. 'Itsa money I'm givin' you, milkman, so you jus' be *cool*.'

And when Bill looked into his numb freed palm, he saw it was the money, the hard cold frightening thing, it was the right money, five bright coins. 'Oh no, he ent *ner-vous*,' the tall one said. 'He jus' feels bad takin' money from us, doncha Dad? He jus' likes us, he gonna make friends nice 'n' *easy* with us.' And the horror was suddenly over, they were gone, they were back in formation, were gone round the corner at a wolf-like loping run: and the big single skull on the back of the tall one's jacket burned into Bill's eyeball a moment after they'd gone.

Bill bent slowly to pick up the pieces, clutched one of the black messy things, then another, then straightened letting them fall. And his hat chose that moment to finally tumble and fell with its bright fighting bobble right into

the milk and the glass and the mud, and his white hair
blew in the wind: and he just couldn't bear to retrieve it,
although it was one of the last things she knitted before
both her mind and her fingers had gone, there was too
much mess, he was much too old, he was shaking, he had
to drive on. Clarrie Dutton, who knitted the hat with the
last of her keen sense of hatred and humour, would have
felt very happy, watching it darken and drown: as all
bright living things (and black jokes) sink into the black
oily water, sink through the slime of dead leaves, go dark
and go down.

28   'You couldn't say this was a leg and that was an arm'   I

Jean-Claude felt absolutely dreadful. And he must
look dreadful. Too dreadful to check in the mirror. Too
dreadful to let it sneak back, as it did every morning, to
think of her dying, too dreadful to *think*. So he sat and
stared out of his window, just stared at the fine bare
treetops of the gardens below. Much prettier, bareness,
than evergreens: evergreens were stodgy and solid, he
liked the bones to show through. On the other hand, he
liked to feel private: the thin screen of twigs in the winter
let the other side of the Crescent stare hatefully back at
you. Harder than usual when you looked *dreadful*, of
course, and were feeling thoroughly *ill*. What was more,
the way the light fell on the glass made the hatred it
beamed oblique. All you caught directly was a flash of a
hand or a face or of something which moved and was

white in the cold dark eye of the window, then curtains were suddenly drawn. Or a strong bare branch in the garden would cunningly blow, and would scratch the white movement behind it away till tomorrow.

He had talked to Mo about the eyes in the windows, half-serious, half as a joke. And Mo understood him as always, as always, had done the same thing, had imagined mute signals flashing across or white hands taking notes on her movements, deftly and watchfully, writing neat figures on pads of black plastic, eyes through the leaves which were noting the hours when she lay on her balcony drowning in blank August sun, too many, counting the fat black birds on her roof which kept flying and flopping and falling, too many unless they were part of the plan. And then too many planes coming over, watching and planning, their sky-trails bright in the sun. With Moira, all fantasy flamed and flew, though the images tended to end up twisting in uncontrolled flames and then falling, charred and sinister, darker and grimmer than his (she was dreaming of flying: then splayed on the cold stone, dead.)

He remembered the fat black birds which had frightened her so in the summer, their loud clumsy tumbles on the blue slate roof just above her, their blundering attempts to fly blackly and fatly in through her window and batter themselves at the light or her face, she imagined, in tears of despair one hot day when she ran round and told him she couldn't go back there ever, one had got in. Black, gross and blind, an unbearable, panicking vortex of feathers and pain. He was frightened too, rather, but poured out a whisky and left her and went round to see, and he stood on the landing for ages, heart beating, his ear to the thin cream door. He heard nothing, and finally took a deep breath and edged in: but the thing had quite simply flown out again. And she was so grateful for nothing, had hugged him and burst into tears all over again when he went back and told her the horror was gone.

She had loved him, he thought, in her way, in his way. In a sense, she belonged to him. All those hours spent talking and drinking his whisky on winter afternoons, her complaining, as always, she ought to get on. All those hours half-asleep in the sun. All those long indulgent dinners in restaurants (paid for by him) where each one expanded and grew evanescent and rosy and brilliantly, volubly, drunk, and the eyes almost meeting in warm rosy twilight and drink said You, you are beautiful, brilliant, and we shall for ever conspire and be young, almost meeting: the long walks back and the awkward touching of arms on the street, at first agony, later a dull occasional ache and finally subject for ribald laughter, though sometimes, lying alone at night, the laughter had not quite prevented the ache.

And Thank God she had never suggested, not even at first before she had known . . . though she once in the first months passionately kissed him, coming up behind him where he stood fixing drinks on the fridge with his shirt undone in the heat (it began in summer), and slipping her hand inside and then over the warm brown skin she had pressed her unbrassièred breasts on his shoulders and said he was gorgeous and licked his ear wetly and hotly, paused to move round. But whatever she saw in his eyes made her stop and laugh oddly and say Hey, that's quite enough ice, and then bite her lip foolishly, moving away. Which was such long ages ago. And for two years now they had discussed his boyfriends with the same brutal precision as hers, or on sober occasions respected each other's emotions, analysed them, magnified them, mixed them with whisky and water and sugar and alchemized them to warm gold. Both knowing the vice and both knowing the warmth and the pleasure.

All gone. And the waste made him *sick* with anger, the hours they had spent on each other, the investment of memory and sympathy and sheer concentration. That whole sweet part of his life just so brutally, *stupidly*, hacked away, so unfairly, *his* memories, *his* sympathy, *his* concentration: splayed on the cold stone, dead. And she had said nothing, had given no clue. If she'd just said one word he could have helped her, he knew . . . As it was, he just felt so *stupid*; the whole thing was over, without him, – excluded, and sick with surprise. It had to be somebody else down there they were grimly, efficiently removing, somebody else in pale glimpses or suddenly, horribly, blood through the heavy black bodies of policemen saying 'Come along, everybody, move along now, please, clear a path' – Brown or Jones, and the big boots blacker than birds on the pavement . . .

30 Black, gross and blind

And he wouldn't have known even then if he hadn't had one of his rare long nights of insomnia, thinking of swimming and waterproof eyelash dye and where he would go in the summer and really how *good* that his job meant he had a real summer and whether he'd manage to bear with the boredom of college meetings for very much longer . . . there were doubts, confided in her . . . and yet, although someone like Moira might giggle and mock, they had to go on. That terrible moment when the Treasurer, out-voted on the Library project, resigned from the committee, and as he stood up he knocked over his glass and it broke as it fell and he openly wept, his pink face in glittering fragments: *not done*: the high room curtained and silent, shut off and discreet: and after he left Harry whispered 'Old Stokes is a broken man' and he nodded back wisely, urbanely, committed to wisdom and boredom for ever by smiling and sitting, shut off from his shock and his pity, his hand very calm on his glass on the dark teak table, the thin smoke waving, saying goodbye to the sun . . . for very much longer, for ever, there were forms, there was work to be done . . . and besides all *that* (and he curled up his toes) in some ways the job, and *tradition* and *form*, were *fun*: swimming and waterproof eyelash dye (blue) which was fit to be cried in and where would he go in the blue skies and summer, Stokes fell from the tree he was pruning and died in the garden, peacefully, two months later, a stroke, quite peacefully, the lens of his glasses broken, the bright blue skies leaking in and the summer, the trunk of the great dark tree stretching up in the last blurred shot to the Library Committee above him, then climbing, straining, fell back . . . and time flew and the summer came round again and his quick drowsy thoughts flew round and a black shadow fell on the trunk of a tree stretching upwards, Macbeth, something hard and erect where two easy thoughts crossed, something angry and real . . . So he'd got up unrested and early, Mo's birthday, he had her present to get and a dearth of ideas and a headache, plunged out in the sun for a walk with an eyelid which twitched and a headache, a headache, to find . . . two yards from his doorstep, *this* – something happening, ambulance, police – and Macbeth pushed up to him, grinning, as Jean-Claude stood still on his doorstep in puzzlement changing to horror as he saw for certain a flash of red sunlit hair and corrected it red matted hair in the sunlight, and knew, almost knew in that flash it was Moira. Time staggered, and fell.

'I say,' said Macbeth, and he took Jean-Claude's arm

with a touch that was even then powerful, frightening, familiar, too many sensations, the sun in that sick red flash: and then down, looking down, on his arm the black nails and the gross silver ring with its blind red stone like blood and the three-inch black watchstrap heavily studded with silver, the jacket was black leather too but the lining flashed briefly scarlet, more black please and shut out the red, I can't think, I can't bear it . . . 'I say, yuh gonna have a *norful* shock, you know. Iss your *fren*', you see. Young *Moy*-rah,' which he pronounced with incredible sing-song viciousness, aping respect. 'She gone an' dun 'erself in. Jumped off. Off the top. Go on, 'ave a look. Got 'er 'ead bashed in. 'Ave a look.'

And he'd snatched off the hand and walked woodenly on in a wide avoiding circle, not looking, walked numbly and woodenly on towards the mad main road and red flashes, the mad buses blindly and noisily passing and skidding through sheets of grey tears, his own, and sat down on the seat at the bus stop and quietly fainted.

31 Volubly, brilliantly drunk

Then two days of savage continuous shock, not eating, too drunk to know whether or not he was sleeping, incessantly ringing up friends and then ringing off weeping, only sobering up enough to walk with slightly exaggerated grace along to the off-licence. Started to drink mid-morning when he finally abandoned his knotted attempts to sleep and had whisky and strong black coffee, leaving the coffee untouched. Without for a moment considering tradition he kept the dark brown velvet curtains drawn roughly across, their rich drapes going anyhow, scraggy dispirited triangles of daylight poking through and accusing the fur on his tongue and the pain in his eyes. Inside this dark tent the amount of time passing was uncertain, the number of times he was in tears, the number of bottles, the number of phone-calls: and whether his rambling laments reached the mouth of the phone or the bottle he wasn't quite sure.

. He grieved and more bitterly still was *aggrieved*. His best friend had deserted him, cruelly, said not a word. And everyone would ask him, everybody, all his friends would expect him to know. But Jean-Claude had nothing to tell them. And of course all his friends would conclude that she hadn't loved him at all. As he emptied glass after glass, he began to think it was true.

But on the third night he slept seventeen hours, having crawled into bed at some ultimate stage of the afternoon frenzy, the street lights just coming, the triangles still faintly grey. He slept like a baby with dry streaked tears on its cheeks until ten the next morning, when he woke with a start and sat up and stared round him, aghast in his sleep-washed state at the path of the hurricane, bottles and glasses and ominous long dark stains. And looking far worse when he drew the brown curtains and let in the morning. Some blessed amnesia – some anaesthesia? – came while he swiftly and neatly, as was his habit, cleared up, automatic and quick, feeling only disgust at the mess and the smell and the dark messy passage of time which his labours with vacuum cleaner and dustpan and brush were dissolving, feeling no grief: until all the mess was dissolved and the records were back in their sleeves and the (eight!) empty bottles were under the sink and the high bright windows were open, and then light fell bleakly again on the hard indissoluble fact underneath the despicable mess of his mourning, Mo's death, and he turned on his heel and away from it, went off to run a deep bath and to shave and to shampoo his hair and be drenched with cologne, with his *Yves St Laurent: Pour Homme*. To be new, to wash it away, to be clean.

32 Everyone would ask him, everybody

On the landing, about to go down, he was frozen, one foot on the stairs, by the sound of Peg talking. In flood in the hall by the sound of it, could be the phone, very loud and excited, his normal, his everyday bane and the new black dimension to life didn't help him to face it, as normal, as every day frozen (but somewhere the new black dimension was aching towards him.) Peg Starr, the old caretaker, talked. And talked, as he found out one ill-advised day when he let her, and heard her arthritis, her corsets, her husband, her womb and her ears: all these spectres invoked by his smiling in vague good will at the carpet in passing, because it was sunny and June. From which moment these dust-covered horrors trailed dimly about her, ghost objects he'd met and was wrong not to ask after, flouting them daily by freezing and tiptoeing back at the sound of her shuffle below, or by charging like three mad buffaloes past her and 'MorningmissisStarrjus-tofftoseemypupils!' he would loudly essay over six brutal shoulders, and leaving her womb and her ears and her husband protruding in dusty neglect, he was gone. He swayed to and fro on the balls of his feet for a moment and realized there were two voices, one of them a male voice, not just the phone: and an isolated phrase, then another,

98

at too many decibels, pierced like a dum-dum bullet the thin bruised floor of his brain . . . As he fitted them into their pattern of harsh-vowelled sound (and the thing was outrageous, *disgraceful*), Jean-Claude swayed forward and stayed.

'Oh yes, 'e was very fond of 'er, very, they was always around together, laughing and doing, they was. Oh yes, she was always round 'ere, I was always seeing 'er. Not that she ever exchanged three words with *me*, mind you, but then 'e's not much of a talker either. Course, 'e's foreign, you see. And they keeps themselves to themselves, which is only nat'ral. Oh *yerrss*, you can give 'im a try, but don't say I 'aven't *warn* dew. And you'll 'ave to remember, 'e'll be in a bit of a state at the moment, so I should go careful. I know 'e's in there all right, as a matter of fact I'll feel better in my mind if you do go and 'ave a look, you see I know 'e's in there 'cos the curtains are drawn and I've 'eard 'im in there since it 'appened, sort of crashing about and playing 'is music and moaning and doing, most unlike 'im, like I say 'e is usually really very quiet. And I was just getting a little bit worried about 'im, you see, because there 'asn't been a peep out of 'im now since it'd be yesterday afternoon. Thass right dear, you go on up and give 'im a bash, thass the best,' and Jean-Claude darted back into his flat and was pressing the catch of the Yale lock noiselessly down as he did so, too slow to avoid hearing Peg's next squawk, up the stairs at full volume, not giving up: 'Do you think I oughter come with you and 'ave a little peep, jus' so's to see 'e's all right? Just a little peek in? You don't think so? Oh well, all right. Well you know where I am if you want me, dearie.'

Jean-Claude sat down in the kitchen in such a position that he could see the man's shadow through the glass. The whisky was there on the table in front of him. With only a second's hesitation, he lifted the bottle to his lips and drank deep, and the fire ran wildly and beautifully down round his throat and his gullet and yes, it would soon reach his bloodstream, making him brave and untouchable, mythic and messless and strong.

33 This squalid little farce

As the foolish feet shuffled and fumbled outside on the landing, the man would be reading his name, his own fine French name which they couldn't ever take away from him, or his money, or his looks, or his brain, or his will to drink more – he took swig after swig after deep warm swig and another, and finally the shadow started knocking, prevented from seeing the bell (as Jean-Claude realized suddenly, drinking the joy of his own alcoholic perception) by Peg's injunction to 'give 'im a bash': a perfectly functional, visible, normal white bell. And the knocks turned slowly to bashes, *go on, 'ave a bash*, and her harsh hateful voice in the hall was confused with the bashing. Then silence: a slightly embarrassed male voice, northern accent, was calling 'Jean-Claude? Mr Jean-Claude? Are you there, Mr Dupré?' – pronounced of course English-fashion, as instructed by Peg, and the slip with his fine French, fragile French, once his papa had been Free French, name – Dup*ree* was too much and in two strides reaching the door he unlocked it and flung it (and hand grenades at the Germans) wide: to find Les, who was looking *too* odious, must be a plain clothes policeman, was seen in a flash to be plump, pink, sweating with grease from the bashes so each tiny pimple shone out, and most abjectly, irksomely, sweatingly apologetic.

'Look, I am awfully sorry to knock so hard,' he began as the door swung open and he saw how much taller the figure inside was than him, in the same split second saw something else, and trailed off in a foolish rush into pathos, eyes down. 'Especially-as-I-see-that-there's-a-bell.' There was a silence. Jean-Claude filled his lungs with air.

'YES! THERE'S A BELL! THERE! SO I SUGGEST YOU USE IT!' – and Peg Starr on the floor below remarked to herself very happily 'Aye-aye, skylarks.'

As soon as the words were out, Jean-Claude's strong sense of the absurd came accusingly after them, and the horrible-looking man recoiled in a horrible way and muttered horribly pathetically 'Yes yes I see now, of course I shall use it' and actually reached out and pressed it, actually! – staring hard at his shoes.

Poor Hawkeye. But what happened next disturbed him still further, his small pink eyes stretching open, his lips coming loose, for the tall dark figure in the doorway was starting to laugh, giving off fumes of whisky and shaking, laughing and gasping so much that he had to lean back on the door for about thirty seconds before he recovered and motioned Les inside. For Peg, thirty seconds of puzzlement. Laughing? Probably gone barmy with shock, done his nut. It was quite exciting. Loony. Perhaps they would lock him away. She worked in one once, as an orderly. At least they were never dull, when they were barmy. You could have a bit of fun with them. She played with her wedding ring, trying to shift it on the grey swelled flesh of her hand, remembering. She and a friend. They had lots of games they could play with them, fell about laughing. Especially at bath-time, both of them. Dirty old buggers, funny old buggers, most of them. The things you could do with them (shifting the wedding ring, squeezing the flesh till it hurt.)

(In a long white room someone helpless, not mad but

too old and too lost to resist, Clarrie Dutton, her eyes darting helpless as mayflies as Pearl Buckle's hands squeezed in.)

34 Mythic and messless and strong I

Hawkeye Hawtrey was definitely nervous when he crossed the threshold, but things very quickly cheered up: there was order inside and not shrieking bedlam, and it soon became clear that this character really just wanted to talk. Things were clear quite soon, but they soon became less clear. Jean-Claude filled up Les's glass as often as his own, which was far too often, Les thought, unless Mr Dupree had money to throw around. Which he had, by the look of the flat, very smart in a low-key traditional way with a lot of cream silk and nice pictures, old prints but no rubbish, thought Hawkeye, generously, blurredly, much later, *if* you ask me. And when at the end of an hour or it might have been less or it might have been more they finished the first half-bottle, he calmly fetched another whole bottle from the kitchen, malt whisky, no fuss and no trouble. Except, when he poured, his hands seemed to be shaking a lot, and you could see, even Les could see, in the clear white light from the window, his eyes were in trouble, red-veined and with heavy dark lids which he rubbed too often. And yet, he was shaved and he smelled of something expensive, and his clothes looked good, very good, even Les who was not very good on male beauty could see that this character was very good-looking, and a very good sort, and he had just at first seemed a little bit short but it did take all sorts, Les conceded, it did take all sorts . . .

Les left after three, feeling pleasantly blotto. He liked this character, yes. And *he*, pondered Les, very pleasantly, *he* liked me. Les had helped him, talked to him, helped him through a difficult hour. They had parted good friends, firm friends. And the firmest friends differ, we differed at first, Les mused, very kind, very wise as he hiccupped and knocked an old trolley hard into the wall of the hall, and he laughed as he thought of that funny old faggot who grabbed him on his way in, and addressed her, her white-flowered wall behind which she was probably hiding, My greetings, old trolley, and gave her a parting tip, which was truth, my old t., and not money, saying 'Whoops!' very loudly and thinking that very good guy on the first floor had obviously loved her, the girl and not Peg, and that, my old trolleye, is truthe, and the waye that this sadde worlde goes, I am certayne: reverting, as Les always did in his cups, to a jovial mock-Shakespearian, acquired long ago when he was doing his journalist's stint in the provinces, and spent all his spare time half-drunk doing amateur dramatics, for love of his blonde and professional amateur Juliet, who was broke but never too proud to share money and liquor, *his* money, *his* liquor, a pro. And Juliet did go professional, finally, getting an offer, went into suburban rep and he never heard any more of her.

And Les was looking to see her name up in lights one day, indeed Les had been looking for years, when alone and just pleasantly tipsy and not staring into the round black pores of Jean, who would never be lost so easily: and the image which always brought sad brave prickings of tears, bravely dealt with, englobed him, the familiar image of himself trudging on (for she was at least far better looking than Jean, and her hair glinted gold, through a decade of gilt, from the balcony), Les in his

trenchcoat, alone, with the collar turned up at the cold
blue night, looking up not at her with her long blonde
(pretty long, long, he refused to remember) – her hair
flowing out, very pretty, *surely*, behind her, but true love
long gone, looking up at her name carved in swimming
blue neon on the front of a myriad theatres towering
above him (she always considered herself, he remembered, refused to remember, above him) – this image of
tragic perfection englobed him, now swimming down the
hall in a blue friendly world of sad truths, worthy men who
were brave but deserted, blue whisky and sad golden
truths.

Within seconds, though Les only seconds but also a long
golden decade away didn't know it, the door would have
opened by magic, the last of the magic, a bright cold
difficult world would be waiting outside it to eat him: his
watch said well after three: time flew, and the sun split
into his head, and somewhere from a high balcony Juliet
screamed and fell.

35   Mythic and messless and strong   II

And worlds whirled, for Jean-Claude, up above him,
adrenalin rushed through his veins and the words rolled
round in his brain and the room spun slightly but
pleasantly round him, unreal, and he wanted to go on
wisely and fluently talking (yet somewhere, behind, black
and dim, something else was beginning.) Two hours
floated by, unreal: floated pleasantly, then less pleasantly,
the dry flight slowing and foundering, the white mad

wings of excitement failing, the route uncertain, asleep in a chair but dreaming of talking and flying, then out in the kitchen with brisk housewifery washing the glasses and making black coffee, then suddenly hungry, then headachey, back in the kitchen much later or not much later and wolfing down ancient delicious nut biscuits once bought by – once brought here by Mo, automatically feeding them into some long dry tunnel of wind and excitement and worry, a body whirled helplessly down it, mouth open and drily working, the white wings broken – found dead on the ground in the morning. For something, it seized him and held him as night came to get him, had just gone terribly, lengthily wrong. And the streetlights came on down below and the cold light steadied and cut him. His consciousness ceased in that instant to flicker and swing.

He had talked, he had revelled, explaining: adoring, extolling, lamenting. Oh God. To that poor professional dolt with his spots and his fake spy raincoat. Oh God, God, GOD. They would quote him, banal and pompous, prolix, confiding and mad. Mo would *die* (she was dead, she was dead) Mo would *die* if she read him, the horribly vulgar and *private* things he had said. He would have to deny it, all of it, take out a libel suit. And the last of the afternoon fled, cold and grey, unredeemable, horrible, trying to hide once again in sleep, curling deeper, don't find me, don't blame me, a broken nut biscuit slipped down in between and held tight by his elegant thighs in grey velvet, dreams aching and crumbling, too cold to wake up and too shameful, his flung neck stiff when it briefly and shallowly woke up, his vile mouth open and dry.

Which was why for two days he had been jerking to a halt on streets or on staircases, whispering fiercely 'Oh God, God no, you *didn't*' and 'Oh no, I didn't mean *that*.' And 'talks to hisself,' Peg was thinking, creeping

105

cautiously into the hallway to check he'd come in on his own, his fancy pink back in that jacket going upwards, – alone. Oh yes, and she smiled so her teeth slipped slightly and she had to suck them up again, smooth and satisfying, tasting of bacon for breakfast, nice. Oh yes, it was always a sign.

36 Horribly vulgar

But it wasn't so bad as he thought. Drinking up in two minutes of high-speed sweating and reading the volume of horror, Jean-Claude found it fifty times less than the sweats and despairs of his dreams. He had failed to consider the vulgarity of Les's imagination, which rendered the thing into comic opera, the characters crudely got up in some ill-stocked prop-room, where the oyster-coloured silk was cream. He recognized dimly his own betrayals, spread out through the text and distorted by Les's own ponderous morals: disguised by the kind pompous tricks of the trade, *as reliable sources informed me* (they didn't), *as friends of the dead girl said*, and he did, how he did. But relief spread joyously through him. His folly and guilt were unaltered, but here he was, back from the dead. Because no-one who read it would know just how close was the whole constellation of pop sociology, crassly banal, to the blurred starry things which were actually, drunkenly, here in this very room said . . . and that ultimate horror, the schmaltzy devotion with which they had parted, Les saying 'Truss' me,' on the threshold, and wringing his hand and indeed his shoulder '. . . *truss*' me,' that ultimate intimate horror had not come over. Jean-Claude hadn't reckoned on Les's tough interviewing image, which demanded that he invent confrontations where none had existed. Jean-Claude had emerged from the re-texturizing process irritable and laconic, evasive, suspicious and strong.

As the comedy went, and it did, he found he quite liked it, imagining all over Oxford that people he knew would be reading, his friends, *too* amusing, *too* dreadful, *too* sad. 'Moira Penny's constant companion.' He liked that. His worst fears had centred on the row in the street the next day between John and himself about the presents, with that pink fellow watching . . . was it a libel to state that someone was weeping . . . ? But it wasn't too bad. What Jean-Claude could not know was how many limp words Les had cut from his first wild version. John's final victorious sally had gone in the bin, together with the 'smooth-talking foreigner' who watched his departure in tears.

But the fact remained, John had won. Jean-Claude wished he had kept his two cards and given them Moira in person later: concealed in a huge loving tree of white flowers which he dreamed in a moment and gave on a sudden inspiration, posthumous, perfumed and perfect, with art and love. And the gift would have grown in the warmth of next summer's sun to a thick woody vine, would have held the slate roofs of their houses together in flower . . . And someone like John, Jean-Claude thought, would have sneered at birthdays for bourgeois formalism, or some such bullying phrase. He was willing to bet that there wasn't a card or present from John in the whole collection (Jean-Claude, of course, was quite wrong. It was seven inches long, it was plastic.)

37 Blurred starry things

Birthdays and tributes were very serious affairs to Jean-Claude. There were certain elaborate acts of grace which quite simply improved the texture of life. Human beings were highly evolved, they were able to choose to love and please each other, they could use imaginative formulae to smooth away the edges of horrible general truths like loneliness, ageing and pain. Or the *best* people could: the *civilized* people, his friends. Jean-Claude put his faith in the particular, in individual compacts, individual kindness, individual offers of love. He had made one to Mo. And yet death was a general truth, and had the last word (someone acidly typing agreed.) Now the whole complex structure seemed – foolish, he thought, feeling suddenly tired, just foolish. His carefully chosen cards looking suddenly foolish, pathetic, excessive to hostile eyes. In a sense she had failed in her bargain with *him*, failed to protect him, failed to inform him, failed to involve him, failed to make use of the rich and elaborate conspiracy which she had helped to evolve. Failed to be there, quite simply, that morning, when his poor cards shot through the door. So that now I am left quite naked, he thought, in a piercing instant of simple self-pity and rage. (John's bent bony form, the blonde stubble, the hostile and humorous pale blue eyes.) For both of the cards had borne welters of fine flying kisses, flying and falling as always in ominous dark formation from left to right, he had always been quite unable to keep a line straight (and his Schools examiner said to him later, in private, offering avuncular advice when they met in the street, that it was obvious to all of them that this chap was brilliant, but why did the young always think it a sin to be neat?) – and such silly, such loving, such intimate, *foolish* messages scrawled in his black broken hand falling hopelessly downwards, the cold eyes following, fleeing pathetically, nakedly down to the right and he shook his head sharply, tried to recall from the bland squares of newsprint before him the first sweet thrust of relief, it was gone, it was lost, he was lost, she was gone, she was dead. 'Go on, 'ave a look. Got 'er 'ead bashed in. 'Ave a look.'

38 'Go on, 'ave a look.'

Two cards in the same black undisciplined hand. It was two months before Felicity, bored and desperate, finally opened all Moira's birthday mail. Beautiful cards and those silly affected messages. Two, why two? And who was Jean-Claude? It was a name from a novel, a name from a novelette. Some other lover, evidently, and John was too proud, of course, to have talked about those – not sexually proud, just pretending it wasn't important. They were almost the kind of cards that a girl might have sent herself, and that silver lily surely was Mo's taste and nobody else's, beautiful, yes, but . . . the Mo she had always felt ill at ease with, the Mo she privately told herself she distrusted, the Mo who made her feel heavy and stilted and flat. And she told herself, privately, often, that ecstasy was easily faked, though she didn't believe that Mo faked it, really, it was just some primitive and dazzling faculty, something near beauty, that she herself had somehow utterly missed. And it wasn't important, of course, but she privately grew to hate Mo, very privately, so tucked away it was hidden even from sane and polite

Felicity, Fee who existed so far from all hatred or ecstasy, Fee who could never have faked.

John would never have left me for Mo, she repeated again as so often, never, no not in a hundred years, and the hundred years which she'd always used as a talisman for their love against loss and death still rang in some far bright room of her brain with a reassuring finality, final, a hundred years' lease on love. But the echo laughed back at her, laughed from that dark little attic where wild chance had leapt in the night and was briefly a long flash of silver, then black and the rooms were locked up, all their happiness, John had gone weakly and helplessly into the darkness after, had left her for nothing, a freak storm of snow and sentiment, left her for four mangled limbs which could never have captured him living. And their house felt empty now, she couldn't afford it, the lease would be given up.

He was happy with me, she thought, Mo and he had started to quarrel, I know he was happy with me (but the world, it was clear, would never believe her) . . . I *know* he was happy with me, tearing numbly into vague floral efforts from relatives, casting their sunshine-and-blue-skies verses aside unread and their humbly offered addresses, to which Mo would probably never have written alive or dead, but now had no option. I know he was happy with me, I did make him happy.

One package Felicity was leaving till last. It had grown very large and very heavy, suddenly. Lying on the carpet, brown paper, with small neat loops of blue ink on it, very neat and innocent, but somehow starting to soak up light and space. The old maid's writing was John's, and the old-maidish double-knotted string was John's, and only John, she considered, was precise enough to put it in the post when he was going to see Mo for dinner that day . . . until Clara phoned, around lunchtime. And had his one suit on, and fluffy washed hair. It had seemed so messy

110

and so awful, the grief and the stuff from his nose and the wrenching noise with his beautiful coffee-striped suit on, everything suddenly, unbelievably changed, a quite new historical period opening now that Clara had phoned. Chaos, his lean and predictable face in horrible blubbering chaos, this swelling, this redness, this wetness and lurching of limbs . . . somewhere just out of touch with the process a cold Felicity coldly remarked, out of order and sunlight, all this. On the surface she met it with voluble, shocked compassion, but deep underneath, in the stillness behind her repeated gestures of love and even the tears which she tenderly, naturally shed, there were two things: anger at all the mess: and then deeper still, shameless and spreading, was hope (Mo was gone, he was *hers*), so dizzily filled with potential for real free pleasure at last she was forced to remove her tenderly, naturally sorrow-filled gaze for fear that the joy which was in there biding its time would flash suddenly, savagely blue, *it is my turn now*.

39   A quite new historical period

And now blue, blue, nothing but blue. In the last six weeks since she gave up her job and had stayed inside with her grief, seeing no-one and darting away from the hall if she heard feet approaching, usually only the milkman or postman, the world's strong sensible axis had shifted and Nobody cares, she told herself, I had to wear myself out over them but now nobody cares. Which was false, and she knew it. And yet, after all these years of extravagant caring and sweating for so many people it came as a kind of relief to turn inwards and pity herself, to feel that the world was indifferent. Just simply let go, after endlessly feeling her effort was needed to keep the world turning, simply let go and curl up in a closed grey world of her own. She sat in a cushion-filled corner and played all John's records, even the pop which she with her classical training used to detest, yet she had grown slowly addicted, fatally, now.

'Am I Blue', 'The Blues Came up One Morning /Without a Word of Warning', 'Billy's Blues', 'Blue Notes for You.' At least it turned bleak grey grief for a while into something which went well with whisky, the fourth large whisky (although she had never touched it before John – died . . . now the last of her careful economy went on whisky), something liquid and tremulous, bottomless, every celestial shade of blue. Something much nearer, Fee thought in a lucid moment, the egotistical joys and despairs she had never gone in for, despising people like Mo whose emotions became metaphysics or poems, things which reached tellingly, tremblingly out to the sky . . .

And the sky became pregnant with indigo, each afternoon, staring back at her grief through the heavy sash-window. Infinitely slowly going dark, more slowly each day as time stretched with the sobs on the record and shivered, that heavenly blue . . . after all those years of briskness and black-and-white effort, the whisky helped her to see it, curled up on her dusty cushions like a limp lost child, like a child who contained the whole world in her tired hand clutching the whisky . . . finding at last and by evening that she was important, and central, and tragic, and wise.

The hangovers were red and dreadful, the bed in the morning was empty, the sheets were mysteriously crease-less and virginal now that she slept alone or alone with the pills, deep down. In the morning importance had gone

112

and the grief had set greyly around her red headache again, set creaseless and lonely and grey.

40 Every celestial shade of blue

It was eleven in the morning and the blues were already playing, drifting through the dust-moted sunlight of early spring. Since John – hadn't been there – she had let the flat get very dirty, most unlike her. Though *he* had been dirty, had left things for days when she was away. And his dirt was at last taking over, now *he* was away. The small pile of presents and cards lay sprawled on the fluff of the carpet, looking violated, filling Felicity suddenly with pity and guilt. Torn edges of envelopes, cards lying anyhow, nobody pleased by them, nobody bothering to stand them up. She started to do so, half-heartedly, told herself she was an idiot, had always been an idiot, a good-hearted idiot, and stopped. Good old Felicity, it had always been good old Felicity, you can trust Felicity, Felicity was marvellous, Felicity, of course, was a brick. (On the other hand, Fee thought viciously, hating the chorus of stupid affirmative voices, they also contrived to imply Fee isn't really very imaginative, is she, of course she's an awfully good sort but isn't she just a bit boring . . . Even John, maybe, thought it, and certainly took her for granted, the fact she was always cheerful and never jealous, the fact she had endless patience to listen to his theories, the fact (they were *none* of them facts – she was jealous, she did get impatient) – she would always be there when he came back from Mo. And she *was* here, kneeling here, now.

But he wouldn't come back to her, ever, and she was the same old idiot, kneeling in pain on the carpet and starting to tidy those stupid irrelevant presents, thinking of him, thinking of him.

Three smaller packages she had opened: one of them cheap pretty beads in tissue paper, tiny glass things of all colours, how pretty, thought Fee, who had not felt pretty or looked at anything pretty for ages, from Jill, who sent love and was hoping to see Mo soon, now never, the music insisted, now never again. And the other a joke red jumping bean with a smiling face and black spots. From Clara, of course, with a note to inform Mo that jumping beans jumped because they had live insects inside them, so if this one didn't, that meant it had died in the post. Of course this was nonsense, Fee thought, who was afraid of insects, especially just recently, rustles in the night and dark spiderous shapes in the big empty flat . . . they would want to touch her, and she who had not been touched for so long had a horror of that. Still the thing looked sinister, lying on the carpet on its side with its blank grin toppled, not jumping. Like a little red totem, grinning bad luck. Yet behind it swam the powdery laughing face of Clara, who Felicity had always liked, always, she told herself, always, insisting, staring at the dumb black grin on the red plastic casing. Clara, who had written so kindly and clumsily after John's death, and Felicity thought of the letter, puffing with effort and powder, rather, like Clara, trying so hard to be *kind* . . . and she realized slowly what the red bean had known from the very beginning, ripped from its packet, rigidly, brutally grinning, dead on its back, that she had begun to hate Clara now in the same way as she had begun to hate Moira after John's death, which was fiercely, totally, now. No, that was wrong, as she *always* hated her, she weakly acknowledged, kneeling there weakly, weakly acknowledging years of pretending that she was self-sufficient and

114

strong. And sat staring, staring down at the vile little human bean with its knowledge of hatred, staring at the scurf of envelopes and wrapping, staring at the third opened parcel, a packet of figs with the sugar gone blue and white and mouldy, disgusting, the card that went with it saying I HOPE THAT YOU WILL NOT THINK ME A FIG-URE OF FUN(!) – in shaky blue capitals: and the Joke, whatever it was, had gone equally blue and mouldy, stuck to the figs by a long brown sugary stain. She was staring, finally, bitterly, wearily, at the little brown package from John, double-knotted, which slowly grew into a huge brown package, impossible, threatening, triple-knotted – staring weakly and wearily, feeling the aimless anger and strength which had helped her rip into the other parcels draining away. And yet what could it matter, how could she mind it, now.

41 'Go on, 'ave a look' II

And her eyes travelled round it. Nothing but wreckage and rubbish, the sun filtered in and saw nothing but trivial mess and wreckage and rubbish, and her with her lank greasy hair and her whisky-stained wrap of flowered cotton. It was all so unnecessary, pointless, and all her life she had hated time to be messy and pointless, and it was all his fault, he had upset everything, pulled life apart. And all because Mo had been *pretty*, that was it really, a lot of it, though he denied it: although they agreed that it wasn't important, sex wasn't important, or beauty. But John was a fraud. He was vain. He loved his own looks and he loved being looked at, blonde and arrow-like, hard-mouthed, striking, like a Swedish spy. And *I* loved them too, thought Felicity. It mattered, it moved you, it tore you, *You're beautiful, darling*, the sun on his hard bones, beauty. (And Fee wasn't plain, by a long way, but she wasn't quite slim enough, not quite. And her movements were neat and deliberate, and her clothes, she had felt, watching Mo like a lithe silver fish swimming down some imaginary sunlit and sea-dappled street, were too stiff somehow, never quite right. But it mattered, as all women knew and he pompously swore that it didn't . . . she knew, and he couldn't conceal it.) The horror was all his fault. And the mess was his fault, the mess she had made of the past few months, and the job she had stupidly left and the tears and the rubbish.

She snatched up the parcel and tore at it feebly, ripping the neat blue writing, breaking her longest (and too long by now and too dirty) nail in a hopeless struggle with the string. Inside was more packing, an anonymous cardboard box about eight inches long, not heavy, three inches across. Felicity stopped in a panic, debating. It was the shape which was odd. Not books, which you would have expected, it must be – some kind of *thing*. With anyone else it might be a cork-screw, or, I don't know, a pen-set, a statuette, anything, but *John* . . . Well it might be something edible, she thought, something nicer than that odd pack of figs, of course, some special delicacy which Mo couldn't afford. Some pickle or preserve, something they would eat together, she shuddered, yes, that would be it, an aphrodisiac, sitting in that dark little attic which she would never enter, although she had often imagined it, laughing and tipsy and him in his coffee-striped suit with his hair fluffing up like a small bird's feathers in the light, little boy, he was just a little boy, with his little boy feelings for beauty . . . and she placed the box delicately down on the carpet, very neatly, precisely aligned with the join of two pieces of carpet, her world would at least now be neat, went out to the kitchen, erect in her thin flowered wrap and planting her bare feet neatly, found scissors and paused for a single untidy second before making coffee: saw the whisky: felt the tears which had formed a few seconds ago lurch and roll in two straight neat tracks down her cheeks, and reached out through her tears for the whisky, slopping a large one, very large, into a beermug, not caring.

The record had stopped as she poured it, a sequence of neat short clicks. She walked back with her glass through a loud empty silence, walked neatly, the vacuum fatuously streaming with sun. She walked to the heavy sash window and swiftly and neatly, just scenting the dream in the whisky, released the Venetian blinds which had never been used when John was – cut off the light very neatly, cleanly, completely, let them right down, let some comfort, oblivion, come. And she piled up the sad blue music, turned up the volume, and tenderly, hopefully let the arm down.

She was crouched with the box and her beermug, taking deep breaths to avert the black pressure of sobs: and deep burning drinks which revived her, set blood running back to her cheeks, made her breathless again, made her gratefully splutter and cough. With the whisky inside her she was real, she was warm, she existed . . . she was there, surviving, surviving, although all the world had gone dark and faded away. When the glass was empty she walked back through the flat very purposefully, pulling her blue flowers around her, very sure and very erect. Fetched the bottle, and this time quite calmly, to a high, absurdly high level, with a slow precise wrist, filled it up, and the record was 'Blues for a Season', cerulean saxes, deep down, drowning down, loud. And the box was upon her, suddenly, easy to open, the string and two sellotape snicks, undone. Even then, she just looked at it, puzzled, then touched it, then stared at it, stared at it, staggered but not understanding, for some thirty seconds was staring and staring before she was able to scream.

At first glance, it was a little pink figure of the Virgin Mary, incredible, plasticky, ridiculous, long robes and halo and demure blue veil. But the face was all wrong. Too pink and too painted, black lashes and full red lips, and the blue robes were stupidly conical over the breasts. Something awful, she puzzled, something uncanny, something about John which I knew nothing about, some terrible private rite. But the truth didn't strike her till she nerved herself to reach out and clasp the cold plastic, and then she caught sight of the other side.

It was a seven-inch penis, a smooth pink cock, quite naturalistic, the veins and the ridge of the foreskin delicately picked out: and she realized that the face and chin of the virgin continued the line of the foreskin, and the neatly crossed arms and flowing robes continued the lines of the shaft. It was a dildo, a dildo, a *dildo*, and Felicity dropped it and started to scream.

42 It wasn't important, sex wasn't important

Fly away Peter. Fly away Paul. Poor ol' Felicity, poor ol' John. Feeling sicker and sicker into afternoon. Half-lying, now, curled round the whisky bottle, spilling it, sometimes, a pity, or else it was practical, watering the blue cotton flowers. Fly away whisky, started off full. That was very good, *very*, and Felicity started to laugh, convulsively, burped and a rush of vomit threatened, lurched and fell back, or Felicity, was it, fell back and be careful, Felicity. Shan't. She had *always* been careful, always, always been loving and good. She was good like Clara, with time for anybody, big clumsy Clara for whom nothing ever went right, poor Clara, big clumsy Clara (she rocked to a rhythm, like a child) poor Clara was good like she was but nobody loved her, nobody . . .

. . . Everybody said that she *understood*, ask Felicity . . . and she did, or at least she once thought that she did . . . now she didn't, any more, and everyone was dead, or else dozing, and Felicity was dozing with her blue flowers drooping in two inches of whisky by her head. Oh, you thought you'd caught me out, you'd caught me napping, did you. You won't fool me, thought Felicity, sharply awake, more perceptive than ever before in her life, knowing all, and they certainly couldn't fool *her* with their foul secret parcels, they certainly never again could demand she be bright and careful and bland and then blight and careful and brand, she burped and she giggled and suddenly stopped with a plan. And she fed it with whisky, warmly, and watched the blaze crazily grow. Not *Felicity*. *Why not* Felicity? Blight and brand.

And she took a box of matches – not Felicity, *why not* Felicity? – souvenir box of last year's Italian holiday, blurred sunny views and a bright one of John's blonde hair in the sun briefly floated in front of it, printed itself on Felicity's clear dreadful hand. He was carrying her in his arms, and laughing. She said that the sun was too hot for her feet, she was burning, their damp bodies burning, him laughing and carrying her to a sheltered spot in the dunes: where the sand was still far too hot, but he fucked her and told her he loved her, the first time he'd said it for years, and they lay on their backs and burned and watched two little boys on the beach who were playing with red toy planes: and he said something strangled and odd about how they would always be friends, and the heat of the sun soaked through her, the safety, the heat of his body, and she knew (and then told herself she was mad) she would never again be as happy, the red plane was flying and falling but always took off again, always, at least while the children were still down there playing, at least for the afternoon. But the view on the box was an aerial view, too distant, a vague blur of sunshine and too many bottles of wine.

And the hand, *not* Felicity, *why not*, took a match and lit it, not catching on the third, not catching on the fourth, not catching – *catching*, was fire, was a flame. First the light on the hand, a hand which was red in half-darkness, a wild red hand which was hers, *not Felicity's, why* not? Be careful: shan't. Then the flame darting downwards, the face glowing mad Halloween above it, a neat face, Felicity's, masked by a witch's face, redly and horribly lit from below: *NOT Felicity, oh no no*. Then a good smell, cheerful, burning, the sad paper wrappings beginning to go, and the fierce light growing, red-gold in the last half-inch of the whisky, and a fierce-faced Indian, brightening, reddening, drank it, a lovely and fearsome savage with red-gold skin, not Felicity, Felicity, Felicity, wake up Felicity, wake up and look at your beauty, Felicity, wake up and look at your game, at your lovely red violent game, Felicity, look how John's neat paper shavings flare up in a great bush of flame and the dildo is stirring and softening, Felicity, smelling of burning plastic or is it the smell of your burning home or of sperm, is he going in hotly after the dildo, Felicity, is he about to come?

Not to Felicity, not for Felicity, not with Felicity, no: around eight she was screaming again and more wildly, waking from deep dead sleep burning hot in an untouched corner, a wild girl shining with sweat and coronaed by clear orange flame, for a second a wild leaping redhead, a beauty, not Fee, that was plain . . . till the first flame delicately touched her, and pictures turned into wild pain.

120

Miss Poynes peeked happily out of her high bedroom window not far from the Crescent, through cherry-pink curtains, she made all the curtains by hand. The house had four stories and all the curtains were covered with bunches of cherries, even the sweet little navy-lined curtains which went round the cage of the parrot (she put in the lining by hand.) She did like cherries: the taste and the colour were happy, and these days they all needed happiness, really, there was too much unhappiness, now, in the world. She peeked down to the left, towards the Crescent, being very careful because she still had her nighty on, which was naughty at this hour, she chided herself, and a rather *naughty* nighty, she prided herself, it was cherry-pink nylon in layers with pink silken ribbons, her birthday treat to herself. It was a lovely colour for clothes, although fuddy-duddies thought it too brilliant. She was rare, it was true, in being able to wear it, with her beautifully contrasting, equally brilliant and young green eyes and they didn't need makeup, although she was nearly sixty, although she most certainly wouldn't have been too proud. She had been painted, by a professional artist, in oils, quite recently, not for money: he saw her in summer, out on her step, and he set her alongside her parrot, and told her she still had a wonderful head, like a bird's, and her eyes were the shade of its feathers. He was charming, she liked him, except he was most insistent she didn't wear pink, and he made her remove the pink curtains from the cage of the parrot. She was sure it had missed all those plump juicy cherries. She liked him, he wasn't long-faced, he was energetic and cheery, with dark curly hair . . . if he had been older, she thought, if *she* had been young, for she did feel young, and she blushed to acknowledge her feelings and *oh I am naughty*, she thought, and kept peeping.

The milkman was late, her nice cheery milkman, her William, she called him, her Worthiest William, her Bill. Well, it was after all – was it? Sunday, she thought and she rubbed a new hole in the frost and then spotted him through it, her Bully-for-Bill. And he hadn't got his hat on, she noticed, and worried a little to see him, his white hair and streams of white breath now huffing and puffing below on the pavement, his milkfloat (she craned round and found it) parked over the way: and of course they don't have any heating, she thought, and she pulled the warm nylon around her, not wearing his gay little hat and no heating, on such a bitter cold day. It made her feel cold just to look at him this morning, oh what a pity, she usually liked it, his cherry-pink cheeks and his bright blue eyes and his nice straight back and his hat, and the whole effect was so cheerful, usually, making her think of the sweet painted soldiers she'd owned as a child, such a beautiful scarlet and gold-painted set . . . and now she stared closer he *did* look exhausted and gloomy, not gloomy exactly but somehow all shrunken, my William, and grey. And Miss Poynes pulled sadly at her ribbons and settled her gaze on hope and on beauty, something distant and happy, something faraway into spring in the green Crescent garden, there would soon be lovely long lambs' tail catkins on that dark tree, such bright little fellows, all chasing each other's tails (but the side of the tree that Miss Poynes couldn't see was in shadow: a shadowy boy in black leather, etched into the lines of the bark.)

That was it, thought Bill, as he plodded on stiffly and grimly, two pints for old Poynes-in-the-arse, automatically, that was the trouble, that was the thing that the nobs didn't see. That however you felt and no matter what happened, you just had to keep on working: you couldn't just put your feet up like *they* did, let everything go and enjoy feeling bad: he was a milkman, and even a thoroughly shook-up milkman had to go on with his rounds. What Bill wanted to do was sit down and think about yobs. Think about what you should do, what the public should do, about what he would personally do to them later whenever, in some brave dreaming or drinking moment, the chance arose.

In the army, it was somehow all chances, because you had power. You drank with your mates and they were all for you, they backed you, they shared the same code. Your fears and your dreams. They knew what you stood for, no-one had to ask. They knew they all stood for the same things. And *that* lot – they flashed before him, briefly and maddeningly, rat pack in leather, grinning and loping – we would have flattened them, me and my mates in the army. What made him laugh was that really they acted as if *they* were army, those bloody yobbos, done up in leather like a uniform, flaunting their skulls like swastikas, keeping in a pack. *We* would have flattened them, *real* army, we were really tough: they didn't know what real men were, these yobbos. We learned to be hard and we learned respect and we learned the difference between them, thought Bill, just dusting his favourite pronouncement to Edgar, who thus learned respect for his big ex-army pal Bill, though he never could learn to be hard, being tiny and wall-eyed and crumbling, his bones wearing down to their final arthritic decay. Respect, that was what they all needed, thought Bill, he would *teach* them respect one day, those yobbos, those yobs, and he pulled back his shoulders too stiffly and twisted his neck.

In the army they had a few drinks and then went out and settled things, settled the lads from the town, fair fighting with fists and you stuck by your friends, and you knew who they were, the whole lot were your friends in the army, one for all and all for one. Bill sighed. Trouble was, it was all over now, and the old good feeling was gone. When you came out you were on your own. He came out to get married, he thought he'd have kids, he believed in the family: kids . . . and to see a bit more of his Mum. But he never got married, the kids never came, and Mum had grown old with the years and didn't even want him to live at home. And being in civvy street, you tried to keep up with your mates, but when you saw them it wasn't the same. You were still good to drink with, any way good for a drink, but you just weren't one of the gang. Things had never been the same, somehow, not since then, and it was thirty years gone. Drop a bomb on it all, blow it up. Because now it had got so those yobbos came up to Bill Dutton in the street, ex-Sergeant Bill Dutton, and walked all over him, bloody well pretty near *danced*. And you couldn't be cocky, you didn't feel brave, he mused sadly, when you knew you were quite on your own, in the world, if you liked, and the power and the numbers were all with the other side.

Macbeth, as a matter of fact, wasn't feeling cocky either.
He felt low. He was reading, with much concentration and
scowling, the *News of the Weak*: bent over the page which
so fascinated all of them, Bill Dutton, John X and Jean-
Claude Dupré. Grab and Lou, his henchmen, were waiting, standing by the window half-heartedly practising
arm-locks and chewing gum. Macbeth was first with
everything, always. Whenever the noise from the arm-
locks got too loud, he just turned his head and it instantly
died (although death wasn't usually half so easy: upstairs,
very faintly, the noise of somebody typing.) Macbeth
wasn't reading about Moira, though that was what all
three had dimly intended to do. He started, laboriously,
running his finger down the columns, making sure they
hadn't got his name, which he had on the door of their
room, not very intelligent really, although it looked good,
the way Lou, who was a little bit artistic, had lettered it,
RICOS, his own real name. And he hadn't been very
intelligent, really – (you had to be intelligent, in this
world, be on your guard all the time) – having his bit of
fun with the man from the newspaper, showing him the
skin-flick picture of Moira, just to shake him up: but old
spotty face hadn't dared come back and ask where he got
it from, hadn't dared put it in his paper, either, it seemed.
It was probably too dirty, they can't use beaver shots,
although she was cracked up her beaver, Macbeth felt it
briefly, the pleasure of folding it, squeezing it, the gloss
finish cracking, and grinned. It was all nice and flat when
he found it, tucked in his wallet, the wallet of her blonde
skinny fancy-man from London, who once had the nerve
to smile at Macbeth when they met on the stairs: which
most evidently meant that he wanted to be friendly, so

when he left his jacket, very carelessly, down on a chair in the bathroom, one hot afternoon, Macbeth knew he meant him to have it, and he kept the money, not much, and the photo, which made him grin whitely whenever he passed her on the stairs, with her nose in the air, not knowing that he'd got her bruised pussy folded up in his pocket, and her tits pressed flat against his zip: and the jacket he tore into three and fed to his rat in instalments, good exercise for it, and its sharp little teeth and steel claws ripped Blondey to bits.

But the story wasn't interesting, really, if he wasn't in it, and Macbeth was just wondering whether to hand it over and give some milk to the rat when his pale slit eyes found the next-door story, and stuck. And this story gave him bad feelings, a tide of bad feelings, like wanting to be someone else, or just wanting, or something just *bad* that he didn't want to know about, but he still kept reading, bent over and frowning and sometimes mouthing a word.

It was a story about the American Space Programme. The reporter had gone to Cape Kennedy and interviewed some of those two-bit moon-men, astronauts he called them, fucking astronauts, was it. It was simulated flights they were doing, very clever, to get ready for some smartarse moon shot, some smartarse adventure like staying a month on the moon. And doing these Walk Into Space stunts, a man going out on a lead into space and pissing around on his own. Fucking zombies, weren't they, Macbeth thought (or tried to.) Fucking zombies, letting the fucking government take them for a ride, weren't they, letting the fucking army fuck them around. But he read on eagerly, trying to remember all the details, the times and the distances, the names of the spaceships and the stars. And there was this crappy bit where some creep who'd already been out on a space walk crapped on about the way you were supposed to feel, it was a bit like they said you ought to feel in assembly, the size of the universe and all that stuff, except it made more sense if you were up there, watching the sun going down on earth. Macbeth drank it up. Only three or four years ago Macbeth would have loved to be a spaceman, up there in the blue in a beautiful silver suit, with your friends down there in the darkness, watching on screens, just tripping for hours on space and stars. He could have been a hero: it was too late, now. And his ma, who was always a soak and had got a lot worse since she'd got too old to get boyfriends, would have been looked after, put away safely for him, if he was a hero, because they didn't let anything happen to screw up heroes. They would probably have sent round a police assassination squad for her, very tactful, instead of some shitty social worker who said that now Macbeth was getting older and a very good boy, she could see, she would love to have a little help from him, and *your mother, you know, would be utterly lost without you.* He could have been a hero. It was too late now.

Macbeth had asked the school careers master if Britain had spacemen, went and asked to see him at break, knocked on the door of the staff room. But when the careers master found out what he wanted he lost his temper, and said he was heading for nowhere but the dole queue with his silly bloody jokes, and sent him away (and he was in the dole queue now, so that bit of it had come true. And his ma went spare when he left, was quite lost without him and went in a loony bin, so he'd been told by a friend, and he punched him and shouted he didn't want to know: and yet it was funny, they fixed it, the odds were all on their side, priests and teachers and social workers, you knew it was crap that they talked and you naturally didn't take notice, but then it just came fucking true.) Then he asked the science master, who he quite liked, just asked for the simple fact: did they have a Space Programme, in Britain? And the awful thing was that he guessed why Macbeth was asking him, and was kind, and said No he was afraid that Britain was too poor to have its own Space Programme, and America only used American nationals, so Macbeth was out of luck. So everyone in class got on to the fact that Macbeth wanted to be a spaceman: *wants to be a spaceman, does 'e?* – and he had to stop the titters with a bit of aggro, over the next few weeks, a bit of knuckles and a bit of razor. The razor went into the science master, not very far, just a warning. Catching him by his back door, and the house wasn't half so well-off as Macbeth had expected, round by the dustbins, one pale summer evening too light for stars: not much, just enough to let him feel it, just to show him who it was, just a warning. And the master was so scared and surprised he was shitting himself, saying 'My boy, my boy' in his thin soapy voice like a girl who was just about to cry.

Macbeth went on reading, three years taller and older, bent over his elbow so hard it was rucking up the page, and Grab suddenly grew bold out of boredom and asked him, nervous, you could hear it, but asked him, 'What they say then? Leave an ickle note, did she, 'er royal fucking Majesty? What she say?' Macbeth looked up and fixed him for a good ten seconds with his narrow bright eyes, the irises so pale as to be virtually transparent. '*You*,' he said finally, bending down again over what he was reading, 'are jus' fuckin' *ignorant*.' Which was perfectly true: since the age of eleven at school, Grab had had the official distinction of being a Retarded. It was all right now, because Macbeth thought for him. It was much too late to change anything, for any of them, now.

One floor above there were pink hands rigidly straightening the folds in the paper: not his paper, *her* paper, C. Hans never bought rubbish, the *News of the Weak*.

On the other side of the landing, Frank still dreamed. Amid yellowing piles of paper, of love and money and murder, where nothing but vague hands pulling and insects eating and breeding had happened for years. It was very quiet in the Crescent, everyone said so, especially on Sundays. You *knew* that nothing would happen, North Oxford stretching damply around you, soaking up tension, soaking up passion, soaking up light and sound. Frank smiled like a baby as he held hands with Moira and dreamed, as they flew hand in hand through a melting and blue-flowered heaven.

And one floor above, in the top attic storey tucked under the blue slate roof, there was movement. Someone survived. It might be the black birds merely, dragging and fluttering over the slates? No, it was here inside.

There were two cream doors on the landing, both of them locked. But safe behind one of them, something lived and was moving, furtively, timidly, brushing against the thin walls. It was something very tiny and old, it was a very old woman, or looked as though it used to be a woman, now a doll, stick-thin, dehydrated and varnished: it rustled on the wallpaper, brushing two papery fingers against it: it wanted to come out and go down. It was Clothilde, it was Bill Dutton's old Duchess, whose gold-top pint was still sitting on the doorstep in the cold thin sunshine, alone.

Alone like its owner, for Mrs Evans was already up and had taken her own two in: deep down to her cosy kitchen. Was happy, as usual, to see them, imagining that first lovely cup of milky coffee. It was nice to be up in the sunlight, stand here a second, nice to see the sun on the branches, and the sun coming out like a searchlight from that funny glass-house contraption on top of Gore-Thingummy's house on the corner, almost opposite. Feeling content. She'd had a good sleep, and she'd put on her makeup, and she knew her little kitchen below would be warm and bright: and she still got a funny little thrill from that stain on the pavement, waddling a little way forward on the thin black ice. And she wouldn't change places with anyone, not really, this morning, not even Pelham Thingummy, Harringay, Gore-Harringay, with his sun-roof and his millions, over the way: and she remembered it was Sunday, which just put the finishing touch to it, Mary had so many pleasures, little pleasures really, but no-one could take them away. Since she hadn't got a husband, and she hadn't got a fortune, but just little things like her comforts, and Sunday being her favourite day. And she poured a cup of milk into the saucepan, all ready, and put on her good green coat and went out to the shops for a *News of the Weak* and that cheeky reporter, wasn't he, letting herself get excited about what she would see.

So Clothilde's gold-top pint stood alone on the doorstep waiting. And she had been waiting for nearly two hours to go down, waiting till nobody moved or breathed or whispered against her, in the tall building beneath her, her black painted eyebrows clamped tightly with concentration, her fine veined nostrils aquiver, head cocked, very patient, for artists, as she had explained to inquisitive people so often, need never be bored: or lonely, although she was always alone: she had plenty to do, for two hours had been rubbing in green herbal cream to the brown freckled crags of her hands as she stood a short step from the edge of her world, on the edge of her worn orange carpet, waiting for silence and safety. And sometimes she waited all day to go down, in the long hot summer, not minding the wait for herself but the milk never waited, went solid and sour in the sun: and it fell back down to the ground from the balcony, brave hands tipping it, innocently tipping it, a fierce white fountain streamed out through the blue summer evening, the black birds flying, the white feathers fell to the ground, and the empty bottles shone bright to the sky in the morning, joining the jewel-bright battlement, shielding the queen.

Clothilde lived her life in a state of siege, feeling safer because she was tiny and light (they were used to looking for giants), because she was locked away here at the top of the house, very near to the safe cold sky. She was only frightened of people, of gross, inartistic people, and there were so many (though happily now they were starting to die away.) She timed her swift scurries downstairs to avoid them, fearing their big heavy bodies and curious eyes and their rude loud voices attacking her, saying Hallo and How are you. Those dreadful great leather-cased boys, so many of them, pushing and shouting and fighting down on the landing, or even more frightening, passing her out in the street, very small and erect and defiant, on one of her rare trips out, in a pack, like dogs on the run. And that big one, to frighten her, turned at the very last moment and said in his common voice 'Good day, Maddum,' and then they all laughed and ran on.

And Frank Drake on the floor below, who had once been so friendly. Until she had seen he was laughing, the coarse pink fellow, and later of course she had caught him rooting in bins (and today he had got up late, making horrible sounds in the bathroom, delayed her on purpose, the filthy and fat Frank Drake.)

And Moira, a loud giantess with her boyfriends, so crude and so fleshy, so big and so horribly close. And pretending that *she* was an artist, of all things. Dimpling her fat pale cheeks and smiling dishonestly, when they

131

first met on the landing and Clothilde had distantly, regally, (foolishly!) let herself be introduced, had said 'Je suis artiste:' – 'Oh how *interesting*!' Moira had giggled, showing her big horse teeth, 'How very *nice* to have found that out. You see I am, sort of, a writer, myself: but I do like to think I'm a little bit artistic, as well.' – and she thought Clothilde wouldn't see through it, the way she was lying and boasting and all the while pulling her messy hair over her face and making believe she was modest. Clothilde wasn't fooled (she was wise, she had lived), not even at first, not for more than a moment.

47   Big heavy bodies and curious eyes   I

There were terrible things, things she had started to do to Clothilde once she realized her neighbour despised her, things so terrible no-one believed Clothilde when she told them. Now Moira was gone, and Clothilde felt much safer up here on her own. No great feet would stamp on the landing, no great pale body would sprawl on the balcony, sucking up sun, no pelt of brown animal hair would flick out at her spitefully, passing her on the stairs. Which she did on purpose, listening day and night for Clothilde's slightest movement, and great noisy feet would rush out when she heard the slight click of the lock which she couldn't make silent, not entirely silent, however long and delicately she tried: for Clothilde *was* delicate, and a lady, and her delicacy had to sustain her, the pride of a solitary artist who lived in a zoo (for the noises which came from that attic, quite often, could only be animals breeding):

Clothilde *was* an artist, had been studying all her life to be an artist, studied every day, every single and solitary, delicately darkening, day . . . and the animals shall not, although she is ninety, prevent her.

Since early this morning there had been nothing but doors slyly opening and closing again with a bang, and the feet had gone endlessly hammering up and down, it was hard to tell on what storey. You could never quite tell, and Clothilde wasn't nervous, but sometimes it sounded as if they were almost in her room, it was so hard to tell in the darkness. And she would sit up in bed very straight in the dim yellow glow of her night light, and switch on her wireless with loud French military music, to show she had spirit, to frighten them off. And they couldn't scare her, not really. Big oafs, she was so much superior to them, and prettier, she thought, inspecting herself in her tin-framed mirror, her tiny yellow face lit up by the life of the spirit, but that was the trouble, they envied her – Moira envied her, especially Moira – for being so swift and so light and so slim. And she pulled down her navy blue beret neatly so only a little grey down was showing, you must keep pretty and neat so she always wore it: and cut her grey hair every week very short and fluffy, and washed it with herbs, so it looked like the soft grey down on the ducks she fed in the park (it wasn't surprising they followed, and watched her with terrible envy): and the blue beret floated on top like a boat, like a small child's boat.

And the face underneath it was also curiously pretty and childish, seen from a distance, out in the street, the tiny child's figure in its long blue coat and the face even smaller, a palette of colours, always the same, in brilliant miniature. Thin clever lips, very red, and a bird-beaked fastidious nose, and the eyes in the child-sized yellow-skinned skull rather large and short-sighted, lofty, artistic, dramatically ringed in dark blue and then black. And the

133

rings went crooked where the wrinkles descended in close-up, in close-up the eyes dreamed out under rainbows of painted yellow parchment, dreamed out above dwarf wrinkled apples of bright red crepe, and in close-up the child smiled or spoke and the lips were pulled back to bare teeth of a brave ancient woman, her own teeth, all of them, baring a black and tobacco graveyard of ancient bone: and this graveyard was barred to the child she had been and was still in her dreams, in a blue sailor-suit, in the paradise parks of green Paris, in love with the future which hung in the haze at the end of the long formal walks and which leaped from the sail-covered water, which shone from the deck of each launched toy boat, the divine blue artistic miasma.

Clothilde was that lost child still in her dreams and her tin-framed mirror, and she looked for the child in the mirror each time she went out, with a last soft feather of powder. She slid back the catch and she waited and listened again. Her main fear lived on the floor below hers, C. Hans. Who was not just a beast like the others: C. Hans was a monster. C. Hans had no nose. The first time she hadn't believed it: her feet almost stuck to the stairs, and she never stopped on the stairs, but she stood and stared like a child who was suddenly burdened with ninety years of horror. C. Hans had something, but it wasn't a nose. It was a shapeless addition, a surgeon's addition, a clumsy and formless appendage of matte yellow gristle, with two clean functional holes. And she'd fixed her eyes on the stairtreads, ever since then, whenever a glimpse of striped suit up above her warned it was horror, and him.

She had heard his door close, she was sure it was *his* door this time, now almost an hour ago. And the lock: she was sure she had heard it. So he would be safely locked in, with his horrible yellow secret. Clothilde had come out, very swiftly and quietly and twittering courage to herself like a bird, and she went down the stairs to her milk at a stiff quiet quick near-run.

She was caught. There was Frank in the hall-way, right by the door which stood open, his pink greasy face very big and very bright in the daylight. And just as she stopped with her hand to her thin bird's chest at the turn of the spiral staircase, Frank looked up. Too late to go back, so with chin very high and eyes misty she sailed on down, and he tried in his womanish honking voice which she long ago discovered to be mockery '*Bong*jaw, Madame' – and she long ago told him, quite kindly, when they were still friends, that she was *toujours* a girl, and should therefore be called Mam'selle. So she stared with great ice-and-mist eyes just over his head as she floated on down, great ice-clouds in fierce black rings floating down to freeze him, and then when the fat pink face had come close enough to astonish her (still) with his coarseness and *him*, she thought, with her frail icy beauty, said slowly and thinly, and coldly in accented English 'Good Mor Neeng', to the wall, to the door, to the sky, to her proud lonely milk bottle, white and exclusive and cold: thus leaving him fat and flustered and foul in the hall-way, his dirty old yellowish mackintosh flapping around him, she told herself, bending very briskly on the doorstep and breathing the clean air in.

She stood on the doorstep for a second or two to make sure he was safely gone, puffing pinkly and sadly, she thought, back up to his room. But she had no pity: the artist couldn't afford any pity, for fools like him. She was lovely, but she could be cruel. She screwed up her eyes at the thin grey sun. Before they had quarrelled, Frank used to ask her in: even then she was careful of going so far, although he was most polite on the stairs and had practised his French with that curious honking accent, always forgetting the persons, always forgetting the Mademoiselle. Not realizing what it all meant until later, she thought, and she slitted her eyes still more sharply up at the wide grey reflecting sky which seemed suddenly vast and sea-like and lonely, and scuttled inside like a small grey stranded crab.

48   Big heavy bodies and curious eyes   II

As she trotted upstairs with her eyes sliding over the stairtreads, many of them worn and dangerous, probably part of their plan, she remembered the terrible day when she discovered that Frank was in league with Moira. Up to that day she had spoken to both of them, warmly to Frank and coolly to Moira, and sometimes let dazzling smiles fly down on him, parting her fine red lips (which had always been called her chief beauty), her lips and her strong white teeth (in France, far away, as a child.) Coolly to Moira, who tried (and failed!) to impress by deliberately talking in French and carrying large piles of papers and books when she followed Clothilde downstairs, by receiving a lot of letters and visitors, men, with educated voices (but Clothilde knew just where it led – she had heard them like animals bellowing with laughter, breeding) – and by typing, very loudly and pointedly, all through the night. It was easy to see through that vulgar and spiteful young lady, who meant to upset Clothilde by pretending that she was an artist also, was not just 'a little bit artistic' but *more artistic than her* . . . Pretending she thought of Clothilde as a friend, though she cooked rich horrible-smelling meats on the ring in her next-door bedroom, liver and bacon and other unspeakable things, on purpose because she had spied and discovered Clothilde was a vegetarian, and Clothilde had her pride, she would rather die now than complain, she would not let her see it upset her: this cunning girl hoping the rank red smell of the slaughter would stop her from painting, would make her die, even, so Moira could climb along the balcony, over the milk-bottle ramparts and in through Clothilde's dormer window (she screened it, carefully, each day, with a pinned-up duster, lest Moira grow bold and peep in) – climb in and stare down at Clothilde on her deathbed and steal all her books and her letters, her valuable coloured inks and her gold-nibbed pen. So Clothilde, having seen through all this, was guardedly friendly, her face when she met her not smiling exactly but never expressing disgust, its tiny wise yellowing muscles performing their delicate rituals, making her wonder, flattering her, sometimes, by making a show of confiding small troubles in French, and the troubles were real though the friendship (bitterly) wasn't.

The Troubles. The milkman, who was dishonest, and sometimes stole Clothilde's token, leaving no milk. Mrs Evans, who was impertinent now when she collected the rent (and was always first for the lavatory, leaving Clothilde on the icy staircase, twisting her fingers in agony: this she would die before she confessed.). The filth that she found in the bathroom, old chewing gum, half-cigarettes, and once something dreadful, it must be those terrible boys (it was Moira – the metal feet trotted), a book with strange pictures of women and horses and pigs. These horrors she sometimes hinted to Moira, omitting embarrassing details, in a sibilant whisper, suggesting she might after all be a friend, if a humble friend, of Clothilde's, that if she gave up her pretences she might even one day be allowed to help her. And then the day came. Clothilde never *needed* reassurance, *ça va sans dire*: but she thought she would like to hear a little reassurance, suddenly, thinking of Frank very hard one morning, very, though she was an artist and naturally interested in higher things: very hard indeed, for Clothilde was beginning to realize that Frank was courting her, blatantly, shamelessly, madly – *or was he?* This silly young girl might help with the answer, although she was practically sure. And Moira would be flattered to be talked to, if jealous (Clothilde licked her lips, she had made them especially crimson and gleaming.) She knocked, but instead of asking her in Moira almost burst past her, the same clumsy giant, saying she was just going out. So Clothilde started talking on the landing, very quiet and discreet, about Frank, who meant well, said Clothilde, and was *not* a bad fellow, but she was afraid that he *smelled*, sometimes, rather, and possibly *made things up* (here her eyes narrowed slightly, the black rings squeezing together, hinting the trap was closing on Moira's own similar guilt) – she didn't believe it was true he was writing a book about Jokes, as the poor chap feebly pretended: pretending that he was a writer, in order to further his courtship. Poor Frank: but at least, he *aspired*, which was splendid, if sad, and her eyes squeezed mockingly down on pretentious Moira.

'What courtship?' said Moira, and blushed or pretended to blush. There was a silence: a door swung shut on the floor below, and above it Clothilde's brain swung for a moment, and then went scampering wildly, crab-like, sideways, across blank vistas of anger and loss. 'It's not a *courtship*,' Moira continued, pretending not to notice, 'It's nothing to do with me, this nonsense, you know, it's really not at all my fault. I think Frank is a little bit mad you see really, or somehow *cut off*, you can well understand it. There's nothing between us, except in his mind: nothing's happened. Except that he left me some flowers on the landing one day, they were actually rather pathetic, it's a mean thing to say but I wondered if he'd picked them

off someone's rubbish. And he keeps on asking me to go
and have a drink in his room, it's embarrassing, and saying
he just has to see me because of his book, and he . . .'

49   Higher things

But Clothilde laughed thinly, and then more thinly, and
backed with immense black dignity into her room, not
saying goodbye, and had never emerged from her room,
or would never emerge from her room for Moira. Her
door was now closed, the charade of friendship was over.
The situation was clear, and yet it was complex. Fat Frank
and Moira had long been plotting against her, hoping
together to bring her down to their level, to make her a
figure of fun (and Clothilde would have spat with rage if
she knew of Frank's feeble and painstaking pun in his
birthday present to Moira, a very rich find in a normally
not exceptional bin, I HOPE (*for I love you, but fear I
shall never say it*) THAT YOU WILL NOT THINK ME
A FIG-URE OF FUN (!)) They had doubtless discussed
her together for hours in their fat ugly language, locked up
in the bathroom together, probably, rocking together with
laughter out on the landing below. On the other hand,
Moira alone had wickedly plotted to ruin Frank's growing
love for Clothilde. Clothilde laughed aloud in contempt as
she remembered how Moira betrayed herself out of her
own thick lips – so Frank had left flowers on the
landing – *who shared the landing? For whom, in fact, were
the flowers?*

For Clothilde. And Clothilde had said nothing, backed

with most perfect dignity, always the artist, out of the way. But she started noting it all in her notebook, or most of it, when she remembered, on good days, that is, when her teeth didn't hurt too much in the night, for the bone she had known since a child cried out to her, sometimes, but she didn't stop to listen, she knew she must sleep and survive. And sometimes she sat up quite straight and wrote in her notebook, for literature, surely, was even more martial than music, sat tiny and utterly lonely now Frank was gone and her writing was *not* quite straight in the dim yellow glow of her night light, dyeing her brave yellow skull in the shadows yellower still. She was noting the facts about Moira.

They certainly didn't read well, as item: Clothilde's best books, her two favourites: the titles would not be revealed: they had disappeared one afternoon in the summer, and Moira was later seen laughing, half-naked, triumphant, out on the roof in the sun. Item, some butter she'd left on the window ledge, Normandy butter, the best: a necklace: a beret, her old one, but good: a handbag which had been her mother's, the leather was old but it still had a pretty silk lining, shot silk, turquoise green: and soon after, she noticed that Moira was carelessly painting her eyes to match it: the flowers, of course, which were hers, and there may have been letters also, or other flowers, roses or orchids or lilies and *C., with my love, from Frank.* Item, the garlic. The garlic she needed *at once* for her three-day garlic cure, which she did once a year (and the girl had been clever, had plotted and noted the date), when she ate garlic hourly, had nothing but garlic and herbal tea, it made the blood young and clear. Moira wanted her blood to go rotten, for Moira liked blood, and she liked rank meat. Item, the tray, the enamelled tray with the gay little boat sailing proudly in blue and silver: sailed away. And the tea, the limeflower *tisane* which was good for her chest and smelled citrous

140

and fresh, singing to her when she drank it of blue summer skies over yellow-green lime trees, singing of youth and of home, now mysteriously gone: and she stood on the landing and sniffed it, her lovely green perfume, now blatantly, bitterly, drifting across from the door of Moira's room.

Then after the subtractions, which were hard, there were the additions. Item, two copulating mayflies insolently placed on Clothilde's pillow. A sauce-pan of uneaten food which Clothilde well knew (they would find she could not any longer be fooled) she had cooked several months ago: they had hidden it under her bed, and the thing had gone horribly mouldy. A small piece of glass poked carefully under her door, so it was difficult one morning to open. They hoped she would feel cut off, and hemmed in. But Clothilde had her notes: she had lived long enough to be patient, Clothilde would survive. In the end, she would win, she the artist. The artist would always go on when the animal hadn't the stamina, brutally, painfully, lacking her patience and dignity, died.

Thus Moira. Clothilde poured a tall glass of rich creamy milk for herself with her blue beret bobbing, and her black teeth peacefully smiled. When they'd met on the stairs in the past few days she had hardly seen her, not bothered to blink or avert her proud head: Clothilde had decided, and *she* was the writer, that Moira was dead. (Yet she heard the typewriter boastfully typing, long after she was in bed.)

For the rest of the day after reading the paper, Jean-Claude settled down to think. It was easier now: perhaps he had simply grown bored with weeping and drinking (or possibly she had grown bored with making him weep and drink . . .)

At last he could think about Moira, and not just his feelings for Moira. The first question was, did he really believe that it was suicide? Did she have enough to survive? Or rephrase it, he thought, like the reporter, rephrase it as the police did, doubtless, as big boots marched through her papers, hideous thought: rephrase it, and you got was she happy? – and he'd been too clever to ask. Which was rational when she was living, since who was happy, exactly, and anyway what did it mean? You're not happy, you just go on. But she hadn't gone on. And the question became in her absence both real and important.

Or another one, even more brutally simple. Was she too unhappy to live? Because of course she was often unhappy, though he was mad to say so to Les. About the death of her parents, the thought of their loved lined bodies in boxes, so far away: a dwarf in the street, little man with a blood-pudding flush to his face and two huge spotted dogs on tight leads, they might whip round and eat him: the birds on the roof: or her terrible fear of the dark, round the door of her dreams, the pink messed face of C. Hans. Or things which were distant and general, now nearer, the movements of great blue glaciers, wearing men down, or violence which came from the skies (now nearer, nearer, the pattering metal insisted.) She thought a lot about dying, not distant or general now.

She was suddenly there in the room before him, grinning. The catalogue left her like him, and the rest of the living. And that in itself was a lie, leaving out as it did most of what he so loved, all the vital, ecstatic, ridiculous, easily-pleased parts of Mo, which she didn't so obviously share with the rest of the living: yet *they* went on. And she would have done the same, he knew it with total confidence, suddenly, seeing her smiling, now. She would have been there: she was here. Fearing the end till the end more than most, eluding it nimbly, growing older and dressing up younger, painting and dieting, writing more desperately always to get it all written in time, doing yoga and losing her temper, drinking too much and eating too little, losing young lovers and finding old lovers and each time a little less resilient, only a little less, still bouncing back. And through all this always his friend, she had promised, her white wrinkled hand was on his and the promise outlived her at last, and his faith filtered back into individual compacts, individual kindnesses, individual offers of love, and his favourite record repeated.

The black mud shifted: the black rings spun. It was just mad chance which had sent her sprawling to horror: he wasn't abandoned, he wasn't unloved. And he saw her clearly before him, aged ninety, in wonderful thick blue furs (yet the cold metal feet said the opposite, equally clearly: she hadn't expected that life or that peace would go on.)

But he walked round the flat, inspecting this bright new version, and found it from most angles solid enough, and beautifully painted. Blue mink, she would choose, with her hair dragged back and dyed silver, the elegant bones of her skull wearing through. She would walk with a silver-topped cane at his side (she was laughing) and tell him of ancient and scandalous letters which he would receive in her will (he was laughing as well.)

In the glow of his bright new confidence, transmuting, he found, to a sense of virtue, a resonant will to be good, to be good *for ever*, he sat down to write to another one of the living. An abject letter to John, explaining his wild accusations as so many drops of water and whisky, saying how sorry he was and how sorry they'd never got on. 'Just whisky and grief', he wrote candidly, winningly, letting the pleasant thought strike him, time for a drink.

The thing would have given Mo so much pleasure, he thought as the drink slipped gracefully down. She like him loved formal treaties and declarations, loved human beings to make overt and elegant movements of advance and retreat (but between the thoughts now there returned the ungraceful image, a white body slipping and dizzily falling) – it would have pleased her so, with her fear of being swallowed up in history, that two men who loved her should shore up her loss with a sacred compact between them, a high cairn raised over love.

Jean-Claude felt exalted, briefly, as he sealed the envelope, gracefully sealing the tomb, ignoring the clumsy intrusion of death and of dizzy blank falling, concentrating vision (amber-filtered with whisky) on the image of the black-clad knights, clasping hands. He had always in any case thought John rather attractive, so hard-looking and lean. He sat on, with his whisky, sur-viving, old and benign.

What he failed to take into account, of course, in constructing his chivalric tableau, – what the whisky, which knew so much, didn't know – was the effect of exposure on the (attractive) human form. He could not be aware of how coldly and carefully Moira was shaping her own alternative image, up in her dark attic room: and had sent John walking out numbly through the white park, now running, running to meet and blend with her cold white dream. Jean-Claude didn't know she was making a snagged cross of blood for John's forehead, his blonde hair a helmet of ice, that the snow would soon whitely, respectfully kiss his hem. He sat on: it grew later and later: John ran, growing colder and colder: Moira wrote on.

52   A high cairn raised over love

That night Jean-Claude lay straight and peacefully in his bed, his beautiful face lit up from one side by the street lamp level with the window, the shadows etched in like the stain of centuries past. Lay like a crusader who had vanquished the infidel, lay like St George who had silenced the snarling dragons, lay like a knight in his tranquil tomb. He listened to the wind which was sighing through the branches, regular and low. Feeling tired, so tired that sleep was a rare firm promise, his whole body slowly and calmly leaning towards it, calmly and slowly letting go. If dying could be like this, he thought easily, just a slow graceful dissolving, limb after limb . . .

Then he suddenly stiffened, recalling. Something unpleasant still lurked at the back of his pillow. A phantom, a phantom in black, in black leather, laughing: Macbeth. Not a phantom, even, but something more real. Something with muscles and sinews and gleaming flared nostrils, something immensely strong. A monster, smiling and snarling and baring his teeth, a dragon not yet laid low. And the memories bled back, intermixing with quarrels with Mo.

For he felt that he'd asked for the fall he had taken, down in the Crescent garden. A quarrel with Mo, one of many, some time last spring, on the same old topic: and the bitterness still dragged after it, uselessly, even now. He wanted her to marry him (putting it casually, always, carefully casually, it really didn't matter to him.) Dismissing the sexual omission as unimportant. She could be happy with him (meaning she could protect him, by letting him be her protector.) But she said he was wrong, unhappily, doggedly, staring down out of his window, both of them watching the thin young leaves on the trees and a child's kite staggering upwards on the spring gusts of wind. It wasn't sex that mattered, she said, but risk and involvement and need. In some ways their friendship was atrophied: too much flattery, too many cushions (unfortunate metaphor, that, in a flat piled thick with oyster silk cushions.) No sense of violence.

'Ah yes,' he cried, defensive and mocking, before she could finish, 'I know what you mean, those strong dark passions, the life force, good old Lawrence. Well no, it's quite true I should never *wish* to give that. For me, quite frankly, sex isn't important. I get it, it's good, and – that's that. Your cosmic forces of violence – they don't and they can't touch me.' But she wouldn't agree, and as ever events proved her right (for she fixed the odds, sitting up in her high attic typing). And down in the garden, a long way below them, a long way below the brave little kite with its wildly waving pink tail flying upwards and out of the picture, out of the hopeful frame (oh how *cheery*, Miss Poynes thought, gladly and gaily observing it, out on her step in a cherry-flowered dress for the very first time that year) – a long way below and in shadow, a dark boy waited to touch him, his long oiled hair merging in with the bark of a tree.

53 'Sex isn't important'   I

The gentle decline towards sleep was arrested: below on the pavement, disrupting the sigh of the branches, a dog was suddenly howling, wretchedly, howling of darkness and cold, not far away. He pressed his lids closed but behind them the boy loomed up blackly to face him, the flash of one earring, not with his henchmen, alone. He was tall and his hips moved like oil, his buttocks rippling with muscle, tight and high. In the sun, he wore a tight black vest with a white satin appliqué skull, so tight that it moved with the swell of his chest, so tight that it could have been sprayed on. And his arms, hanging loose with their cords of muscle at the ready, the black studded watchstrap threatening above the wristbone, the broad brutal hands with their big silver functional rings which flashed from the knuckles as he ran, one with a blind red stone.

And with Grab and Lou he always moved at a loping run. Seeing them coming, Jean-Claude would get off the pavement, walk on languidly, his eyes fixed hard on some neutral point ten yards ahead . . . mustn't look at them.

them. In the end though, when the light feet and the faint swish of leather were almost level with him, he had to, had to, throwing a quick hungry look at the face in motion, the full scarred lips slightly parted, the sun glinting off his white teeth, unnaturally pointed, the fiercely dilated nostrils, low forehead and terrifying glass-pale eyes which would catch him staring and beauty would call at the very last minute from the side of the mouth near the earring, *Hi Fairy* or *Hi Pretty Boy*. In those two years since Jean-Claude first noticed him they had never spoken. There were just images, snapshots, frozen, darkening . . .

Sun on black leather, a long flexed muscular thigh. Then once on a motorbike, loud and triumphant, a wonderful centaur-like creature, savagely real and yet dreamed, greased mane and bright leather and steel. For a second the slit eyes cut him, severed the nerves of his stomach with their slivers of hard light glass.

But the times that he saw him in pubs were the most important. Only twice, and on neither occasion was he drinking. He was on his own, and he was playing the fruit machine, both times glimpsed from behind, the skull, the long athlete's legs in studded denim, the high tight balance of his bum and the greased hair waving to his shoulders: it had to be him. But it wasn't the simple physical beauty which made Jean-Claude stiffen and stare and much later, in the quiet of his room, grow big: it was the pub in question, which was a recognized gay pick-up spot, the most famous in town. Each time, when he turned back from ordering his drink, the fruit machine stood there stupidly, the boy was gone.

Then finally something had happened, down there in the garden. It was late August, a warm summer evening, and he had decided to go for a walk. The Crescent was utterly peaceful, the air smelled of flowers and cut grass, the birds (and somewhere a gentle piano) still sang in the gathering dark. He breathed in deeply, crouched in the leaf-mould under the trees for a moment to savour the sense of being a *creature* here for a moment, being alive and alone: feeling the joy of his young crouched body, his eyes and his ears and his nose. Rocking back on his heels he stared up through the leaves at the sky. Between the branches isolated stars were coming, and that was a plane with its red light winking a signal, carrying tiny human beings bravely across the cloudless and bridgeless and netless, nothing to save them, sky: so far away. Planes were birds, to Jean-Claude, and all human flight was a poem: to climb so high . . . he could never feel Moira's vast fears, of how death would come from the sky . . .

Someone told him the end of the summer was the best time for shooting stars. He didn't think he'd ever seen one, or that if he did see one he'd know. And then suddenly saw one, a faint far brilliant explosion at the corner of his eye and the edge of the universe, surely, dazzlingly far, shooting and dying before he could turn his head and make sure. It was almost completely dark now and behind the trees he could see the lights of the Crescent cheerfully burning. He found a patch of grass just out of the trees which was springy and turfy, and lay down flat on his back, deciding to stay there and watch for an hour or so.

Another plane. And that high humming ache going with it which always moved him, suggesting vast distances and the pain of crossing them, suggesting the infinite numbers of stars and faces and fates he would never know. Strange bodies above in the aeroplane, each one perfect and complex, suspended in a shadowy network of fears and dreams, each one with a detailed and difficult journey in the thirty or forty years to go: the end of which he knew nothing. The grace of the arc was enough. Or again, if that busy light suddenly now as he watched it staggered and plunged, spinning through miles and miles of regret and black screaming panic, so many, to the dead black earth below, he would read their names in the paper perhaps, and some photographs, maybe, blurred, taken many safe years ago . . . he could never hope to know. Yet they swam through the sky across his life as he lay there, drawing his eyes and his sharp luxurious longing with them, and then they were gone.

He watched another star flash, and compared to the plane it seemed bare of significance, now. Then another, a glory and instantly gone. He was definitely cold, and his arms were getting bitten through his shirt. He sat up and looked at the lines of bright glowing windows through the trees, promising civilized friendship, the comfort of scale and immediate order restored. He got up and shook himself, kicked through the grass to the gate, going carefully, picking off leaves and feeling the way: it was pitch dark under the trees and hanging twigs reached down and scratched him. He ought to be close to the gate. He could see the street lamp shining brightly through the netting, very close now, and he reached out his hand to the netting, glad to be back in the light.

But a hand reached out and touched him, nonsense, it must be a tree: and he turned and saw in the golden light from the road the long oiled waves of the boy. Jean-Claude made a silly little sound between a scream and a gasp. Macbeth held his arm, not tightly, he just had no strength to get away: couldn't really believe this was happening, didn't even know that he wanted to get away, for even in his frozen panic, the stars and the quiet and the black-leaved sky made it like his wet dreams of Macbeth which were always curiously idyllic, waking him high on a wave of spoiled bliss which would slowly, sadly subside and the sea of the dream would be lost. Only now he was here, in the garden, beside him. Macbeth spoke first (as he always spoke first, as he did in the street that morning, the broken body behind him: as he would on that very last night, the very last time he would see him. Macbeth would speak first, and move first, and would have him.)

Macbeth spoke first. 'You wan' somethin'', he said, not asking but stating, and his hand moved down to the wrist. Jean-Claude thought he would twist it or snap it, briskly. He stumbled, oh stumbled again, with a tongue like tinned meat in a sandwich said 'No, I'm just walking . . .' then realized, knife-thrust of bliss, that Macbeth would not snap it. The boy held it, lightly but firmly, his fingertips, yes – a caress. And he guided the hand he was holding down to the front of his trousers, quite gently, then pressed it against him as soon as it touched, as it touched, as Jean-Claude could not quite believe he was touching, the edge of a great hard bulge . . . They went into the middle of the garden, where it was darker, where there were only stars. They took off their trousers, the process as foolish as ever with its clumsy stepping and the erections coming out of their bandages: and then not foolish, Jean-Claude couldn't think it was foolish, seeing the pale swollen shaft sticking up at the sky.

There were stars, still stars and even one shooting, as Macbeth lay down with a fluid motion and pulled his legs back and apart so his knees were framing his strange cruel head. In the waxy light of the stars, with his jacket on still and his legs oddly naked, he looked like some savage and complicated idol, the parts re-disposed in a formal and rhythmic ritual, something repetitive, savagely real and yet dreamed . . . then that image vanished also and other rituals began. And the rhythm, after the rituals, was simpler, now, going home, it was coming, was coming, was his, he was in him, fucking him, killing him, making him scream, they would *come*, he was *coming*, oh *come* . . . oh darling: and the fucked boy screamed like a dog and his warm sperm splattered Jean-Claude's thin shirt and under his chin. For a second he rested, his mouth hard against the black jacket, breathing the smell of the powerful animal in, exhausted, still in him, oh darling: but when he raised his head Macbeth's face was possessed and impassive, metallic with sweat and the slit eyes looked through him, past him, cut a pale path to the stars.

56 'I get it, it's good, and – that's that'

Then finish. The big rings dug into his neck and his head was flung backwards. 'Gerroff!' growled Macbeth, and his voice was straining and furred with anger, 'Ger-*roff*!' Jean-Claude pulled out, feeling stupid and vulnerable, suddenly, in his half-undress and his limp cock's pathetic retraction. Feeling frightened, suddenly, groping for his trousers, bending down. Macbeth leaped on him from behind, his arm going under Jean-Claude's jawbone and forcing it viciously back. At the crotch their limp flesh still touched. Macbeth hissed 'Look whar I've got, Johnny.' The expected, somehow expected terror, the end of the dream: the long cold flash of a knife, very long, very thin, very near him, waving, very near his vulnerable lips and eyelids and nose, and his mind flashed to Hans, C. Hans and his vile white pretence of a nose: and he kept very still and his breath came shallowly, waiting, waiting to be cut, for the edge to go in on a great jagged wave of white pain.

The voice, with its muscle of hatred, was a relief. 'You gonna gimme' yuh money, Johnny.' 'Yes – oh yes. Only – *please* don't put it so close.' Jean-Claude tried to speak without moving his lips: the point was an inch away from them: it would go plunging suddenly in, breaking his teeth and tearing his tongue. '*Please* don', *please* don',' the boy crooned, mocking him, moving the point very gently to Jean-Claude's chin and then along the line of the jawbone, just touching, his lips, very cold, just touching, his nostrils, very very delicately just inside, then the worst horror, tickling his eyebrows and down round the socket of bone so he suddenly, vividly thought of the two gaping holes in the painted skull on the jacket, just sketching them in. Then it was over. The pressure on his jaw was released and the knife moved away just in time to avoid his reaction, his head slumping forward. Macbeth moved round, more animally horrifying now he could clearly be seen with the contrast between knife and leather above and bare legs and pendulous cock below, yet another variety of mythical monster, an ancient and terrible story repeating, the nightmare lesson repeating, savagely real and yet dreamed: and a girl in an attic up under the stars was savaged by dreams, dreamed on.

But 'O.K. Johnny,' he said, very flat, very mean, not a demon, a brutish and criminal boy with his cock hanging down, and Jean-Claude crouched down with his trousers round his ankles and felt for the wallet, feeling only the beat of his frightened heart as his ribcage pressed his bare thighs, then Thank God, the wallet, thank God, it was fat, yes there must be yesterday's twenty-five pounds in it. He looked up. Macbeth had his clothes on now and the knife was back in his hand, held at crotch level, obscenely pointing up. The faint light snaked in the curls of his hair and glanced off his rings as he took it, the blind red flash from his finger, checked for the contents, took it. 'You hadda goo' time,' he said, very softly, and laughed, very softly, a murderous laugh, and kicked Jean-Claude hard in the stomach, doubling him up with winded agony, head down hard in the grasses coughing and choking for breath, and in the middle of it was a regular pattern of rustles and cracks growing fainter, going away. The gate swung, and then metal-tipped shoes on the pavement, walking, not running, away and the pain and the panic, a miracle, ebbing away. Jean-Claude stayed where he was till he was certain, his arms curled round his bruised stomach, shivering, shivering. When he finally made to stand up his trousers tripped him, and he lay sprawled down the bank with his fingers clutching at leaves, being violently, lengthily sick. Looking up at last he confronted the same fixed stars.

Now safe in his still warm bed he allowed his clenched lids to open, the horror lived through yet again and now done. But the horror might not be done. There was Moira's death, which changed everything (and Macbeth had been there on the pavement to make the connection), leaving a warning, an aching gap: that she meant what she said when she talked of a permanent sense of threat, of trapdoors to violent death in the regular surface of the pavement. And she didn't even know about Macbeth, or at least he never told her. Didn't dare tell her, afraid of her terror . . . for him it was just an anomaly, somebody breaking a bottle of ink and the ink falling random and black on the smooth bright patterns of life which were pledged to go on. And then after it happened, the patterns reformed and everyday comforting habit blotted it quietly up.

But she asked him, desperately – trying to wake him, trying to warn him, *her friend*: and again now up in the attic typing, trying to keep him alive and warm – didn't he notice how all the characters kept dying off, how before death there were complicated disasters: how long people worked and how hard yet their long-planned holidays ended in Naples, and the courier at the hotel (which was not the same as the snap in the brochure, surely, though no-one remembers) had a glass eye, the wrong colour, and knew too much about Clara: how all the package tours had the same end on their tickets, whatever distractions they offered from nagging quotidian pain like doorsteps to fall off and baths to drown in, distractions like tulip fields, vineyards, alps not to fall off and seas not to drown in, white dreaming beaches and brown naked bodies stretched peacefully wide: much more distracting, the hard-working coach-driver's fingerstalls, not to be looked at, the hours of driving too long, the nagging quotidian pain in his ten black stumps (which no-one remembers) finally sending the solid black wheels sky-crazy, and last stop is white naked bodies (which no-one in workaday England remembers) stretched wide over hoardings of vineyards or tulip-fields, carefully enlarged from the brochure, rotting or burning, a foul blue wind blowing down from the alp to the desolate beaches, the coach on its back like a bug, one wheel still turning, the tickets blown free of the flames and the names of the owners are black but the end of the tour reads clearly, DYING IN OTHER WORDS, ALL TOUR MEMBERS . . . And over this death looms another: the death which might come quite voicelessly, senselessly, steel death come from the sky, and nobody asked for their tickets or read them, DYING WITH *NO* WORDS, *NO-ONE* REMEMBERS . . .

All this dismissable, mania, Moira, there were experts, treaties, laws which would stop things happening, bad things, things out of turn . . . Yet her solitary death changed everything, carried him into her world. It couldn't be his world, a regular world where very little chanced to go wrong any more. This was Mo's world of cholera germs in the stripes of the ice-cream and poisoned beaches and towers not leaning but falling, cracking the lens of the camera, and Mo's thin body crashing to wreck through black air was the first broad hint of the end of the tour, on the stone something pale and broken and too much, much too much, blood.

Leaving a warning, an aching gap and a stain on the pavement, a warning. It was starting, the blood had begun. And Macbeth emerged blackly from under the pillow, looking for someone, for him. Jean-Claude turned his face from the wall with a tired tossing motion, trying to toss off the fragments of vague fears and threats and precise white splinters of bone, they said she had broken her spine, what does it matter what else if her skull was broken? – . . . precise white splinters of light on a lifted blade.

58 'They don't and they can't touch me'

He was there, Macbeth with his knife, looking black and enormous against the street lamp. Jean-Claude gasped a terror-struck breath before he saw it was only the curtain, pulled in a swathe skew-whiff across the centre of the long window, and the breath leaked slowly away as he shivered with shock. He was hopelessly awake now, every limb restless, his head aching. He thought he would like hot chocolate, but there was no milk. Five minutes' walk from the Crescent there was a milk machine. A cold boring walk, but then a hot bath and hot chocolate. Sensation, action, anything but lying in the dark with his thoughts. Mo's nightmares dissolved with the light on. You only had to try and keep the light on. Life wasn't so bad (it was dying, in other words, somebody said.) There were the visible comforts of his room, soft light on the oyster-coloured silk, his feet on the soft thick pile of the carpet, the cool silky stuff of his shirt slipping over his skin. He looked round before leaving. Light gleamed on the tassels of shades, on the spines of his packed walls of books and the edges of frames. Life was there, rich and factual and pleasant, and he was secure.

As the front door clicked behind him, the streetlights started to die in a communal flickering spasm. It must be exactly midnight. The night seemed very much colder and wilder when they had gone, and somewhere the wretched thin howl of the dog had started again (for she tried: she did try, in all conscience, to warn him: *dying, in other words, dying,* each warning and hair of the miserable dog is numbered, but no-one remembers.) Clouds covered the stars.

He was cold (since he would not be frightened) and started to run past the garden towards the main road, where the traffic still rumbled and big neon lights were still on. He was sure they stayed on all night as the giant container lorries thundered up and down, propping up tired little men in their cabs who were bloodshot and weary, half-dozing and dreaming of flying with out-stretched arms and of home, and he saw in his mind's eye one of them heavily, sickeningly overturn and the tired little body was squashed in its tin and one wheel, very black on the neon, continued to spin.

On the main road the lights shone all night but Jean-Claude never reached them. He was found in the morning at the back of the Public Lavatories, dead on his back with his keys and his coins beside him, normal and bright in the sun. A neat six-inch slit had divided his throat from his chin and a great beard of blood poured through it. The doctor found evidence of anal rape, described by the coroner politely as 'a certain deviant sexual act' for he took the view that such things were a small black part of the picture, and best swept under the mat. Fortunately, as in hanging, evidence of orgasm was not taken to imply consent.

Macbeth hadn't taken his keys or his money. The flat, with its elegant oyster-coloured fittings, its books, its engravings in grey metal frames, had no interest for him. He had killed what owned it, what had dared to have *him*, the sneer and the lah-di-dah voice and the buttocks dancing and taunting him, spread them and viciously had them, holding him down like a dog.

158

He had killed the bad luck of his name. When he was thirteen and a cocky and only half-criminal virgin, a rich man began it, paid him ten pounds for the first tight pleasure, liked it so much that he did it again and again: and he said he was perfect, a real little wrong 'un (yet five of those first pounds went to his mother, trickled away on gin) and called him Macheath, playing Brecht very loudly as his hot stiff cock went in, again and again . . . and Macbeth, who was then plain Ricos, got to like it, secretly, hatefully, never lost the habit, and heard the name as mac*beth*, it was a good black name, it was the name of a play that the top stream were reading at school (Macbeth read only accounts of slow Nazi atrocities, very very slowly, locked in a fat red book in the library), the name of the hero, he could have been a hot stiff hero, briefly, then. But the man got bored and some dumb kid told him the king got killed and it wasn't so easy to get it, in secret, again . . . and it puzzled and hurt him, somewhere, although that dumb kid must be wrong, the thought that the hero of something would not be protected (shot in the back, he expected, by some fucking policeman or sneak, as he rode away . . .)

They had ridden like dog and dog, and he made him die like a dog, made him howl with terror and crawl through the bushes, begging to be let go: and the blood from the neat quick cut in the end went everywhere, soaking his fine silk shirt.

And Macbeth wiped the blade on the grass and was gone like a wolf through the bushes, clutching his weapon and ready to run for ever if necessary, ready to run like a wolf through the night of the world for ever. Cut off by his wolfish birth from the white metal path to the stars he had only the wild dark side of the world to run through, his blade and the points of his teeth flashing sometimes out of the night as a warning, like lost stars shooting, flying and falling, burning the earth and themselves wherever they fell.

(And Pet wept, when he never came back: she had practised a lot, with her finger, and gone to her lady doctor, who refused to give her the pill.)

59   As ever, events proved her right

Lou and Grab were removed the next day by an army of policemen, Brigadier Brown and General Jones. They were found sitting utterly blankly in their room on the first floor of Number Fourteen, divided by only a few sparse inches of brick and lustrous inches of oyster silk hangings from Jean-Claude's luxurious flat. The room was filthy, as Mrs Evans had always been much too frightened to enter. Their furniture was orange boxes, and three sleeping bags. A glittering sea of empty bottles spread out from one corner of the room: in another, a tottering pile of papers and comics, also two books which turned out on inspection to be porn, hard porn, one mostly girls and pigs and stolen by Grab from the bathroom, the other the tale of the Beast and the Teenage Virgin, a photo-essay co-starring a frail and pretty blonde who didn't seem to need much urging – the latter impounded by Jones (who was rumoured, unfairly, surely, to fancy the kid in the paper shop) for ruthless in-depth analysis, later, at home.

On the window sill was a rat in a cage, Macbeth's rat, not fed this morning and frightened and savage with hunger: crouched in a litter of something which looked like a shredded jacket, eyes burning out like stars, red stars, or the lights of a small red plane, someone lost, someone dead, a few hairs from a light blonde head, a few bodies flying and falling, and Brown said 'Here we go again' as he read what someone had scrawled on the base of the cage, 'Evil rats on no star live and Macbeth couldn't live there either'. It had to be *her* . . . and yet she was supposed to be dead and these other deaths just to come tumbling illegally after.

Between the patches of damp on the walls there were life-size pictures of nudes stuck up with yellowing sellotape, corners curling: and a newspaper picture of the girl, old-fashioned and coy with a cheesecake smile and her blouse knotted so-called casually, anything but casually, under her bra. But the coyness was countered by somebody's pen, which had scrawled in a long pubic beard of blood in flamboyant red biro, and a crudely accurate penis cutting through. *Fuck Moira.* On the floor was a mixed scurf of chewing gum, burnt-out matches, cigarette butts, hairs, many of them oily and curiously waved as Mrs Evans was to find when she finally got in there with her dust-pan, two of them long and blonde with a teenage ghost attached which she didn't even notice, moping and weeping, old condoms, labels off thousands of tins of baked beans, and a few baked beans, or they might be baked beans, gone mouldy. 'They live off beans, these kids, it don't do them no good,' she thought sadly. After all they had only been boys. By the time that she swept up the beans, Grab and Lou were dead.

They were both outraged when asked if Macbeth had been homosexual (somewhere like a wolf, running.) 'Caw snot,' said Grab, '*Caw snot*! 'E was always screwing birds. Ooever 'e wanted, 'e got. 'E 'ated fairies like poison, did Macbeth.' And Lou, who was chewing a last bit of gum and of comfort pulled from a rather dusty part of his pocket and stopping every so often to spit, said ''E *couldn'* 'ave been, we wos almos' always wiv 'im. We used to shag birds togever, too, all free of us. Macbeth always used to go firs', 'cos 'e was boss.' Without a boss, Grab and Lou

161

were lost. He had made them part of a unit of three, a black spearhead, swift and invincible, fearsome in flight, now fallen. The point had snapped off. They felt useless, punctured, winded, unloved. Their godhead was gone, and big feet stamped about them in boots saying *Show some respect when you're talking to just for example Brown* and Brown said the same for Jones: and whatever the scared boys said was recorded, and blinding lights shone (somewhere utterly else, under cover of starless darkness, Macbeth still moved at a loping run.)

And they killed the rat on the first afternoon, two men in big boots with white coats on, Herr Doktor Jones and Herr Doktor Brown, though it managed to savage a finger, the sharp white teeth going in at the base of the moon on the nail and its jaws snapped shut on the surgical white of the bone (Macbeth on the run, with his sharp teeth smiling.) But it took four weeks for the boys to finally hang, by their belts, in their cells, from the torture of too many questions and no leader. And boots of all ranks were sorry, and took for a time to savagely kicking each other (Macbeth, not smiling, surviving, still ran for the moon.)

60 Surviving I

In her attic, Clothilde grew gayer as the tall house emptied. She had pinned Mrs Evans to the railings one cold brilliant day and extracted the story, or some of the story, for poor Mrs Evans, who was afraid of the fierce little woman with her long black teeth and her frothy foreign pronunciation at the best of times, had been left by recent events in such a state of ginger wine and vibrations that her story lacked everything but an end, which was that nearly everyone was dead and gone. At this rate, she felt, *she* wouldn't last long, nor want to, with the back of her high blonde bun pushed uncomfortably back against a spike of the railings in a desperate attempt to avoid the bright jets of saliva which Clothilde turned on, aiming carefully upwards at the coarse pink face in the sun. The old English woman was fat and stupid, and understood nothing.

Clothilde despised her for making her shout and crane upwards, hurting her throat and her eyes in this vicious and dazzling English winter morning. She despised her dyed puff of blonde hair like a horrible yellow meringue. She despised her for cleaning the house and not cleaning the house, she despised her for smelling of drink – at this hour in the morning! – and for living down under the ground, she despised most of all those white regular teeth, clicking plastic, so clearly false and this creature could only be sixty. Clothilde was the only person who knew she herself was ninety. And all those young ones were dying! She drove herself fast up the stairs, past the empty rooms, through the deep empty stair-well which echoed with somebody typing, echoing louder and louder as more of the rooms were empty – but she never heard it: cackling with shrill cracked joy as her kettle was boiling, surviving, surviving, surviving, leaving the boots and the black metal feet and the heavy black birds far behind.

Mary Evans, the distance of Moira's fall away, wasn't happy. She sat in the kitchen by the fire with her feet in a bowl of hot water, trying to set her hair to rights by the wobbly reflection in the glass which covered her favourite snap of her husband, hanging debonairly on the chimney breast at the age of thirty-two, which was what he was when he died, with a thick head of wavy brown hair and a centre parting. Mrs Evans pulled weakly at her own thin back-combed scalp and thought how long poor Harold had been waiting. I really loved you, Harold, she told him, stirring the soap about in the water with her chilblained foot and watching the clouds uncurling, feeling sad and sentimental and old. No world for the old, this violent and horrible world. But then Harold had been so young, well almost as young as some of these young ones, gone far too early, you couldn't deny it, without a line on his forehead, gone under a lorry of lavatory pans of all things, tripped over the lead of some passerby's poodle and rolled straight under it, didn't have a chance. Which left Mary, and though everybody was kind to her face she had a good idea that behind her back they were splitting their sides – lavatory pans! But it didn't make death any different, she reflected, however it happened, it was still serious, it still took people away. She looked down at the slack blue veins on her calf, and her thickened ankles. She felt no use, that was it.

If she'd had Harold's baby it might have been different. So long ago. Your kids had to listen to you, anyway. After the first excitement over what happened to Moira she found no-one wanted to hear what she had to say. The boots of the police and the deaths and the typing up in the attic went on regardless, the journalists wrote what they felt like writing, you understood less of it all every day. And with all this tragedy, life for a woman on her own was frightening. The ginger wine and the telly couldn't quite keep the horrors at bay. Why take all the young ones, since she was so useless, wasn't it time for *her* to be taken away? Behind the glass, in the faded sunlight of twenty lost years, Harold seemed to be smiling, saying *Come on Mary, I've waited.* Yes, take her away. But it wasn't like that, thought Mary, all sunlight and clouds descending to take you away. You had to go one way or another, and none of them was easy. After all no one, she told Harold

164

firmly, would have wanted to go *your* way. And then poor Moira. She shuddered. She'd never understood how anyone could bear to live up so high.

She stood up on her painful feet stiffly and reached out very very carefully for the green bottle just beyond her fingers on the flowered tablecloth, *still* just beyond, and she shifted her foot very slightly and very nearly slipped on the soap, very nearly, and her heavy slack body would have gone headlong and her forehead struck hard on the edge of the glass-topped table, probably hard enough to do it, and the unlined face behind glass with the sun slicking down his centre parting was just for a moment laughing. With spite, not with joy at the end of his wait, for he'd never much liked her, to tell the truth, and the poodle had belonged to his pretty little ballet-teacher mistress, with feathery eyebrows and little boy's hips, who had mourned him sincerely and married another within the week, which was explained by her dying in childbirth seven months later with the head of Harold's son pushing out too early and brutally hard from her small cervix. So Harold had not for the past twenty years been entirely sad or alone, which Mary for the most part had, but she still struggled gamely to regain her balance and made it, triumphantly clutching her bottle, dropped heavily back into her chair with the warm ginger smell in her nostrils: and she whispered to Harold, with a last vague pull at her hair, that things could be worse a lot of the time and after all *she* didn't know what things were like up there. So if he didn't mind waiting, she'd thank him not to take what she'd said too seriously, at any rate he needn't try and hurry things up for her. The wine in her throat was lovely, as strong as fire. She thought about lunch. There was the steak and kidney: and she'd pop out and fetch some nice cream to go on the rest of the tin of pears. And she'd call in on Emma for a chat on the way and ask if she'd help with her perm.

Don't worry, Harold, said somebody up in the attic, presumptuously, up in the clear cold sky, she won't be coming to join you up there or down in that vast double grave for a very long time, two decades exactly come six o'clock tomorrow. Arthritis and disease of the arteries are nicely on their way, coming nicely. But these heavy babies will go till she drops, full term. And her spine will be so doubled up that at least she will not have far to fall to the pavement, not fall in the dark with a long icy way to scream . . . Harold's wife, unlike Harold and the poodle, will be taking a short road home.

61 Surviving II

Clara spent hours on Felicity's letter. Ash covered the pale pink paper, and the phrases she was trying to find coiled stupidly round in the coils of smoke. When she had finished and eased her stiff spine and picked up her compact, her white powdered face was transfigured with pearls of sweat. She re-read it and then re-read it again and then in a panic before she could change her mind she folded it and stuck it hard down, leaving her usual broad finger-marks, reddish this time, the inkiness tinged with lipstick. She had never found it easy to keep herself clean, though she worked at it gallantly, as she did at everything, wiping and straightening, combing and powdering, refusing to accept her appearance lying down. Clara loved to be active. The letter to Fee was a brain-wave, the first bit of hope in the last few days: at least to do *something* for *someone*. She glowed, she believed, as she looked at that fat inky package, in kindness and love. She felt strong. She felt strong enough for a bath, the first one for far too long, and she flung off the quilt she had round her and marched in her bulging unsoldierly body to run it.

But the hot tap trickled unwillingly, the cold tap dripped and whispered, couldn't be stopped. Watching the weak threads falling, the question returned – what was there left? What was there left to be done? All that was left of Mo was her writing, and Clara had never felt easy with that. There was Jean-Claude, she supposed, but she didn't see him accepting her comfort (the body lay closed and cold in the morgue, though poor Clara wasn't to know that.) He made her feel clumsy and overenthusiastic, too fat: and she saw her big gestures reflected in his pupils, saw them grow instantly actressy and unreal, regretted that her nails were (suddenly) filthy and that she was wearing this (suddenly) foolish hat.

And she knew she had understood Moira as *he* never could have: from the depths of Clara's own hopeless chaos, mosaics of noisy emotion and glittering junk. They were both outsiders, too, in the sense of being poor, Mo always on grants and then later on the dole queue, herself making do with the tiny wage that she earned teaching drama and art to mentally retarded children, from the odd sale of a picture or an extravagantly sequinned cushion, and then from nude modelling down at the art school when she was desperate, and that was real suffering. Sitting there shivering, heavy and pale, stripped of her brave layers of scarves and patchwork and beads, unable to throw up her habitual screen of noise and gesture and vivacious movement. Still, it bought her some eggs and potatoes. And because they were both outsiders, outside the well-lit and well-off world of – oh, Pelham and Jean-Claude and their parents – they felt inside something much more labyrinthine and shady, a world which was infinite and devious in its pathways through the dark.

When Mo talked about the dole queue, – the blonde girl, bottle-blonde, with beautiful legs and big eyes and a gross hare-lip, always there with another blonde who could have been any age, could have been her mother, tiny legs like pipe-cleaners in patterned black stockings, long boots and a short tight military coat in black rippled plastic – and her hair was bushily curled and was coming uncurled in places, wild and split: underneath this bright chemical ash her face was so pale it looked greenish-yellow, she wore no makeup and horror, she had no teeth: and her jaw moved constantly as if it were still adjusting, as if she were mutely complaining that she had been beautiful, honestly, done a good business, had suddenly looked in a mirror one morning and found it was way too late, – Clara understood. Because this was the real world, this was most of the world, with no money for teeth or new clothes or extending their short lease on youth or on beauty, dying, in other words, dying, and cheaply, in their mute queue. She and Mo had somehow managed to slip unnoticed out of the shimmering nets of their class and their education, managed to slip through a blistered door to the other side.

62   Shimmering nets

Or had they only been tourists, loving the stimulus of strong colours and abject and freakish disasters, laughing and telling themselves (this was Mo, who was more of the theorist than Clara) of course it will happen to us in the end, in the meantime letting her lens zoom in on the others: and of course in the end, which was sooner than Clara expected, Mo's body was found in the Crescent one cold photographically brilliant morning, the shutters flashing and flashing, her hair, which had swung so freely, now caught in the shimmering nets of blood and black ice and her features hopelessly, bloodily confused with the pavement. That day, Clara thought, they both ceased to be tourists. Mo had become a resident for ever, while Clara was filled with agonized faithless yearnings for warmth and safety and home.

She sat in her flat for days with too many fires and lights on, gorging fudge. So sweet it was anaesthetic, so sweet that it filled her head with its shimmering nets of sugar, and her jaws were absorbed with chewing, unable to sob, and her fingers methodically, ceaselessly pulled off the wrappers and dropped them like snow on the floor. She went to bed early with a hot water bottle and too many covers, woke up in a sweat in the middle of the night and again began to eat fudge. In the end she felt so fat that she couldn't bend over to scoop up the litter of papers. Even when she sat up straight, her loosest skirt hurt her stomach, digging brutally in, saying Fatty, Fatty . . . So she let things lie where they dropped, threw the skirt on the paper-strewn floor and sat draped in an egg-stained quilt, with her tired jaws chewing and chewing. And yet, she wanted to live, she believed in action and kindness.

Then down at some ultimate level of panic and self-disgust something surfaced: the thought of a letter to Fee. And slow hope came leaking back with the salving mechanical motions of searching out paper and stamps. Slow hope, and before she began she scooped up the pieces of fudge which were left and carried them bravely off to the bathroom, ready to drop in the bin. She smothered the too-long neglected shine of her skin with powder and carefully painted her lips. Then again, when the letter was finished, with hope leaking into the form of

a long hot bath, she fluffed the white powder over the
doubt from the cold tap, unstoppable, trickling in. And
leaving her hopes and her doubts to run she came back
and addressed the fat envelope, pressing very hard with
the pen, more vigorous than accurate: yet only the
postcode was wrong, so Brown and Jones posted the
letter, much later, convinced from a careful reading that
she was all right, not a nut, for the nutters were found
smashed to bits on the sensible pavement. This one was
bright pink, and All Right. Clara wrote *We all have to go
on, we must think about work and the living.* She wrote in
a sweat of conviction, quite sure that Fee also believed it
. . . (somewhere a wild girl, sweat like the wax of a wild
orange candle, burning, then paler, dying, dying . . .)

63 Surviving III

Surviving, she thought: that was it, as she stood on one
foot in the scalding bath, inspecting the huge soft world of
her stomach. She wasn't a tourist. In poverty and the
bizarre she could rest unnoticed, knowing the landscape,
knowing she had no further to fall. It was different for
Mo: she would never appear like Mo in a journalist's
standardised prose 'an attractive redhead'. Clara, of sheer
necessity, hated anything standard. Like ordinary, handsome men, the kind with good teeth and bronzed skins –
they were never for Clara. The pain (as she slid in the
other foot, now her whole leg, the broad flesh flushing
with blood) of those first college dances, attempting to

wear pretty clothes and careful hair-dos, attempting to look like the others, and failing, failing. So now she chose other freaks freely and boldly, or boldly, apparently freely, now sinking too quickly and burning her bottom and thigh. Old men and married men, foreigners, painters with habits, drop-outs, petty crooks and psychiatric patients, anyone down on their luck. She reasoned quite rightly from her own case that these would be sure to be grateful, that she could appear as a fairy godmother scattering beads and feathers, scattering small brightly-coloured totems of love. She believed, she would always believe in it, kindness and generous love (yet her voice sometimes skated too high when she talked of her lunatic private life to Mo, *too* bizarre, *too* fantastic, but (honestly) *real* and *tender* – the 'attractive redhead' looked back. It was all quite different for *her*, and somewhere that high laugh choked and went under.)

The water was up to her nipples now, searing but glorious, one line of pain where the burning meniscus edged upwards, the rest a great furnace of bliss. This was safe, this was warm, this was living, Clara thought, this is mine, I must hang on to this. So warm and so sleepy: to live in a bath for ever, the solid world cupping you, holding you, keeping you warm and safe. A small piece of fudge, lodged under her tooth, floated free to surprise and delight her, making the hungry juices run . . . but she clung to her hope and her virtue, the fact of the small heap of fudge on the seat of the lavatory, waiting to go in the bin, the fact of her brave new beginning, the day stretching out full of Brillo and Vim, a new model Clara, one of the living, Clara come back and declaring her faith by being endlessly slim, she thought dizzily, letting her leg float free, for one warm lulled moment imagining lightness, a state of perpetual radiant vertigo, surely, a sexual storm, all her zany wrappings blown off her, the dazzling imago blown out of its thick cocoon.

But the leg floated back to its fellow, bubbled with cellulite, hopelessly reddened and fat . . .

. . . and her eye travelled evenly round to the small cache of fudge on the lavatory, someone was offering comfort, deep inside Clara her kind voice informed her that she was still warm and living and sensual, the bag was soon wet from her short wet fingers and she was soon floating on pink clouds of sugar, on fat clouds of sugar, her chins on the water, the last of her life in her hands.

As each granule of sugar burst and the sweetness rushed through her, she felt she would drown on these great swells of greed and their resolution in sharp crests of pleasure filling her brain with a sweet golden tide-race of sugar and butter, squeezing out, blotting out, melting out thought and her head dissolved back on the water, her hair floated out in a halo around her, her spine too deliciously loose and unsprung to support her, drifting and drifting, only her jaws and her ravenous spatulate tongue still moving . . . then suddenly something was stuck: everything shifting and bucking in great slapping roller coasters of water, flooding the floor and the walls and her pink limbs tearing through blockages, thrashing and kicking and bucking through terrible noises of choking, one broad hand trying to clutch at the side of the bath and the other one clutching her throat with its fatal brown stoppage of sugar, the red of her face growing deeper and deeper beneath its glistening powder, the big mouth sucking and working, working and sucking, the eyes bulging out at the dirt on the walls in blind panic, the faces she made in the dirt for amusement now set there to laugh at her big pink body for ever, now tiring, now quieting, now nearly still, lying sprawled to the ceiling on offer to anyone, anyone liking a freak will enjoy this huge plastic inflatable woman, her special attraction a gross red terrified face, the whole sliding gracefully downwards into the heat till the raw red skin of the face lies under the still clear skin of the water, which glazes it kindly, the eyes, which were noted by many in life to be kind and thoughtful and loving, open on nothing. For they are all gone.

High up, on dry land, in the attic, someone typed on.

64 Kindness and generous love

Few of her splendid articulate friends were left to mourn Clara, but others turned out at her funeral in force, a group of Retarded Children straggling after a teacher, not understanding but loving the flowers and the priest in his surplice, connecting it somehow with Miss who was kind and taught drama, and this was another cheerful play. A crowd of old lovers eyeing each other discreetly, wondering whether that odd-looking fellow could also have been a lover: one with a stick and one who kept laughing and screwed up one side of his face at the early spring sunlight, laughing and muttering, one very handsome in some kind of (phoney, the priest observed angrily) cassock, purple and black, very handsome except for the mad fixed glare of one glass eye. He had been very fond of Clara, a fine free girl who would jerk him off in his robes and hungrily lick his socket, a girl who was ready to hide the books that he (fairly frequently) stole and on one occasion some package tour tickets for Naples, not asking, or getting, a cut or a trip on the ocean, finding the bath was enough to drown in . . . he hoped that his fine free friend would be waiting in (phoney) heaven. And then at the back of the queue, in a wheelchair, sniffing up every two minutes at the cold bright air, with the frost, not grief, for she'd seen

173

too many, and hoped to see more – Hetty Sear, the old lady two doors away who Clara visited, going in regular bursts, and if she didn't turn up for a week or two Hetty never minded, for the next time she came she was loaded with guilt and presents.

And Hetty preferred the presents she made herself, little bead mats and embroidered bookmarks, colourful nonsense, since Clara bought all the wrong things at the grocer's, all doughnuts and biscuits and sugar, and Hetty had never quite managed to tell her she didn't like sweet things. So while she did a flourishing small-scale business selling Clara's handiwork to Alfred her ex-husband's cousin, who ran a little trinket shop, all sorts of silliness, in Chelsea, the food just sat in her kitchen to rot, since she didn't believe in wasting and Clara went on believing in loving-kindness, whether the cold world proved it or not (it did not.) Hetty told Clara she set all the pretty things out in her bedroom upstairs where they cheered her up: *oh how lovely it is, my dear, when you bring me new ones* (her voice on the quaver.) Now all that would stop. But Hetty didn't mind, she didn't need comfort. She never felt so happy as she did in a graveyard, watching a new one go down, especially a young one, knowing that she had outlived them.

But one of the young ones is watching her, up in a dark room some kind of justice is typing. The rats and the mice are at work in her kitchen as Hetty sits out on the hill in the high pale sun, and their sharp teeth tear at the lush glossy packing, their strong feet stamping and scampering, bringing their friends on the run. She will die two months later of rat poison, drunk by mistake for her cheap patent medicine, and big helpful Clara goes soberly casketed into the ground and *Well*, Hetty thought as the chill wind exposed her pale freckly scalp like an egg to the sunlight but no proud mother-bird sang, *Another one gone*: and she shivered triumphantly, and pulled down her ancient

174

sombrero, for which Clara gave her a beautiful peacock-feathered pin that she wasn't, however, sporting, as it had already been sold. She regretted it slightly, being only a little more greedy than vain: but she reflected that peacocks were always unlucky, and Hetty had always been lucky, and now she was eighty she needed her luck to hold.

Mary Evans went along when the day turned out fine, for she liked a nice funeral and she'd always liked Moira's pretty friend, to her taste prettier than Moira with that lovely big smile and always something cheerful to say to you, and wonderful clothes she wore, really exotic things, not what *she'd* wear of course but lovely and fancy. Dramatic, that was it. Now Moira was a different type altogether (the type coming thinly and coldly, not smiling or nicely talking, the type coming louder and louder high up at the top of the house which was emptying, darkening), always looked peaky, half-starved, and unless she was actually smiling she never looked happy, not really, not to her eyes, and with all that was said in the paper no wonder. It never did any good, not with married men. She didn't condemn, she felt sorry for the girl, but you also had to think of the wife and the marriage, didn't you. She'd have been shattered if she'd found Harold out carrying on, although Harold, of course, just wasn't the type, so she never had to worry. In the end it would turn out well for someone. That blonde man John (who was a wonderful snowy-white angel by early next morning, but nobody told Mary Evans that he had already gone home, his white curls streaming behind him) would go back to his wife (a wild girl shining with sweat and corona-ed with clear orange light as the first flame delicately touched her, but no-one had told her) and they could settle down and be happy, with Moira gone.

All the same, it made you think, standing out here in the lovely crisp sunlight and watching someone go into the dark wet ground, and she wouldn't want to wish it on anyone, not her worst enemy, not that she had one. And this funny crew left above it, she thought, looking round, it was quite a shock to find that nice Clara had such peculiar friends. The only normal-looking couple she supposed would be the parents, they looked quite well off, the woman very buxom in a tight black coat with a nice bit of fur to it. And a hat with one of those short dotted veils, it was really a very nice outfit, the kind of thing she'd choose to wear at a funeral if she had a bit of money. She didn't see any tears though, behind the dotted veil. They were funny things, parents. She'd have *died* grieving if she'd have lost one of her own. And indeed all her life she'd died grieving because she hadn't had one, not anything but Harold of her own. Mary Evans enjoyed the sad thoughts brought on by funerals: they made you feel quite exalted and church-like and solemn, when you got home, and she thought of Harold's face by the fire and her ginger wine, waiting for her, life wasn't bad (which was dying, in other words, someone in the attic was trying to remind her): the wind in her one good ear, Mary Evans took a short cut home.

65 They could settle down and be happy, with Moira gone

And the tall house was getting rather church-like anyway, solemn and empty, stretching up cavernous and damp to the fortress of Clothilde's room. There weren't so many feet on the stairs at the moment, though sometimes the typing hammered like feet, and Clothilde was a little less careful, a little less delicately cautious before shooting the bolt. Because one of the pairs of feet which remained belonged to Frank, and Clothilde was perhaps not trying to avoid him, entirely, thinking of him more kindly than of late as she boiled her chick-peas and lentils: she had outlived her rivals, now. Not that Moira was ever a rival in the sense of being an equal, that much was clear. But Clothilde knew how shameless she was and how bold, how her big body leaped down the stairs and wriggled and flirted (and now, even *now* something rhythmically battered, hard metal on paper, grew bolder, an army of echoes: and the ghosts in the house locked their doors and covered their ears.) Poor Frank knew no better. And she, Clothilde, had been cold: no wonder that he had been tempted. Perhaps she was hasty in thinking he'd started to mock her. Perhaps he did it in thwarted fury, biting his nails in his lowly room, rushing hopefully out on the landing whenever he heard feet coming, retreating, doubtless, too late when he found it was only that gross and noisy girl. Clothilde had been cold because she was not quite ready. But now she began to feel ready: ripeness is all, and she sat in the glow of her oil-lamp painting her cheeks into fruit . . . her cheeks which reminded her now, though they were not always so pretty, of perfect apples, which had to be stored in the dark through the winter, acquiring a sweet dry perfume and soft wrinkled skin, so much prettier then than those hard bright young ones, all pale acid colours and skin so smooth that it looked like plastic: Clothilde thought of Moira, and her black teeth bit through the plasticky skin and the pale citrous flesh to the hard core of metal and paper, and under it pain.

And then red on her lips, like holly berries. When she practised smiling in the mirror, she always kept her lips pressed together, not showing her teeth. Of course she didn't need to, knowing them to be her own, and of finest bone, and well-born, and antique, and lovely. The skin of her sharp little nose and chin and her high proud forehead was yellow, the forehead cut into three tiers by its lines like a many-storied building, a palace, she thought as usual, my fine yellow palace, the house of an artist. A lovely autumnal yellow, she thought, quite natural, which was why she became so angry when she saw that hussy in the basement with her silly dyed hairdo. She knew Mrs Evans was trying to copy the tints of her own superior beauty, was trying to copy the lovely sun yellows which only survived near the sky. And it took a strong character, an artist, a person of some refinement, to bear to live up so near it, so very alone and so high. Then her eyes, which she rimmed in mystery, darkening the two tiny sockets till they looked like tunnels of blue-black coal, leading deeper and deeper back into the skull. When the long excavation was finished, the mirror proclaimed her entirely beautiful.

66 Ripeness is all

If she could meet Frank *now*, she considered. If he would come to me *now*, up here in my room. And she cocked her small bird-of-paradise skull to one side in the glass and listened for feet on the stairs, but the sound that came back was only the sound of hard metal on paper, metal on paper and the type pattered on and Clothilde stayed locked in her dream. If he came, she would of course be frightened at first. It was a very long time since Clothilde had a lover. But once she did have one, a man with a wonderful highwayman's name, Jack Gilpin, or formally John: three or four decades ago or down some dark half-decayed passage between them Clothilde had forgotten, life changed.

Yet someone remembered and minded, the metal feet tapped down the passage recalling that just between Thursday and Friday some three or four decades ago life changed. And before, there was money for sherry and time for birthdays or memory days or days when she thought she was writing or flying and sat up in bed in a terrified young excitement, trembling slightly on the edge of the glass, sipping herself to sleep with the light off, her green hopes sprouting in darkness, a bud, a flower . . . but slipping into tomorrow where generally there was nothing, dead leaves and dry petals, the bottle (which she checked daily) mysteriously lower, hope less. And then only a little later, not very far down the passage, there wasn't the money for sherry or things like expensive underwear, not that it mattered, of course, what an artist wore, but a child, it was nice for a child to look pretty . . . but the ageing child could no longer afford a brassière, and her thin breasts hung behind modest layers of wool, dry and yielding, the first part of Moira, and later Clothilde, to die.

Once her nipples had grown big and hard and ached with pleasure when a man licked and chewed at them, someone, John Gilpin, it felt like the head of a baby pulling beneath her nightdress, and she thought one evening, which was a memory evening, properly speaking, not for John but for her mother and father, borne off by cholera down a more distant passage and into another locked room, far away and yet still alongside her, – thinking of John who did always push in, sitting and sipping her drink with her buttercup yellow nightdress pulled tight down over the two hard points of her knees which were locked round the clean empty cage of her chest, – he was pulling at her heart, he was trying to lick my heart. But Clothilde was afraid that her breasts would suddenly grow milky and leak into his mouth as he mumbled and licked her, and after a minute or two she said stop it, don't be so peculiar. For two or three decades and somewhere between she recalled the sequence, – the head of the big rough baby, the hardness and heat in her breast and the stupid sound of her voice – with astonishment and grief, and more and more rarely. And the days and the years in the passage pushed up between the pieces of memory, forcing them apart, and essential fragments were lost on the endless cliff-walks before sleep, when the sheets stretched down in a long sheer fall down her long falling body, chalk-white, then the dull black water, very far away, which was ice or pavement or sleep or perhaps if you fell very far would be death: and a thin child afraid of the dark would be trying to climb up the cliff though each spiral path ended in panic, and the message it dropped on the way had been blown beyond dreams into black oblivion, into the hands of great policemen and under the hard metal feet of rivals and pattering spies.

One night was the very last time she remembered, erosion by sorrow and not by design or it was not she who designed it, sorrowing, losing the thing that evening when sleep came finally, lying there sipping at the warmth in the dark with her yellow nightdress over her knees and with one hand fondling her dry soft nipple, thinking of John and his child or himself like a child who had made her believe they would break into blossoms of milk and tears, and as the tears finally two decades later came trickling under her thin veined lids she again and again and in darkness and silence repeated he pulled at my heart, he was trying to lick my heart, and the empty white cage round her heart was gently and finally shaken with sobbing. And now she could not remember. The passage had finally crumbled and gone and she climbed up slowly and surely, surviving, remote and alone, mounting stair after stair in the high yellow house of her brain.

And yet now after all these decades something was stirring, down on the floor below. She was frightened: but if he should come she would have to be kind, for Frank would of course be eager and nervous. Perhaps he would care to move into the room beside her, thus driving the terrible noise of the typing out of her head. Of course she had never been lonely, but now she would never be lonely again. Something dimly assured her that life had not always been drawn in so tight and so thin at the top of high buildings, drawn up at the very far tip of this cold Crescent moon. She remembered that once there were faces which loved her and talked to her, not just the chattering beaks of the birds. She remembered a child which had pulled at her, nearly crawled out of her shrunk yellow womb. Or she was the child and quite simply got lost one evening, got shut in the park after dark in the moonlight, the people (her mother and father, her lover) all vanished, and she had been terribly frightened because she could hear in the bushes quite near her dogs barking, big black dogs, she thought she could see them, baying the moon. And the heavy boots followed her, followed her, crushing her tracks in the glittering grass: and the little girl climbed a tall tree to avoid them, climbed higher and higher towards that round radiant bowl, but it shrank before long to a Crescent, was empty, and Clothilde could never get down.

And yet now after all these decades something was stirring. I shall have to help him, she thought, for a shy man needs help, as she sat down to work for the evening: perhaps I have been too cold with him, maybe this evening Clothilde will go down and raise Frank up. And she started to work as she did every evening, sat down in a stiff cane chair at her orderly table, her small pad of paper before her, her scissors, her feathery brush which she washed every day and her jewels of coloured ink: and the little tin mirror propped up on the wall before her, the bracket also supporting an oil-lamp which haloed her fluffy grey hair. And the face of the ancient woman looked back from the mirror as always, as clear and as bright and as small as her bottles of ink, and as bright as her bottles could make it. Solemnly, taking the first clean sheet of white paper, cut carefully into the shape of a clean white heart, very hopeful and empty, the lost child started to paint. Every night was the fourteenth of February: her card was so gay in the light. She was waiting for Frank, she was ninety. The end was surely in sight.

67   The end was surely in sight   I

In the room below her, twelve feet precisely below her, sat Francis Drake. He could not be seen from the door: the room was crowded from wall to wall and from ceiling to ceiling with crazy yellowing towers of papers, most of them apparently just about to fall. There were moths and beetles and whopping black spiders in there and the pages never stopped rustling. Frank thought he would kill one, every so often, but never knew where to begin for you never quite saw one clear. Grey spools of mist and cocoons of insect bodies past killing blurred over the gaps between decades of newsprint (the pages never stopped rustling: somebody read in a hurry: the end of the novel was surely, surely in sight.)

The pages never stopped rustling, somewhere secured in a far dim room at the end of a blocked-up corridor, somewhere secured in memory, covered by grey spools of mist and the dead insect bodies of days in Frank Drake's somnolent brain. Which had once been employed in an office, held a responsible job where his public school voice was respected, worked for a Company, worked for a very respectable wage. But the clock got ahead of him somehow, the great gold Company clock, and the hard metal face ground down on his gentleness, said he was soft, too soft, he was slow, he could never keep time. And the grey seas of Company paper mounted all round him, rustling, whispering, hissing that he would be lost soon, drowning in Company paper, locked at the corridor's narrowing end where the carpets are darkened and shabby (darkening, darkening, driving him down to the end.) And Frank had escaped or believed he escaped with the last gallant Joke he could muster: the Company slogan was TIME IS MONEY but Time, he insisted, IS FUNNY, IS FUNNY. Escaped, or believed he escaped (yet the metal feet stamped him *rejected*, kept down and locked out just as all of the soft and slow are rejected, not worth the money, get down.) And now he is locked in his room with the rustling papers, and only the carpets, and memory, and time, are going, going and gone, for his Company watch is not going, something gone wrong. And maybe the joke is concealed further back in the story, for surely the (darkening) end is not funny, not funny, not funny (yet Frank has a Dream, and his gentle heart, and a Plan.)

But today Frank was gloomy. He sat on the bed with his feet up, mainly because there wasn't any room on the floor to put them down. His socks smelt so bad that he couldn't get used to them, and he'd been with them now on the bed for a very long time. Frank was mourning, and how could a man who was mourning get on with a book about Jokes? Frank was mourning for Moira, who left him so cruelly and suddenly, just when his suit for her love was beginning to go so well. He knew better, of course, than to rush her. Those others had rushed her: . . . he'd heard the terrible scenes. But at last he was sure he had started to really make progress, watching her face when he came boldly out on the landing to meet her, watching it slowly succumb to his own peculiar charm. Not smiling, exactly, but – gripped by it, even a modest chap hadn't been able to miss it. His charm worked slowly, but once it had worked it was fatal – in this case, literally! – which was a Joke: and he smiled a slow sad smile.

Her interest began, of course, when he told her about his work. He had followed her into the bathroom, seeing her come downstairs with a bowlful of washing up. And he offered to help her, but she was too proud to accept it – he liked her for that. And he warned her against the sink, the basin was safer: you never could tell, after all, what the sink might be used for. (She didn't accept his advice, which was foolhardy of her. He *knew* what the sink was used for, but naturally couldn't tell her. The lavatory was, after all, a long way down.) Frank wasn't discouraged, the reverse, by a bit of *hauteur*, and observed in a casually gallant way to the smeary sash window that he liked to see spirit in a woman, he liked a bit of fire. She said nothing, but he saw by the set of her head that the point had reached her, the way she tossed back that pretty brown hair. And he started to speak of his work, an analysis of The Joke, scientific, a study along certain lines which were not yet precisely worked out. He was still in the early researching stages, so if she knew any good Jokes she need not feel too shy to come forward. How vividly now he recalled that flash in her eyes – it was impish, surely – as she turned from the sink with her bowl of clean pans (or as *she* thought, clean) and said simply, putting her face quite daringly close to his, 'I'm afraid that I DON'T LIKE JOKES. Now will you excuse me, please?' And she'd gone, leaving Frank in a spin of delight and excitement.

Though nothing so blatantly hopeful had happened again, a new phase had followed this first one of intimate Joking rapture: a new phase of watching and waiting, so feelings, he thought, could deepen, before they made open and joyous contact again. But the end was surely in sight, he was sure it was right this should happen, was sure right up to the day of her death that the thing was about to burgeon, and yet he had sometimes (unfairly) felt somewhat put out that she didn't answer his debonair offers of wine or acknowledge his flowers, when he had spent hours at the back of the restaurant sorting out specially fresh specimens stupidly cast in the bins (I shall not be down in the dumps, however, he Joked!) And then suddenly dead, and the Joke had gone sour, his Moira. So now there was no-one at all to help with his life's great Plan.

68   The end was surely in sight   II

For years he had lived in his room with his project, quite happily, watching the raw materials pile as his system of lines to work on (which aimed, in the fullness of time, for a point) (and time in the office was thin and unripe and deceitful) evolved: all the best things were slow, like thinking, and love, and history: the end was surely in sight. He sat in his room in his stained fawn mack with a system of marking the papers with Jokes (by a small neat cross in biro) slowly evolving, and since few papers had Jokes (though he took a selection of papers, removing the egg-shells, and some of them came from a very good quality bin), there were many hours left of the day for evolving the system, so Frank didn't force it, but sat on his bed in the afternoon sun (in the early years, before the papers piled over the window) and read the rest of the papers. Then at the run-down end of the day when this grew boring, or all day when something like Christmas cropped up or a journalists' strike, he would try the back numbers, distinguishing vaguely, and by the next day not at all, between items he read in the current papers, and horrors which jumped from the piled yellow gloom at the back of the wardrobe, Berlin and Cuba: which made the years seem even dimmer and vaguer and quite unimportant, to Frank, since if Cuba frightened him every bit as badly today as it had the last time a decade or so (or something between ten years and the gathering damp, surely twenty, half-stuck to the wall) ago, and he found that that damp yellow wall divided Berlin and was older, but just as alarming – then what was the point in hurrying? Outside the damp on his walls, the world would continue as ever, roll round as ever, and wait: or else it would stop this time at Berlin or Cuba, with Moira just one of a crocodile tear of young girls with blue hats and red hair in the sun in pigtails, whereas what Frank liked was maturity, fire and *hauteur* – in which case there was even less point (and no point to his system, as yet) in haste. (And yet somewhere, high up in the roof and above him, someone typed on in a hurry, death comes from the sky and though Berlin and Cuba passed peacefully something will happen, exploding your system, he'll get me, you'll be too late – the end was surely in sight.)

But Frank thought it over, curled up on his bed with his gloom (at first) and his socks. And a few hours' thought about Cuba made him feel sanguine, his worry dissolved by the soft rotted light from his full file of jokes, quite full, not to worry, just waiting: for Moira, like everything else, he considered, must come round again.

(And Bill Dutton drove faster and faster on round the Crescent in crazy repetitive circles, what did it matter if spurting bottles flew off and killed more and more people in regular showers of fragments, the milk still arrived fresh and white every day and the milk-white morning papers, Les Hawtrey span round and round on his black leather chair in London faster and faster, recording in regular cut-glass prose the crazy repetitive murders, and tidy pink fingers curled round the (ever-so-slightly-yellowing) papers each evening and threw all the deaths in the bin: and so death came round to Frank Drake and the soft blind blossoms of evening, kiss them, kiss them, kiss the poor circular pilgrims, now flying and falling, please kiss them . . . and somewhere, in lovely and random kindness, a brilliant filament broke and the blue dark kissed Clarrie Dutton, sleep until dawn and your author will dream you back young) – the world didn't hurry, and nor, he supposed, would glory. He wasn't quite ready to rush with his work, not yet. It was human nature to mourn, and the Jokes, he decided, might gracefully follow the mourning. And so he would lie on his bed with his mack pulled over him, long after noon, peacefully shifting and snoring, his hand in Moira's, his heart at the top of a tottering tower of grief and bliss, ignoring the cold metal feet in the attic typing a warning, – peacefully waiting and dreaming. The end would be love and glory and warm shared laughter at Jokes: and now, he was sure, it would not be long in coming.

Yet something, an insect under the blankets, an incorrect series of biro marks, something disturbing the system, something still irked him, just beyond consciousness, something which threatened the dream. Not a rival, surely, for she had been (secretly, tenderly, certainly) faithful: but something which threatened to do them both harm, do *all of us* harm as the hard metal feet in the attic insisted, something which woke in a temper when they were all dancing or painting or peacefully sleeping, something which toppled them out of their towers (which were anyway growing transparent) and ended the pilgrims' dream. C. Hans, just across Frank's landing, lying there blackly, noting the time.

69   Something disturbing the system

Frank's one little difference with Moira arose from a conversation he'd heard on the landing, couldn't help hearing, couldn't help seeing, also, just as it happened, from where he was standing, on tip-toe, his eye to the open crack of the door. It had tickled some very old part of him, something tucked far out of reach at the back of his heart, not a whisper from it in ages, his honour, grown pink and flabby and buried in lustreless fat. Though he knew it was only one of her marvellous ploys to conceal from the world the site of her budding affections, the way she stood outwardly talking and smiling and intimate, even, with putty-nosed Hans upset him, asking the name of some record she'd heard him playing: for Hans came in (Frank was witness to that, every day, unwillingly) each wretched day of the week at precisely six-thirty, making more noise on the landing than necessary, much more, making his point, that respectable people came home at six-thirty and rose in the morning at eight, very noisily, revving his beastly electric razor up to a daily scream (which was the nearest he could get, thought Frank, very daringly and Jokingly, to driving his car round the bathroom, the monstrous gunmetal Volvo which he polished every Saturday, the giant grey regular insect which waited for Frank on the doorstep, its powerful limbs and probosces gleaming with mirrors and memories and faces of clocks on the dashboard, frenziedly polished but darkening, darkening, gleaming with Company chrome: so that Frank shrank past it, regularly, shrank down some narrowing corridor, shrank back guiltily into his fearful memories, into his small dark room . . .) and when Hans came home he played classical music, no wonder she'd heard him, announcing The Worker Is Home.

Hans said, did she mean that she heard him because he had played it too loud, and Frank cried out in his head behind the safe door, *Yes, Yes,* rising higher on his toes in excitement: but Moira said No, not at all, of course not, how could he imagine she was complaining, and other such stuff which made Frank subside with a frown . . . the walls of the house were thin (and now growing transparent) so sound did carry, but since it was music she liked that was simply fine.

Only Hans didn't leave it at that, and Frank's honour began to throb feebly and pinkly, something disturbing the system. It knew, or perhaps it knew once, that a loved one should be protected: and yet it knew also, he needed some definite sign. Hans explained (insincerely and spitefully, simply not playing the game) he was sorry if it seemed he imposed his taste upon everyone, – especially since his taste most certainly *was not hers* – (quite true! muttered Frank to himself in the shell of his room, he's seen through her there, she plays nothing but dancing music, transparent) – but she would appreciate, possibly, even perhaps be so kind as to tell all her *friends*, who were mostly, from what he could see, in her own highly enviable state as regards *not working* (the bastard means me, thought Frank, but his anger mingled with quivering joy, now dissolving, at the sweet term *friends*) – that for people like him, and most of the world was like him, who were forced to work hard in a decent job which had regular hours, great importance was attached to relaxing: unable, like her and her friends, to play music and dream all day long, he would just claim his right to relax in his own chosen way in the evening! The sound of his voice crescendoed: his cream door banged. And she stood for a second on the landing, her slim back (stemmed like a flower, he marvelled) turned on Frank, who was feeling quite gay now the milk of feigned friendship had soured, and his honour succumbed to a frantic desire to wink – stood staring at the cryptic card on his door, C. HANS, old putty-face probably thinks the initials make him more mysterious – Ha, thought Frank, not a CHANCE – and then Joke! he acknowledged, a good one, marking it gaily, and sniggered so loudly that her hair swung round and he hastily, rather too loudly, closed his door.

So the thing was a triumph, really: a Joke derived from a Rout – only Frank felt a little uneasy, long after, in bright warm circular dreams where suddenly something was moving, uneasily, somewhere under the sheet and it sometimes seemed that the hand he was lovingly holding in sleep was slipping, clutching and slipping, slipping away from the light . . . there was something disturbing the system, some horrible end was in sight. And he woke, and uncomfortably wondered if honour had not been right, saying pinkly but firmly Get out on the landing, Frank, and protect her. And lying awake through the (plenty of time into) afternoon, into evening and still into night he heard nothing but small feet rising and falling, messages flying and falling, and since he read nothing but papers they couldn't quite reach him and Why do they all have to hurry, Frank thought, she would soon be back, she was back, for the system was circular, everything came in time and the book and their lives in the end would come out right . . . yet a metal voice somewhere said Hurry, Frank, hurry, he'll get me, you'll be too late.

C. Hans was a mystery to everyone, even Mrs Evans, even after all this paper and time. She had been in his room once or twice with her dustpan, but hadn't seen anything there to explain why he chose to live *here* (for this house wasn't much) when he wore nice suits, and drove that expensive car. And his room had some lovely stuff, one of those stereo whatsits and doings, speakers like wardrobes, all gleaming, controls like the front of an aircraft, everything else but the wings and the volume was flying and falling and only at ten o'clock (bedtime) finally falling, all evening. Which Moira well knew, but it didn't unravel the mystery, the only one left when the walls of the other rooms turned into mica, transparent, the delicate trembling and travelling creatures inside revealed through their shells, and as daytime went on (and she knew she would finish it soon) more and more of the shells of the pilgrims came under her hard metal feet and were broken. But not C. Hans. And the walls of his room (Mrs Evans remarked) were lined floor to ceiling with road-maps, the whole vertiginous world (her creator remarked) reduced to a regular series of numbers and unbelievable labels, a fiction through which no light could come flying or falling (and yet: each page of her novel was numbered, each chapter was numbered and labelled, and she would bend Hans in the end to her orderly will . . . make the map not quite right so his Volvo drove right to the edge of the grey-green cliff and then fell, and the grey map fell from the wall . . .)

(but *Moira* was screaming and falling, could not control Chance at all . . .)

C. Hans had his nose, and that nose was a mystery, for certain. The only thing certainly known about Hans was his nose, but the reason behind it was not. Moira glimpsed him quite often, by daylight, but never quite managed to see him close up till that day of her brave failed ploy on the landing, attempting to quell the revulsion she felt (which had brought the nose softly, uncertainly round the dark edge of the door of her dreams in the night) – ashamed of her silly aversion, determined to be polite.

polite. But the gesture, of course, had failed, and his face at close quarters was solid and neutral and pink, refused to admit any light. The nose had in fact been neutered, one living index removed and this clumsy inhuman addition put in its place like a fingerstall of pale putty, an object, a random query, powerful and blind and opaque. And the rest of the face betrayed nothing: blue eyes, the bright passionless glaze of a blue summer sky behind glass: coarse skin, slightly gleaming, too pink for the nose: wire spectacles flashing reflected light-bulbs and hiding any more human signals sent out by the eyes, digging in (oh repellent, she tried but she couldn't help thinking repellent) – and their thin wire bridge digging in to the bridgeless mound of the nose. There was something disturbing her system. C. Hans and his mystery remained.

70 C. Hans

But the mystery could not be allowed to remain. She was tired, it was late in the evening, the house of her brain stretched up aching and empty as each of her little constructed inhabitants dwindled according to system, their images growing more bright and more clear and more tiny as each tiny pilgrim's portion of clockwork ran down. It was almost finished, her head and her back and her fingers ached from sitting so long in her attic, typing and typing: her sense of existence had dwindled with theirs but her face unlike theirs was devoid of makeup, her long hair opaque with grease. Now the end was in sight her whole body began to ache in a different way, for

attention and pleasure, for happiness, simply, existence
with textures more complex than paper, in three dimen-
sions, in bed, in the park, in the cinema, up at the top of
the arc of a swing. She ached for a view of the sky, who for
so long had only seen ceilings, ached to get up into space
or down to the ground. Solid ground, icy ground, she
would splay out her palm and feel it, cool crystal shell of
the world she had lived in and loved.

Tomorrow would be her birthday, the cards and the
presents and John (in his suit, in the evening) would
come. The result of her careful timing, the end of her
strenuous plan. And the answer to C. Hans came.

C. Hans was an undertaker: that must be it. And a rich
one: had a big house in the country, but lived here on
weekdays because he was mean. There was money in
bodies. His sober suits were essential, of course, for the
job. But Hans was no ordinary undertaker, Hans under-
took to give personal service to corpses, his big pink hands
pushing greedily out of their cuffs when the body was laid
before him, the face painted freshly in readiness, limbs
splayed out limply, unable, of course, to resist. Which
explained his obsession with neatness and order and time:
for what could be neater or cleaner than death? – the eyes
not crying, the skin not sweating, the lips hygienically dry
and the passive display of the whole accepting that this
was all timely, the proper order of all things human was
death (yet her corpse in the end was a mess, the straight
spine shattered, the face in a bloody confusion of stone
and ice.)

She was happy. In seconds the freakish details would
pile. The spectacles, probably stolen, in some locked
cupboard mementos, false teeth and nail-clippings kept in
a small black oilskin bag, and a bright lock of hair from a
wig . . . it was easy: it leaped, with its own momentum, on
to the end. But she mustn't stop thinking, she had to press
on. It would soon be dawn: she drew a deep breath and

got up and went down to the bathroom, leaving the straight tower of paper piled deep on her table, each chapter in order, each orderly chapter numbered, and only one final stanza remained. She was happy, happy to leave them, happy that only a bath and shampoo and one final victorious stanza divided her now from the morning, and back from her warm scented bath with her hair raining glittering drops as she ran up the stairs she was sure it would be a glorious morning, a brilliant morning as frosty and fresh as her body, and she would be out in it, there in the sun.

And the final stanza had come. From the next-door house came a galvanizing burst of pop music, triumphant and loud. In the next-door room, so it must be George whose flat was above Jean-Claude's (and Jean-Claude never ceased to lament it), home again late, very cocky and drunk and intending the kids and Rita to know. And Mo thought, even now at the end as the round vertiginous world closed down into one-dimensional order, of Rita in shuddering tears, peering out at the sun on the balcony, spilling the tangled insides of her soul: which was packets of seeds bought at Woolworths', *quite chancy, but beautiful colours, I've got this window box, see, from the jumble, I thought that something might grow. But he did it again, the bugger, I went in the bathroom this morning and there they all were in the toilet, my lovely geraniums, all sorts, floating face down*: and the world closed down into order but hate was abroad in the bathroom, the roots reached out and the seeds of horror and human hatred would grow.

Yet the music was lovely to Moira: all pounding rhythm and joy and unhinged sensation, everything *she* felt now that the other tight rhythms were tightening, closing, done (someone woke in a temper, just across Frank's dark landing, lying there blackly, blood pounding, noting the time.) It grew louder and louder till the walls and the walls of her book and the very thin walls of exhaustion and

194

somewhere a long dark sequence of chapters of ordered time seemed about to come down and the rhythm went pounding and pounding on till she realized the pounding was at her own door (someone knew it was *her* playing music to spoil his sleep and to make him wake well after eight in the morning, someone was coming up pinkly and angrily, clutching the key of his room in his big pink hand, coming up once and for all to lay down the law, someone pounding and pounding but nobody answered and finally someone, C. Hans, jabbed his key in her door in a temper –

and to his surprise the key turned (for the key was the same to them all, and she made the pattern)

– the horror was in, C. Hans in pyjamas; the nose, the nose and the key was the same as her own but the face was so different, she scrabbled to open the window in terrible, agonized fear, and the icy bars scraped at her soft washed skin, she would edge down the balcony, knock at the window next door until George, stupid normal drunk George, let her in, get away from the horror, anywhere, please, and she prayed to the ice on the air for she wanted to live: but the windowbox, put there last summer by Rita his sad normal wife who just wanted some sort of a life of her own and a garden, was blocking her passage, a hand, two hands, big pink hands, were clasped round the bars behind her, and it was so cold, and she sobbed at the thin pale moon and the dawn for a second, she climbed on the frozen parapet, sobbing, and started to edge very carefully away from the terrible hands and along past the blockage and down, and then right on the edge she looked down for a second and over, and up at the vanishing moon and the blood in the sky for a second and down, and the distance between made her heart lurch sickly in panic, too high and too far, and alone – she slithered, she clutched for a long last stanza of pain at the stone, and she screamed at the end to nothing and no-one, and then Moira Penny was gone.

* * *

It was time for the book to begin.

The naked body of the girl was found on the pavement by the milkman . . . a frosty brilliant morning . . . blood and black ice . . . (she was ended, the book could begin)
   The papers were found on her desk in the third-floor attic . . . so that was all right (single-spaced: typed badly, but carefully corrected, each phrase rewritten again and again: page-numbered throughout, with each section demurely titled: no passionate last minute scrawl of ink at the end) . . . so that was all right (as the funny Moira doll – not worth a Penny, which Frank didn't realize (Joke!) – slowly dwindled, and blood and confusion set tiny and hard on the pavement for more funny dolls to look at, tiny and clear)

But the papers stayed real and full-size on a desk, it no longer mattered on whose desk as long as they lay to be read on someone's . . . someone with brains and a heart, someone living (dying, in other words), someone less rigid than Brown and less moderate than Jones . . . the world which supported the papers had (randomly) opened and closed: and a face with its pleased self-invention, a name with its bright self-invention is no longer needed to hold the fiction together . . . all that is needed is somebody else's hands: for the hands which have sculpted a world must be first and last self-destroying.

Reach out and touch me, reader. Flying, flying and falling. Other chance hands will support me. Take Moira, take me, take these pains.

THE PAPERS

i

Earning a living, dying, in other words:
ten dead ends.

1 Engraving   [*Handwritten note:* C. Hans, all of them.]

Pilgrim walks to work each day
from his tall yellowish-green building to the next
where he turns right by a dead triangular bed
of supposed flowers and walks straight by
three more identical buildings of greenish-yellow
to the next block of four identical tall buildings
with its typical dead triangular bed of supposed flowers
in fact wall-flowers, of a yellowish-green colour, dead,
and walks
straight by the flowers which might well be walls and
arrives
via a third brick blockage of greenish-yellow fitted
with sour green deathbeds of dull flowers
at the fourth order of four orderly buildings and the fourth
bed of supposed dead flowers and walks
into his tomb where daily Pilgrim works
building four walls of wood of a suitable size
for a tall obedient man (which Pilgrim is)
and he crouches patiently to smooth the edges
and he lies as a dead man does to engrave the hinges
and he sees that the longer he polishes his work
just as he is supposed to, – the longer he works
at the dull straight-sided box of death beneath
the fourth straight-sided box of yellow bricks
and death which is the place where Pilgrim works
and where he daily walks from his own box
via three other boxes (life being the shortest line between
four boxes) –
the more the wood takes on the pallor of flowers
the colour flowers for the dead are supposed to be
which is yellow, the colour of all tall obedient cowards
carried

towards their death in a coffin of greenish-yellow
which is what their life has been, an orderly file of walking
blocks
which are greenish-yellow, as death is yellowish-green,
and he daily walks the distance in between.

2 Breeding

[*Handwritten note:* Bill Dutton.]

Willum is training for the wedding ring
he is training on roaring meat and gold-top milk
and he flexes his finger nightly at the dark
and strains to strengthen his knees against the sheet
and he thinks in a frank and full yet reverent way
of the marvellous girl with her fabulous female glands
with her oviform breasts and her monthly opuscule
girl of most wonderful fibrous feminine flesh
with her lustrous nether measure for his ferrule
which he trains on raging meat and jissmic milk
which he trains with nightly laying on of hands
with strenuous yanks performed in a reverent way
Willum is training for his wedding day
where the date of spasmic bliss is doubly marked
with a cross very like the kiss he presses on it
and a ring very like the ring that will hug the groom
which Willum nightly pants and floods to be
and he trains like a balletstar to be a dad
trains for the ring where the sad promoters wait
who will score against or for his heavyweight limbs
which Willum madly fattens on milk and meat
he is training against the odds for the valiant day
when he will emerge like a god from the anteroom
from the darkened bachelor room where he saves his sap
until he can no more and rises up
and leaks into his love in piscous dream
where his milky bride has ovum-brooding thighs
opening viscous lips to drink his sperm –
not knowing the ring is at her fertile centre
the rubber ring that the sad promoters fit
the wedding ring that all Willum's spunk can't enter.

Osric has a homicidal eye
a pale and casual eye with a slanted lid
and a suit of tactical clothes which the welfare boys
in the well-stocked stores of his practical employers
supply in their sets of four and the sets comprise
a leather suit lined with suitable sanguine cloth
and a functional murdering tooth and nail and eye
all of which Osric wears with sober joy
for Osric is a man who loves his job
and he never takes his white-skulled suiting off
for he loves its lining of soft sanguineous silk
and the sewn-in strangling handkerchief pale as milk
and even at nights he sports his carneous eye
his pale slit eye in its bloody and starlit bed
and his nightly ladies writhe therein and die
the ladies which the welfare boys supply
and Osric lays with aptly monstrous joy
which the welfare boys supply and every day
Osric arises from his littered bed
brushes the feather from his leather suit
fastens a buttonhole rose with a casual stab
such as his practical employers advocate
and prowls in a classical way to his well-loved job
yes Osric lives as peaceful as the dead
which the job requires that Osric should supply
in return for the suit and the homicidal eye
and the nail and the tooth which all employees enjoy
which Osric gladly dons for good and all
once and for all takes up his set of four
a lovely life for Osric till today
when his tooth and nail unseat his welfare eye
and farewell Osric time for you to die

4 Doktoring

[*Handwritten note:* The policemen, Jones and Brown.]

Modred's chosen mode of life is hard
he carries brine for his nerves in a hard black bag
(supplied by the medical firm of Jaws and Bone)
scissors to cut the cord and a surgical flag
to reserve the spot where the ill describe their pain
and pain is hard, but it is Modred's job
and when he bends beside the groaning bed
he stoically preserves a pickled smile
and files all details in a metal file
and Modred wears black boots with studs of steel
and a blue serge suit with creases stiff as board
and the boots have iron tablets in the heel
and the gloves have shots of steroid at the cuff
and Modred prays all this looks hard enough
and the sick are much impressed by the hard black bag
and the ferric grace of Modred's opening flick
and the hard-edged medical things he takes from it
and the way his working knuckles briskly crack
and the rigid medical curve of Modred's spine
as he firmly bends to knead a flagging back
or click a sagging tendon into line
and Modred has a handsome steel-grey wig
and a flash of steel-grey dye at his eyebrow bone
which gives his head a frank and surgical shine
especially pleasing to the chronic sick
who weekly swig the tonic of his look
the steely look of a man who deals with pain
for a medical man cannot be made of lard
a medical man must be of sterner stuff
and he worries lest he is not stern enough
till Rigor Mortis hardens Modred's brain
and carries Rigid Modred stiffly off

5 Gardening

Rita has made herself a wooden spade
sporting a splendid head of stainless steel
and she stores it against the spring in her wooden shed
by the rack of assorted packets of dahlia seed
daffodil seed geranium seed *et al*.
which Rita is storing in a regular row
ensuring that all the coloured pictures show
and they burn from their paper earth by the shining head
of the splendid spade which she stores in the same small
shed
which she dreamed last summer to hold the seed and
spade
which she planned last autumn to dig the blossom in
to dig it into the garden which grows in spring
(for as yet the gardener has no ground at all)
at the end of the shed at the back of the wooden wall
as she is warned by her regular gardener's manual
which she keeps in the regular rack by the burning seed
which is patiently waiting for the apparently annual
(so she is told by the grave oracular manual)
miracle which will make her garden grow
(for she has no garden yet, but in time she will)
Rita is honing a wonderful wooden hoe
with a beautiful blue-steel blade with a regular hole
which the astral earth of her garden will pour through
and dissolve in stars against the gardener's heel
as the manual recommends and she doesn't know
as she swings the hoe in the shed with a sunflower zeal
as she practises the swing with a primular grace
which the prose of her miracle manual recommends
for the dizzily hopeful days before spring begins
that her stellar swing will slip and tear off her head
and in spring it will swell to a star-dropping fungus bed
which is what her solemn manual always said

6 Property-owning

Pelham owns quantities of saleable things
which means that Pelham is a man of property
which Pelham promptly owns himself to be
for he knows there is nothing finer than a landed man
he knows there is nothing grander than a man of means
so he knows there is none more grand and fine than he
and he crows like a propertied cock on a heap of gold
like one of the hundred roosters in his stock
on one of the thousand heaps which Pelham owns
for Pelham likes to be like what Pelham owns
and whatever Pelham sells he soon gets back
for he understands, as a circular man of means
with a circle of circular heaps of circular coins
that life is a rounder run on well-ruled lines
and the straightest lines run on till the two ends join
which landed Pelham fully understands
owning several volumes of this philosophy
bound in most valuable leather and gold-inlaid
and in other volumes are lists of saleable things
young boys with yellow skins as cold as coins
sallow old crones with twisted yellow bones
which Pelham buys and sells most profitably
and lists of prices which must be promptly paid
for Pelham sells the fools who cannot pay
this man so much more grand and fine than they
which Pelham promptly owns himself to be
and the lists include such quantities of things
old men with crusted eyes like yellow gold
young girls with yellow hair and wasted thighs
that he finds an unlisted man with some surprise
and the man has put poor Pelham up for sale
for Pelham does not own himself at all

7   Ringmastering

[*Handwritten note:* Rawdon at
St. Giles' Fair, The dwarves.]

Rawdon nightly roars the bears and beauties on
and nightly Rawdon sweeps the big top floor with every-
                                                    one
then huffs the sawdust from his rubicund moustache
reglues it to his smooth ferruginous cheek and goosesteps
                                                        off
blaring *I am the terrible tophat master of the circus ring!*
                                                which shows
the dullest dwarf just who's the big top boss
and two dull dwarves remove each high gloss boot
and he nightly chews on salamander meat
and he nightly takes the best plum brandy neat
six shots of brandy lit with a handy taper
(which the cannon man puts ready to light his paper)
and his tungsten tonsils dowse the flame-spiked liquor
and *Safe as Houses* he roars and the band strikes up
and his whip hand snakes and the timid notes trip quicker
and Rawdon looks to his right with a lash of a smile
for the spangled girls to wind their navels in
and their powdered dimples quiver with fear of their lover
and Rawdon roars for the dwarves to follow on
and they tumble humbly by in enormous hats
in houndstooth suits of the most enormous size
with huge unlit cigars and big white grins
of whinnying terror and great pink hangdog tongues
– flanked by the muscular Mr and Miss Trapeze
who traverse the air with masses of nerve and ease
with plump thighs winking thirty feet apart
but they bounce past Rawdon on rubbery ropes of fear
to the rhythm he beats with the brimstone brim of his hat
and his whiskers flare and his patent boots ignite
and after one *Final Night!* they won't come off

for the dwarves have stuffed their toes with a petrol cloth
and he dies in tears in his igneous fatuous hat
in a ring of flame which nobody dares put out

8 Scavenging

[*Handwritten note:* Poor Frank.]

Francis likes his food and likes a lot
in drooling dreams he licks the cooking pot
the stewpot with its oyster's skin of grease
curling round nacreous strips of rabbit meat
the frying pan hand-deep in eelblack fat
smacking of frittered fruit or battered plaice
the saucepan fresh from boiling *moules marins*
with lukewarm brine and glistening onions in
he nightly dreams of licking out the lot
and thin economists applaud at that
for Francis Drake was planned to clean things out
and Francis is a man who lacks false pride
he likes the bacon trickling down his chin
he likes the warm congealing on his chest
and loves to scrape it later off his vest
joyfully feeling the whole world is fried
And Frank is not too fine a man for bins
and thinks What Fun! to root about for bones
the well-fleshed bones that smell of oily bliss
wishbones of pretty chickens thick with rice
crackling of pork with prunestones, *grenouilles'* knees
lacking the legs but thickly flecked with cheese
Francis is not too fine a man for these
for Francis likes his food and Francis knows
lean-faced ascetics helped to organize
his brooding love of broken cakes and pies
over-ripe *Bries* and torrid Tartar Sauce
and planned his larderous belly and buttocks and thighs
his sausage fingers and his suckling eyes
which rake the pile of cores and pips and shells
and track delirium in smells of fries
and make a jelly meal for gourmet flies
when gaunt administrators think it wise

9 Motoring

C. Hans thinks of himself as a motoring man
and likes no company but that of cars
and will drive happily in his for hours
on the tarmac *Road to the Coast* which he takes for choice
because he thinks to himself (as a motoring man)
that since all roads lead *to the Sea* or *the Hills* or *the Sun*
if you can trust the legends on every sign
and since none of these legendary things has ever been
                                                        seen
by the unemotive driver and he's not blind
it stands to reason to the motoring mind
(of the most phlegmatic and pneumatic kind
for C. Hans' mind is a seasoned motoring mind)
that the ends of the roads have wizened over the years
and this is the state of affairs which Hans prefers
since he only likes to drive in the company
of cars and would think it a simply priceless nerve
were he expected to actually arrive
at *the Sea* or *the Hills* or *the Sun* as he might have done
had he been such a sucker as to believe the sign
so he chooses to motor along the *Road to the Coast*
for the sake of its signs of ochre-yellow and green
and grey (and a classical tune on his seasoned lips)
fanciful colours supposed to resemble *the Cliffs*
and this is the sign that he disapproves the most
for the yards of sign could well have been scored in red
Fine Tarmac Road With Wizened End instead
but as a motoring man on the *Great Coast Road*
he is never bored for he runs each false sign down
as a seasoned driver who knows the way things are
with his gunmetal car mows down each fancy sign
and runs over the last grey-green and ochre thing
to find it *Cliffs* and a long way down to drown

211

Pilgrim is saving for a holiday
saving his pay in the form of paper leaves
of green and blue which he carefully folds in three
and gleefully hides away in a locking wallet
which Pilgrim invented for the purpose, Lock and Key
being safer for holiday pay than pleated leather
and for inventions he earns extra pay
which he saves for a holiday in the form of additional
leaves
and in the autumn all the leaves turn grey
and through the winter weather Pilgrim saves
slaving away at a lucrative invention
as he describes it to his envious friends
who take each year the regular five days
upon the regular sun roof with their wives
Pilgrim slaves away from eight a.m.
in the form of a regular slave but Pilgrim knows
and is therefore smiling that he and he alone
will have leaves to burn at the golden liberation
so he slaves away at his overtime invention
a leaded box which has trebly-welded sides
and a wildly jangling burglary device
walls that are six feet thick
and an electrocuted lock to lock it
and coils of best barbed wire to coil about it
and Pilgrim smiles when they come to fix a price
which will be in the form of several hundred leaves
which will be of many wonderful fresh colours
sure to be yellow as sand and green as waves
blue as the sea on summer holiday
and he locks himself in the box with the coloured leaves
and when summer comes he is as black as they
for saving life's the quickest way to die

ii

Living inside: love is the seed.
The voice inside Moira/Clothilde

(inside/who fail/who hide/
who fear outside/inside/
who analyse the glass/
inside the window glass/
who fall into the mirror/
felled by the fatal error/
living inside/afraid/
of flights outside the head/
inside/until it died/
who feared/the light outside/
until the heart is killed/
felo-de-se[1]/Clothilde/
who feared/ a friend/ no friend/
the end/ who feared/ the end/
or learn to love/ another/
a message came/ together
or learn to love/ another/
outside/ it asked/ it cried/
the end/ is love/ outside?)

[1] '*Felo-de-se*. One who deliberately puts an end to his own existence . . .
Also *figurative*' O.E.D.

They are letting me tell my own story, although it is perfectly clear to me that they will not read or believe me. But still they have given me piles of neon-white paper, wonderful luminous paper reflecting their five bare luminous walls which I must not write on. The paper is free but the walls are solidly jointed at ninety degrees. In the end my meanings will hang together likewise.

For seven wet years I lived up in the roof of the Crescent, a quiet little room pushed up close to the fat black birds. But the battered stairs still led up to me even with regular kicking – I just couldn't kick them away: and seven years after I climbed there the Valentine Killer came for me up them, or did I go down in the world and down them, *felo-de-se*?

Here at last in the pure white light I can set my tall house in order. The Doktors insist that I tell you all just what I mean, and their smiles float up like tentative moons to remind me. The points (which are never fullstops) that require explantion are three, so they tell me, the Crescent, the murders and lastly the Valentine cards. Hearts and flowers: I wanted them once but the desert winds blew them to paper, to streamers of paper which straggled and vanished like tears. And the rain in the Crescent had no other meaning.

The Crescent meant two rows of houses curving towards each other like brackets. A sour little garden they called ornamental (or I did) grew up in the brackets, we grew in the brackets of brick of a yellowish-green. The colour reflected the wild frayed garden, or I did, and also the gangrenous sheen of decay: and decay wasn't simply a

215

matter of bricks and mortar, the mortar clamped down on the sour square faces of bricks, and someone had painted some of the windows brightly – one of them fresh blood-red: and the paint was still bubbled and sticky, or somebody bled by the window, or I did. Decay, in my case, was *only a matter of time*. Will Frank forgive me and pay me a fleeting visit? I drowned his papers in blood: I was dying, my art was sinking.

The architect meant her brackets to curve towards each other in love. There were four floors, carefully counted, and each line of windows stared out at the curved line facing. Although the blank glass was designed to beam love across, eyes grew behind the glass and small bleak repelling faces: the hands did not wave or beckon, and sharp eyes hooked on a lamplit heart behind glass which fluttered, faltered, then died. The saplings would never grow strong in the poisonous soil of the Crescent, too long enclosed. (Yet the dictionaries still insist that the *crescent* is *growing*!)

For most of the tenants my Crescent was only a dark fog of numbers, and this each attacked in his blunt and mysterious way. Somebody left and the shape of a heart had been carefully burnt in my greased orange carpet. Somebody's bright row of milk bottles strung on my balcony catching the rain in their curd. Such tenants don't care what they do, or else I did. Yet please do not blame me for boldly displaying my jewels to the air. I poured the sour milk on the earth in great dove-feathered fountains.

The landladies lived in the basements, away from the wind on the upper stories and murderous tenants: the white rain splashed them sourly. Seven years in the Crescent bred armies of greasy spectres and vegetable ghosts, though at first and at last it was lonely. My landlady dyed her hair yellow to match my skin: she was fat and her breath smelt of dark green basements and wine. I of course did not deign to be friendly. Miss Poynes whom I might have befriended turned into a shell. But was something left in the shell, was it something like love, locked in?

The living things locked in the Crescent were not generic. Each room was of slightly differing volume, each room had its separate keyhole and key, each head had its differing number of hairs, and I used to believe that each hair on each head was numbered. Seven years ago I rejected the general sentence, moved into these lunar brackets of yellow-green brick. It was built for the old and the rich and fell into pieces of ice and apple peel, oddments of watered velvet and dust and sleep. Though they ask for a meaning I only give it in pieces. I wanted to gather the oddments and sleep in peace.

Poor Frank kept all his belongings in packing-cases. He wore his packing-creased suit when he came to visit. Forgive me, Frank, if I bled on your piled-up papers. Your packing-cased room was a desert to die in, a desert. The moon shone in on my blood on the black of your headlines.

It is possible that Miss Poynes will read my story. Some say she crept out at night and sat faintly singing, her deep faded eyes on the moon, and by day I have seen it shining back from her sockets, two fixed lunar slivers of iris, icy and thin. I loved Miss Poynes, although she did not support me. I asked for love: she said nothing, and went inside.

I think she would speak to me now if I walked past her doorstep. Yes surely the hennaed line of her lips like a single hair is moving, or mine is. And then I look back at those floating eyes and wonder. Someone has quietly knifed through the roots of her irises, leaving her vision cloudy and wholly detached, floating out of my mirror, floating up out of the frame (something flying, which fell.) And yet, I have found you can never cut yourself off entirely: the desert sends Doktors to stop you detaching your heart. But my scissors cut hearts out of paper so well and so neatly.

(I laugh when the Doktors say I am missing the point. I feel that suspicion is marching squarely upon me. I hope I have not revealed too much of myself in this letter, shall not again offer my one good breast to the Doktor. *Yes, if there was one.*)

For all of the murders were mine. *Yes, if there was one.* For seven years nobody spoke, but now there are voices: Doktors and policemen, Brown and Jones and Brown. They are decent and moderate men, and they state that they do not like murders. The State, they inform me, decently, does not like murders either. My attic was tiny and innocent, I was also, both of us bare of incriminating detail. My table held only my art and my strictly creative equipment – my scissors, my squirrels' hair brushes (not numbered), a bottle of indigo ink, one of saffron, some deep burnt oranges, black, and a large size of Emperor's Purple. My bottle of scarlet began to look too much like blood as it darkened and thickened. Did someone once ask 'Have you Blood or Ink in your veins?' I shall not reply if they only try to be hurtful.

Seven years ago someone laughed at my Emperor's Ink and said wittily 'Perfect dear lady for purple prose,' or else I did. Since then I have scarcely spoken to anyone, made few Jokes. After seven years' study I could make nothing of life. I could not make love if my Doktor would not make time. (I hoped that in time we should make it: but later he said he was Brown or Moderate or Jones, and the name and the helmet destroyed it.)

The heart which I burned cannot stop them letting my attic. And now I can never return to the clean simple forms of the Crescent, the saving rectangular forms of the structured brick (yet they crumbled, and did not save me.) Only brick and stone does not suffer when houses crumble. I thought that the walls curved together in love, that the green was the faint acid bloom of young stems, I believed that the walls made a cavity for a heart, that the word in the brackets was *hope* or a *future*. But hope wears thin, and the walls were so thin that nobody should have been lonely. All day the great feet beat the stairs till I thought my heart would stop beating, all day I heard great fists knocking at other doors (and later the feet were in boots, and my heart, my art was in danger.) And loud juices ran in the sour yellow belly of the bath, and I fear that Frank had begun to urinate in the basin (or I did.)

His window was painted blood-red, the surface was bubbled. He did it himself and then asked me inside to see, or I saw that inside him a red-blooded heart was asking. The room was a panicky yellow and piled with boxes and cases of jaundiced wood, and long leaning towers of paper which leaned (and I panicked) towards me. He had to tug at my arm to get me inside, or else I did.

We never found happiness there together, though I would smilingly say to my mother 'I write and he paints, so you see it's a very happy ménage.' And my mother was happily settled at that time also, packed in a long quiet case of yellow-green wood. And the wood is the colour of flowers (there are few in the Crescent): but cholera, scarlet in Naples, sounds like the name of a flower and the red flowers bled on the head of my poor dying mother, so sick and so far. It is true that she liked to imagine that Frank was my suitor, but truth for its own sake is sad and barren. I thought that the Crescent would stop life from being so flat and straight on to the end and so sad and barren, I understood wrongly the curve of the young green parentheses. And it seems that my life has got stuck in these cold tall brackets, has lost the flow and the sense of the sentence outside. I escaped when the brackets closed murderously together, but lost my life and my seven bright hearts in the process, my lovely anonymous Valentines.

Yet I hope that in seven long years I grew more objective. When I had grown used to autumnal tempests of feet through the walls and the floors and the rushing of tears and blood through the echoing pipes of the bathroom, flying and falling, but never came near, grown used to the fat birds' thunder above me, the guilty hiss of the urine below me . . . I saw the truth, which was dying, in other words, dying, the child inside me was dying, for all my painting. They told me they cared for each sparrow which fell, or a girl. But I found it a lie, or a sin, and my hairs were fluffy as feathers on birds and none of them named or numbered.

The moon flows more brightly and I have grown lucid again. I feared I should have to refill it. Only bricks and stone and white bars do not need renewal: the body may bloom but in time the mind will wear through. The veins of my nose and cheeks bloomed out into veins of the wonderful orange creeper which grew on the final house of the southern curve of the Crescent, and later the blood of my face and of Moira's face was confused with the stone of the pavement, the line between us worn through . . .

(our bents, in the end, must be straightened)

. . . and after the police have finished their logical march on my murder the road will stretch curveless and factual behind and before them, on either side of the house where my body lay. The ultimate Valentine showed it, the loved white breast transfixed by an arrow, the breast I had bared for the knife or the lingering look of the moon. The tint of my skin in the moonlight was greenish-yellow, a bleak sad tint, but I knew they would find it lovely, or I did. Down on my bared left breast the shape of a bleeding star was ready to flower. I was glad to be opened, I knew I was locked too long in my room in the clean close air of the Crescent.

Seven years ago I should have been less objective. Or someone says more or *amour*, but I know they are joking.

220

My visual sense has been sharpened by endless looking for beauty or hope (Well you would have done better to sharpen your scissors!) *Do not make Jokes.* And the curved exoskeletal brick slowly grew transparent, and I have had curious glimpses of pale private beasts in their shells. Yet I never spy like the Doktors: who set dogged scientists tracing my exquisite inks and the ghosts of my strenuous handprints, set men to analyse mystery and death from the pulp of the paper. The Doktors do not like Jokes and would not even laugh as they pointed at me, my own Valentine Killer, *felo-de-se*.

Each year her cards grew more sad and obscure and elaborate, each year the warning of madness became more clear. A girl (I was always a girl) was found stabbed by Frank's window, pierced through the chest by the severing blades of her scissors: she felt cut off. Yet they say I must not make Jokes. After seven years of love she was killed by the Valentine Killer – *yes, if there was one*.

At night it is hard to distinguish a bloodbath from water. The snailstrail of symbols led over the midnight red of the sea, but the light of the factual dawn was greenish, the crescent moon trembled and melted and finally fled, it was flying and falling, now fled. For years I had not seen land. The path of the moon on the sea was a wonder of complex elliptical motion, and yet it led straight as a die to the red horizon. I hoped I should die straightaway. A straight road is what the Police Doktors insist on: I yield to my fear of a straitjacket, *felo-de-se*. But I do insist on the faces. They hang all about any scaffold of branches or bricks and mortar like torn scraps of paper or slowly deflating signal balloons. All I know is that somehow I never received the whole of the message. I lost my view and later I lost the pattern.

Forgive me Frank if I bled on your piled-up headlines. Their yellow partings must have been sodden with blood, I could never stand partings. The evening before the murder I opened his door for the very first time just a fraction and peered through the crack at his cases and boxes and him standing there with the pores standing out from his nose OH I DID NOT WANT FRANK IN MY MURDER. That evening he stared with his pores and did not even ask me my name, which is not unattractive. Again, though they tell me my breasts are mostly still there, they were firmly turned down by the Doktor. Turned down I fell to the ground, past three brilliant levels of window, fell hundreds of feet to the ground (or she did, or we did.) And hundreds of hard metal feet went on flying and falling, without me.

I painted for years with coloured inks stoppered in little glass bottles, and sat with my beautifully tinctured face at the glass of the window. Of course I was happy there living alone, or else I am lying. Or else I was lying there weeping alone, which admission at this stage is scarcely so happy.

A page curls up in a tiny flame, can be torn out quickly. But here we are not allowed matches, and shielded from pain. The light fittings here are all flush with the ceiling, the feet float on rubber and do not batter the stairs. For there are no stairs: we are going nowhere, and blind screens shutter the arduous path to the stars or the moon at the top of the trees. In the Crescent the tenants booted each bone of the ribcage, and somewhere a long shattered column of vertebrae ached, or I do, or I did. The ribcage was once intended to shield the lungs and the heart, oh wasn't it? Shut in my long shattered cage in the end there was nothing living.

The mirrors of attic rooms have intelligent eyes, your own, and they look at your life growing older and strip off the paint from the skin from the bone. But still I have always loved painting. With indigo ink I marked shells of deep blue for my eyes in their soft pained sockets, and the curve of my cheek caught the light with its saffron shading, catching it, losing it, darkening, darkening, gone. And someone smoothed tenterhook black where my thin brows climbed into feathers, and flew (I was brave, as a girl) at the fat black birds. There were celandines by a black pond in my childhood graveyard: and boats on a lake in a park, but the indigo sea of my eyes is too dark now for boating. The Doktors say too much morbidity does me no good. They are moderate men and quite right, yet I do not think they are bright: it is brightness I need for morbidity does me no good. I was making an art of my life, but the light was waning, and so I decided on something easier, death. Still I could not make it, the police and Doktors made trouble. And now they snigger and talk about lies or false colours. They wish me to stay on the ground, and demand a much shorter sentence.

The lines on their criminal forms are too rigid and narrow. I always found it a penance to write on the lines. And the lines on my face have lately obstructed my painting. A woman once said that my writing was lacking in form (or I did.) My murder however was simple and forceful and pointed. I thrust the blades in where I thought that my lungs and my heart were, the fluttering wings of my lungs and my long-lost heart.

When I could not write, I could always use scissors and paper. With seven years' training my left breast tore like paper. Poor Frank had been snoring from every slack trumpet-mouthed pore. It was not fair to *felo-de-se* in Frank's room, but mine was so lonely. (Of course I had never been lonely: but now I should never be lonely again, with the Doktors and Frank making honks like a goose or a girl and the fat black geese and the police in their boots all round me, oh never *amour*.)

In one stab I was married anew to your world, a new beauty, and policemen and doctors and poor flushed stertorous Frank were all round me at last, although

223

nobody knew me, and now you are round me reading. But do not expose me.

The Doktors will never expose me to life in the communal desert. All paper up here is quite bare: no headlines, and no towers fall. The walls too are bare or too bare and too high for the trees and the faces. To sleep in pieces, I shall, where no towers fall . . . But unless you are ready to sleep now, end now, beware. The Doktors are coming, their boots (Brown and Moderate and Jones) are coming, you do not need them to see you. Escape while you can.

I am smuggling out this message between two saucers. The word in their cracked yellow brackets is some sort of order: all art needs command over life, all life needs not art but an order. The order is (Live) or (Love), and I in my dead art give it. The brackets can finally close now, the Crescent can flee or dwindle. If you choose to believe in metaphors, live behind them: in symbols, then messily die in symbolic decorum. Or *Live*, or *Love*.

(a message came/ together/
or learn to love/ another/
outside/ it asked/ it cried/
the end/ is love/ outside?)

iii

Living outside: men in formation
The end of armies. The end.

Committees

This is the control box. In fact from the outside you can see it is one of hundreds of thousands of control boxes. The control box stands on four tall legs. All the other control boxes also stand on four tall legs. But the length of the legs of the different boxes varies.

From the inside, where they fear to think of the sky, there seems to be only one control box. The legs seem enormously long and the sky very near and confiding. There are ten men in the box. They wear pinstripe suits and the stripes extend skywards. They sit at a table, a big round table of teak. It is teak all through with a modest veneer of plastic. They think this is democratic. They call it their global table.

The table is round so that all men will be equal. They think this is democratic. Committees also are obviously democratic. From the inside at least this is obviously true. From the outside, you see the control box. From further outside, you see hundreds of thousands of boxes: their legs are of different lengths and the boxes are larger or smaller.

Inside the same scale holds true. Committees in bigger boxes have longer titles. The stuff of their pinstriped suits is duller and richer: their breast-pockets sport more solid gold biros and pens. When they break for refreshment, lean waitresses lope in with trays, their legs in black stockings as tender and tense as the legs of fine race-horses.

Under their black lace dresses with frivolous black silk frill front-opening detail they wear body-moulding erotic corsets, with special modesty trapdoors at nipple and groin. In the largest boxes of all, the gold will be fourteen carat.

The trapdoors are democratic, allowing for peeping. If waitresses stand at the central point of the global table, an equal chance of peeping is given to all. At the end of a tiring session, the pin-striped men from the fourteen-carat boxes are permitted to stick up to seven of their maximum fourteen solid gold biros and pens in the modesty plackets which buttress the modesty trapdoors (in all spheres of life there are proper procedures.)

In smaller but nonetheless big-league boxes the ten tired men at the end of a session perk up when politely asked to insert their carrots. One waitress is said to have neighed like a racehorse in pain when ten carrots pierced her at once from all parts of the global table: the chairman explained after climax that everyone thought this was more democratic, moreover that painstripes suit her. The legs of the box after climax remained erect, so the ten limp members retained elevation. The girl had to go to the knackers: her knees and her spirit were broken. Ten donkeys were fed from her ten-carat genital region.

So even control boxes play, and their long legs kick in the air, although never unwisely. Inside them the fat black legs of the occupants tremble with pleasure, though never above the respectable global table. The pinstripes quiver in safety beneath the veneer and the waitress brings each one a large pink gin in a glass in the shape of a woman with round pink vitreous breasts, which committee members may keep as a souvenir.

Yet the pink glass woman is mermaid-like, lacking real legs, on the premise that tails hold more liquid, and knees get broken. So the fishy and blood-tinged eyes of the ten men swivel and stick and swim bonelessly after the lean and marvellously separate legs of the girls in black stockings dispensing the febrile gins, their slim black shanks like the dancing shanks of fine horses.

So even control boxes dream, though a man of substance may also insert his pen at the proper moment, apply through the proper channels, sigh through the proper and far too limited solid gold trapdoor responsibly backed by a solid gold placket. In all life's spheres there are proper procedures, procedures determined by proper committees. So even control boxes work for some part of their living.

This is a control box in the morning. There are no windows, lest members look out and perceive they are merely one box among hundreds of thousands of similar boxes. It is believed (a belief determined by careful committee vote in what is perhaps the tallest control box) that this would be fatal. When flinging themselves through the air at a very great height from the ground men will bleed and die, and the pinstripes be no protection.

But this is the morning and there is no time for jumping or bleeding. Moreover there are no windows. The sun on the bright steel outside of the box may shine like plate glass, but they cannot jump through it.

At first one or two thought it odd that the box had no exit. The hatch at the top of the ladder is marked in gold: ENTRANCE ONLY. In red underneath it says PENALTY DEATH. One or two had presumed it was joking and yet they were cautious. The men who ascend to committees are always cautious.

The men who are flung through the chute marked EXCREMENT ONLY are dead: they are always dead. One or two of them died when they grew less cautious: the rest of them died after years of cautious and loyal years in committee and miles of pink gin and with thousands of souvenir pink gin glasses fashioned like round pink one-legged women stacked under their well-sprung Deep-Asleep pink satin *Toss-U-Off-Put-U-Down* (finally) beds.

Death in bed is usually said to be quick and easy. And this was a judgement arrived at by one of the highest committees, determined by careful discussion and formal vote. The soft pink beds of the voters were naturally some of the widest, and yet in the end the pink seas panted and shrank and the rose-pink valance with concealed pink *Suffer-Kate* no-legged girl-shape mechanism all came down and the pink concealed *All-Nite* lighting sank down and grew dark and the pink piped music grew louder to hide any panting at first and at last the wild waterless voices of old men stifling and calling like babies from under the warm dry murderous valance which held them, and gagged them, and hugged.

Never let your small child near a window. Committees on children will always emphasize this. If the child is stifled with boredom, he may try to jump. Together the broken window and child will be messy. But if your child stifles at night and away from the window, disposal is quick and discreet and hygienic. In all spheres of life there are proper procedures. Please use them.

And such is the public decree of this morning's committee. The stripes come together and spread all around the teak table. The first waitress enters formally weeping with morning papers. Another one follows with free reversible paper hankies for laughter or tears, for committees must not be unfeeling. Another one follows with a large satin-ribbon-bound bin to collect any surplus emotion or crumpled hankies.

Another one enters and reads out a brief polite speech (whose form was determined some ages ago by the proper committee) requesting that crumpled members collect themselves. This is owing to temporary shortage of personnel and for this another one comes and apologizes together with three other idly weeping and waiting waitresses and all their weeping and waiting waitress friends.

The committee chairman offers them coffee. They show

230

their tempers to peepers to great applause and a loud unanimous cry of 'Encore' and 'Knickers', believed, as the minutes opined, to refer to the fate of the mythical waitress sent to the knackers and eaten by donkeys, beloved and mourned by all. The reference was generally thought to be tactless. A motion was passed deploring the offer of coffee. Three hundred black-stockinged waitresses bolt from the room, to the principled cheers and neighs of the mere (this due to a temporary shortage of staff) two million three thousand four hundred and five young mares remaining, hemmed in on all sides by ten men who are frightened of riding and dreaming and dying, for time runs out.

When teak tables crack in the morning under the pressure and millions of panicking mares stampede with their black legs kicking and kicking and some flying out and connecting with panicking pinstriped flesh, rather softened and swollen from years of committed and democratic sitting, when gargoyling silver-plate coffee pots spout and tip and the wet brown liquid boils over and up and two old red terrified eyes will reflect their own colour of blood and the hot bloody liquid boils over and fills your best brogues with wet panic and dark stains spread on your trousers and even the pinstripes begin to quiver and blur and dissolve and are horribly littered with shreds of pink satin like torn pink skin saying *death* and cascades of cacophonous breaking pink souvenir glasses like one-legged women with round pink vitreous breasts torn open, a broken pink mouth saying DEATH as the strong steel floor of the box sprouts cracks and the dreadful green earth begins to show through, oh ultimate horror of greenness after grey steel: look up at the grey steel ceiling and see that it too has a gross blue spider of cracks on it crawling and stretching, a spider of terrible morning celestial blue, oh horror of infinite height after years of safe steel ceiling: when the morning convulses, and ordered minutes fly up and spread out like feathers and time fragments and the years of sitting stand up and have heavy cruel hooves to most cruelly wind you where you have grown dreamy and fat and the feathers fledge horrible birds with a savaging razor of sun in their spurs and their pinions, their wings which will bring down all heaven and horror and horror and horror upon you:-

– then wasted the pain of the climb: wasted the slow industrious scaling of ladders, the sweating in gradually more and more opulent pinstriped suits up the narrow steel ladder alongside the ever more slender and dubious leg of the distant control box, – is it for me oh is it oh bullet of bliss in the frightful but unavoidable blue of the void blue skies, and he climbs to a steel simulacrum of earth with all earthly and heavenly comforts, he climbs to control of the globe in a round teak table: he clutches the steel though his pale pudgy fingers all ache and the trousers are stiff and unpleasantly tight and he pushes the great bulk of fantasy tables and cushions and well-kept minutes and solidly-minuted hours on up (for such lustrous and glorious fun at the top awaits him) on up to the next narrow rung: he must hurry, for time (and time to have fun) runs out –

– the wind lashes and cuts him, his small eyes mirroring dreams of souvenir glasses grow pink and vitreous, redden and run: and the wind takes the leg of his trousers and whips him. He kicks at stray fingers or anxious myopic and wind-reddened faces of climbers behind him, finishing all but a few. When the few and himself reach their distant (but nearer! and *Nearer!*) objective, these stressful occasions are never discussed. In all spheres of life there are proper procedures, and climbers must always obey them, climbing with lethal decorum on up to the top of the globe. But the globe of the world rolls round and it's suddenly *All Fall Down* and all of that murderous pain will be spilled on the wind and wasted . . .

For this is the control box in the morning: the long legs

gradually starting to crumble, the long legs as helpless as unnerved legs of a dying insect trémbling and circling, the long legs jerking like half-severed limbs of a terrified dying mayfly and finally falling, toppling like towers, dizzying out of control and falling as all towers finally do, for in all spheres of life there are proper procedures, falling, falling, the proper committees are falling and screaming inside as their bald heads crumple like eggs and yield to the thrashing hooves of the mares and the hooves of their horror of falling . . .

> (THEY WILL BE NAKED
> THEY HAVE NO TABLE
> THEY WILL BE DEAD)

It is all unfair: it should not take place in the morning. Unfair: for the other control towers remain, and to see there are others and others remaining, their long legs steely and slender and cold and their boxes smaller! and *Smaller*! bullets of bliss in a giddily spinning and vanishing heaven – to see this and know in the terrible battering greenness and blueness before the end that they sat in committee in one of the smaller boxes, easily tipped, with four of the shorter legs and the less precipitous ladders, makes strong men weep – (this a cliché approved in committee, in all spheres of life and of language there being proper procedures) – and know in the end they were weak.

Companies   [*Handwritten note*: Frank, poor Frank. C. Hans, keeping time. And all of them.]

This is Reception. Above it and opposite, a large clock whose face lacks all expression. The hands are golden: the clock keeps perfect time.

This is the Receptionist. Every time anyone enters or leaves, she looks at the clock and smiles a dazzling smile. Her teeth are of gold, four golden teeth at the front affixed to the rest with thin gold wires. The hands of the clock are fledged and tipped with thin gold. She wants to befriend it. The face of the clock however stares back at the wide gold smile and lacks all expression.

The gold belongs to the Company, so does she. And every Company year she completes successfully, blackly recording the hour when each member of staff arrives and departs and arrives and departs every day of the year (although one of them never departs any more from the narrowing corridor), blackly recording the small excursions for sweet cigarettes and balloons of laughing gas and a bag of despair to bury the head in at tea-time, for contraceptives and heart-shaped humbugs tasting of love, – she is fitly rewarded.

The Company Dentist comes in a long white car. The receptionist sits in her plush pink chair in Reception, and all of the staff who are all good friends are summoned to drink pink gin which may well be the Company dental mouthwash (but hush) and watch.

The dentist flourishes a large white cape and behind it she crows three times in a sky of red pain like a neutered cockerel, the Company crest. The cape comes down, and the sun of a new gold tooth comes up with her smile from behind it. Applause is not merely formal. Some offer their fingers for her to bite, and the Company lechers queue up to French-kiss her, to cow-lick the cold gold tooth and exchange rosy clouds of pink gin. They are nearly all jolly good sorts, yet the large gold clock looks down and lacks all expression. The clock belongs to the Company: so do they.

Parties take place in Reception, around and among the attractive Company plants. They have sombre lustrous leaves and responsible stems which delegate buds and functions. Each leaf is a glossy dark green with discreet gold veining, to match the leaf-green Company carpets and echo the chaste thin gold of the hands of the clock, which belong to the Company. *Time is money* (but time, someone says, runs out – but hush, for *time is money*.)

And this is the Company slogan. In gold and green it adorns the head of the Company notepaper, curves round the crest of the Company cockerel: is also the strong first line of the Company song, which is sung very clearly at parties and savagely later in offices, howled with a wild jazz tune and obscene red words. And the Company smiles on this, if a thing can smile which lacks all expression, knowing derision goes hand in thin gold Company time-keeping hand with love and need, and the gold needles puncture the skin and point to the time and stare blankly at workers and slackers. The Company covers its face with its hands but the face behind them also lacks all expression.

The Company covers its face with its carpets and tropical plants in holiday pots and desks with a plastic veneer of good dark teak and wastebins in daffodil yellow and grey wasting seas of waste paper, waist-high, waist-high in one room which will shortly be battened for good and the weeping and stifling executive also inside it, for not all, alas, were jolly good sorts although nearly.

And this one, alas, poor Frank, is weeping and stifling and sits in his darkening office and thinks of the face of the clock. No-one visits him now, only Bubbles, the office junior, Bubbles who last year was thought so sweet and called Bubbles because of the bounce of her breasts and the float of her curls in a cloud of the perfume of rose-pink bathrooms in rose-pink dreams.

But Bubbles is big now, and slow now, and fat. She brings him cold coffee in a baby's cup with a technicolour mouse on the side. Cigar stubs float in it like slugs. She stands over him while he drinks it. Sometimes she brings him sticks of rock, slightly soft and with dust or crumbs on them. His hands shake but he can still break them, with a soft dull sound like the breaking of limbs. By now all his limbs are broken.

The hands on the Company clock never shake: they are firm and cold and they sail on the clock on the wall far above all the offices, *Time is money*.

Down in the darkening office along at the far blind end of the green-and-gold narrowing Company corridor floats a soft sound like the breaking of limbs and the limp rock breaks. In the centre, the Company slogan, TIME IS MONEY. The more you attempt to break it, the more it repeats with a dull sweet sound like the breaking of limbs in a darkening office or gold coins falling and falling on rubber pads. The pads are of clean green rubber and carefully made to avoid any vulgar chinking of coins or chains, he is not quite sure of the difference.

His office is padded, but still all his limbs are broken from beating against the walls which are almost dark now and drowning in waves of grey paper, which rustle with cartoon mice in the dark and the sound of fat Bubbles escaping. But soon she will find it too narrow. He thinks of the face of the clock, far away, which lacks all expression.

The office is lit with fading and flicking fluorescent, with what were once sticks of white surgical light, too hard for his eyes and now broken, time runs out. In the larger offices you will find green and gold filters and piped adaptations of *Time is Money* the Company song by assorted first class musicians of every colour and creed. There are armchairs of soft simulation leather, a gold simulation of luxury piped in green. There are ashtrays stamped with the Company crest in synthetic ambers and jades, too large for the fake teak tables, the mad cock preening and crowing.

In offices far from Reception the ashtrays are smaller

and overflowing with tears and the drowned pale moons they have stripped from the ends of their nails which reflected the moon on some long-lost waters, reflecting the pink private moons at the base of their nails. Yet notices over the desks can be read quite clearly, RE-FLECTIONS SHOULD BE DISPOSED OF OUTSIDE THESE WALLS.

There used to be windows admitting the sun, one remembers. Another forgets, and the sun shines bright in Reception, glints from the hands of the clock. And each day another one forgets. They are all good sorts, and they all forgive and forget, or nearly. Or they are forgotten, and die.

Which only occurs at the corridor's narrowing end, where the carpets are darkened and shabby. Nobody visits but Bubbles, puffing and heaving, sluggish and spiteful, bearing her slug-filled big baby's cup. And he never goes out past Reception, the blank-faced clock and the splen-did Receptionist's big gold timeserving crocodile smile. If he tried, she would run out and bite him, sink her gold Company fangs in his papery neck.

He feels all of paper, waste paper: he feels he is darkening now and he thinks of the points of the clock, of its gold hands feathered and tipped with thin gold which transpierce him there at his desk as the waste and the darkness thicken and windows recede into dreams of windows and dreamed-of windows transmute from glass to thin paper, and paper thickens and darkens above him until there is no more light.

He remembers that once he was told the point of the clock but now he forgets it, blurs the gold point which belongs to the Company, TIME IS MONEY, IS MONEY.

On Monday the end of the corridor will be sealed. Informal weekend noises will be erased (such as rustling, breaking and weeping alone in the dark while the jolly good sorts leap about outside with their gold-haired wives and their nimble green dogs and their jewelled green-and-gold beetles on chains and their Company Freetyme Joke Books, gold letters on green on the green green grass in the sun, which is golden as money, which thought it had bought it. The Company slogan is FREE TIME IS FUNNY, IS FUNNY. Yet somebody wept and would soon be erased, back in the offices, rustling, stifling and beating alone in the dark.)

On Monday, the dead grey waste sighs finally up to the ceiling: the passage is sealed. A fatty, a rose-cheeked woman with dyed rose curls is employed for the sealing. How easily she will stick and she burns like a fat perfumed rose-red candle, she burns like a rose-red dream.

In offices far from Reception, don't look in the ashtrays. One of them is stamped with a foot, a foot kicking, the foot and the ashtray broken. Another is overflowing with ashes. Gold fillings have been removed from the ash.

Armies [*Handwritten note*: Bill Dutton, Macbeth. They want to be heroes. The future: dying in formation.]

Men in matching silver suits: hundreds of them working together, quadruple hundreds of matching silvered limbs. This silver army is making machines. The machines will fly to the moon (so they say) and the men on hundreds of monitored silver screens will watch them.

There are no trees for miles, but only cement and glass and bright metal in buildings. There are canteens, very clean with a filter of cheering music: the meals are sealed in clear plastic cases. The girls have been trained to smile, and are dressed in crisp shiny smocks which reflect this. There is a choice of pale violet or pale lemon. Everything has been foreseen.

238

At each table, trimmed bunches of daffodils or bluebells look almost real. Though the floors feel warm to the touch the air is kept fresh and bracing. Sometimes it smells very slightly of lemons, sometimes of pine. The music is thin and insistent and clear and it too is bracing. There are no windows, but every wall has a mural worked in relief: blue stone for the sky, bright metal for something flying.

The men think them very modern. This is what foreman 227 told Design Committee when they asked him. Modern, they said, but do the men like them? He stubbornly repeated his invention.

The men all move to a rhythm. Not to themselves but to their masters in the various control towers they appear to imitate machines, speaking rarely, smiling rarely, moving slowly and smoothly in their heavy silver suits. The heavy metal stuff insists. Yet each one feels himself to be himself alone inside the pattern. Each one looks at the machines and dreams from time to time of solitary flight, and coming back to bland-limbed girls and bleeding crimson garlands.

They are glad in the end to be pinned to the ground by the weight of their mediocrity and silver uniforms. Because men die. Only men without dreams will be chosen. But somehow, alone in extreme cold, drunk with the horror of white stars growing and growing and flowering and flowering, very high up in the frosty sky, the dreams of men on the ground of wings and of flying and falling infect them: they start to bleed and kick and the crimson floods anticipate the garlands.

Those on the ground are abashed and glad. In their work on the great machines they bend nearer the ground, ever nearer the grassless and treeless ground, and their movements are slower and surer than ever and more careful.

Yet each man drinks his sleeping draught at night and

dreams of flying. There is a single scratch of silver in a black bowl. Without the scratch the bowl would be much safer. But without the silver, the black could not be born. The remnants of the drug, not quite dissolved, gleam whitely on the bottom, a base imitation of the mercury of flight: the sleeper has wings, and on dim fins and feathers and soft confused plumage of sleep swims across the deep heavens, swims up through the ice-streaming stars and is drowned in the drug and the silence. His wings thresh once, and the black bowl falls from the bed on the floor and cracks: but he will not wake until morning. Over his head and the heads of hundreds of others dreaming of flying in the cells above and below him, the black bowl rests and is safe.

In the morning, sunlight enters the camp in clean definite cubes, slotting into spaces between buildings. The music plays: it is cheerful and bracing and thin, they have washed the sky out of it. In the canteens the men talk. Some recount their dreams in loud voices, stories of football or fighting or sexual outrage. They eat their bacon, pink as that lush accessible mucous skin. And their eggs, more yellow and well-defined than the morning sunlight, more round than a football, more round than the safe round earth or the clear plastic cases they came in. Someone whispered the plan was not flying but dying: dying, in other words, carrying death to the rest of the world, that the plan was *The End* in triplicate. Hush, carry death, carry on.

The girls flutter by in a rustle of lemon or violet nylon. Their eyes go nowhere. They smile and smile, they are full of beneficent mornings and music and waking pills. They are very efficient and clean and they smell of freshly-picked violets or lemons. The air this morning is pine. The girls are a base imitation of flightless butterflies, cut out of nylon, mounted on wires and sold in a novelty shop. In a novelty shop there are no surprises: everything is foreseen.

When the girls hear a dream with a sexual content, they giggle and flutter their short fleshy wing-stumps of labia under the nylon. They straighten their knees so no space can remain between them. Their eyes go nowhere.

If anyone says he was dreaming of flying, they smile and smile and gently nudge him and say he is naughty: their arms go round him, strong manicured fingers close on his groin and they lead him away to a chorus of envious titters and jeers as he grins, as he grows, as he hardens.

Round the corner, long nails in his balls restrain him from heaven, from fucking, from flying. They take clean scissors and cut off his limbs for wings and his rosily hopeful naked sword, its poor hopes, its poor redness, they cut off the rind for breakfast. Their eyes go nowhere. They spray more pine and work wonders of hygiene with mops and buckets of stainless steel on the safe close ground: and with tissues of lemon or violet, later crimson. They spray more pine. The tissues are later crimson, and sodden with blood. But their eyes go nowhere, are white and stainless.

If you look closely, you see that the yolks were removed long ago and go round and go round for breakfast, go round and go round in the gleaming canteen, more round than the safe black bowl they were cracked in, round and round. And the dull robbed whites of their eyes go nowhere, smile and smile, and the dull cracked shells of their hearts leak uniform horrors under the lemon or violet crisp bright smocks.

The men think the girls very modern. This is what foreman 228 told Personnel Committee when they asked him. Modern, they said, but do the men like them? He stubbornly repeated his invention.

THIS IS A HAPPY CAMP. In letters of silver stamped on labels of black enamel, hundreds of labels large and small. Each silver suit has its label and each machine and each part of a machine. And the outside of each of the black-lined bowls which contains the men's sleeping draughts has its label.

The bowl's outside is quite black, as if burnt out. It is black enough for the dreaming index finger to scratch it with silver, black enough for the snail track of human flight through the hurtling vastness to mark it with slow and delicate silver, the gleam of the soft suspension of flying or crawling or floating things which hover and glow on the dull vast breast of the dark. But each morning the bowl lies broken.

Each morning the bowl lies cracked on the floor and men walk away to the happy canteen and the very nice girls and the fresh scents of lemon or pine and the clear white eyes and the clear white smiles and the very modern murals, worked for relief. Blue stone for a firm blue daytime sky: bright metal for a corporate missile, blindly and firmly flying, safely relieving the dangerous corporate dream. Someone says it is death they are dreaming, although all they wanted was flight to a strange bright home.

For this silver army will soon be making machines (they can carry death in their bellies.) The machines will fly to the moon with picked athletes aboard (so they tell them), men who can manage their dreams, and the army on hundreds of monitored silver screens will be woken with sirens and shaking and shaken with helpless envy to watch them (they did not know it was death they were bringing back home. All they wanted was myth, a steel vision of manhood and freedom, a fine free flight to the moon . . . but flying and falling, the steel hope always loops earthwards, and communal death clamps down on the hero's dream.)

Solitaries

[*Handwritten note*: Running down. Falling out of the army. Falling to earth. Bill Dutton. Frank, falling further. No possible way to return . . . but alive, and a man?]

This is a bench. On the end of the bench is a bottle of VP wine, half-empty, and under the bench are another two standing together, empty, beside them another one dead on its side with the bottom smashed out. There is sun on the broken bottle, and somewhere the sound of singing.

This is a bench. In the middle of the bench is a parcel of yellowish paper, coarse crumpled paper from which spill pieces of batter and half-eaten fish. On the yellowish paper are spots of red. When you walk up close, which no-one is eager to do, for the straight-backed old couples who walk in the park with their dogs to admire the sun on the bright blue glass of the lake and the orange and gold of the flowers do not care for the tasteful deep tortoiseshell curl of the sun in the glass of the bottle – but if you would like to sit on the seat quite close to the parcel of crumpled yellow, which no-one is eager to do since the fish smells strongly, you notice the red is not ketchup, but blood. Only no-one is eager to look, because next to the bottle of VP wine (half-empty) which stands at one end of the bench and the yellowish blood-spotted parcel of half-eaten fish which spills over the middle, there is a man, and the man is singing. He is sprawled at the other end of the bench from the bottle, and if you look closely which nobody does you will see that the sprawl of old clothes is a man, and bleeding.

There is a man on the bench, but it does not look like a man, it looks like a sprawl of old clothes at the end of a fight with a man-eating fish or the bright jagged jaws of a bottle, under the bench. Yet he seems to be singing of love, though no-one is listening.

The clothes are an old black suit with a rusting of damp and an old blue torn plastic mac and a scratched brown jacket of leather with the sleeves ripped out and a slug in the right-hand pocket: and an army overcoat shaded from yellow to green where the rain and the rot have long been and are long past fighting: a pale canvas hat with a hole and a brim all rippled like uncooked pie-crust, and next to the skin or the layer of dirt which lies over the skin is a nest of old sweaters, their long ends of wool of impossible colours all gently unknotting and whimsically knitting together and fading to soft shades of mice in a soft nest of field mice, but only small insects crawl there. And somewhere under all this is a man.

Underneath the warm nest there is skin, although no-one looks closely. The skin is not clean. Although no-one has seen it or touched it for days which have blurred into months and the years are no clearer, small insects live there. And sometimes they bite, or they hop and they skate like children.

Once he had children he thinks or else he remembers he was one. Now he hates children. At four o'clock when the school day ends they will come and surround him. Like insects he thinks and he makes vague terrible gestures under the nest which he hopes will get out and be bold and black in the sunlight.

He thinks of his skin. For years or he must not exaggerate days which have blurred into months he remembers he has not seen it, or has he forgotten. And yet he believes it is there, and it covers some marvellous intricate construction, and watching the girl who runs past with her dog and her thin legs pumping he thinks it is probably much like hers: though it does not exactly function. And yet, when he doesn't forget he can often hear himself singing.

We all have bodies he thinks and his face cast up on a black sea of fluttering rubbish smiles. Underneath all the rags and the waves and the mouse-coloured tatters of vague time passing he knows something beats: something

244

bites, something moves, something scratches. The lost face smiles.

But now it is frowning. He thinks of the bottle. He looks for the bottle, first in the sky, where it happens his face is then looking. Blue glass, and then sunshine, and empty, and mocking, and huge. Looks hard, and suspects a red aeroplane climbing, or is it the sun in his eyeball, or is it a bird. But he knows (and feels proud that he knows) there are no red birds in England.

He went to Paradise once in the army, and there there were birds. All colours, and fountains of feathers (a bird, or was it *abroad*?) He remembers he watched one for hours, they called it a Paradise bird and he sees it again for a second all dripping with turquoise and orange and flaming impossible reds and the long wings flash in the sun and the colours bleed fiercely together . . . Recalled by the Sergeant-Major. *There's a war on, haven't you heard?* he looks at his hand which has risen and claws at the sky and he thinks *like a bird* for a moment and thinks he is clever and giggles, or croaks like a bird: but he suddenly sees that the clawed hand is dripping, and bleeds in the sky like a lead-filled bird, now falling.

He knows he was once in the army, abroad, and his one bloody hand grips the other.

He thinks of the children, who hate him: much better shoot them. His bloody hand grips on the trigger: screaming and squawking and dropping. He thinks of the bottle which cut him. Somebody smashed it to spite him. A hole between somebody's eyes, as red as the plane or the sun.

He thinks of another bottle, and suddenly, horribly, smiles. Still full or maybe half-empty, he cannot precisely remember. The red gums stupidly gleam. It is somewhere, and shining, and lovely. Or small red planes, and the sun and the drink and the flies are a small red plane on some far red horizon which buzzes, and yawns, and is sleep.

His eyes slip down very white in their sockets of dirt and

stick. At the far park railings the legs of the thin girl running and running away, and the green gates swinging behind her. He screws up his eyes in the sun but too slowly to catch her or see if the bitch had his bottle, running away.

All bitches and tarts, all women. Yet he had a woman once too he remembers and closes his eyes and remembers, the red-and-black gates swinging blindly behind her and closing. For minutes or has it been hours he forgets the lost bottle and shelters behind his closed lids and the patterns now red and now black as the leaves of the palm tree above him sweep over the sun, or it might be the red-and-black wings of the lost bird of Paradise passing. But lost. He wakes up and remembers the fire in the bottle.

The legs of the woman were also pale like the legs of the girl in the sun (now running away) but the legs of the woman were round and soft and slow-moving, and he went softly between them, and hard, and hard. And such peace in the redness and wetness he found there where red ugly heads of dead babies came pushing out later, or else by cold instruments pulled. For now he remembers. And now he forgets and thinks only of drowning in wetness as they must have drowned and he stretches his hand for the bottle.

And then there were thousands of women, all bitches and hard. They drank all his money and left him, as she first hardened and left him. But she had not taken his money. And said that she loved him . . . then later she hated his drinking and gave him dead babies, his son who would fly to the moon, if she let him: but no, he had died. And afterwards cried.

He remembers the sound of her crying and closes his eyes to forget it and afterwards cried, and for minutes which might have been hours and the years too blurring is crying. And blind years of water under the lid feel the afternoon sun stare through them, heavy and red as new blood: pain, and so much time gone. He is singing again, of love.

He has it. He picks up the bottle, half-full and his own, and he lifts it into the sunlight, carefully, carefully, joy in a slow brilliant arc of brown glass and the fire inside it which lives and is found and his own and the hateful dead babies and schoolboys and birds not steal it, nor even the years: for as everything else has grown less and the contacts between his head and his dim drowned body have dwindled, the number of bottles has grown and the radiant rainbows of sun in brown glass have redoubled, or pools of pale fire in brown rain and the real red fire deep inside it and swallowed and seeping through each dry and ever more distant vein which goes shrivelling into the lost grey regions of flesh: where possession has passed to the tiny silver-grey brainless and dancing fleas, his children.

Yet the fire makes his head feel better, his body slightly less far. And he finds it and lifts it, warm to his warm found hand and a warm found bottle to hold it, and burns in the sun and drowns as the fire pours down.

And it pours and it pours. In slow intermissions with bright blurred edges and red pools of sun in the eyelid skin. Into hours. He can trust it for hours. You cannot trust a woman: the hours became years and they left him. With bright blurred edges, the sun on their hair. When she bore the dead baby, his son, who was planned as a hero, her hair was all dripping with grease and black sweat though the first time he saw her it hung down as blonde as an angel. The doctor had said things looked black and her hair when it came fell in black chains of tears to her shoulders, and something that was not a baby (although the whole building was full of babies angrily crying) howled and cried. Their baby was red and ugly and silent, and only the mother was weeping. And the hours slipped by into weeks and she still sat staring and weeping.

The baby was his and was born with a mouth and a

247

brain, it would fly to the moon; but its wings were broken, not moving. Possession had passed to the ground and the slugs and the insects. And now all the schoolchildren hate him and come and surround him who lost his own children and tease him and stick to the skin of his fear like insects, his fear they will come in a swarm and seize him and take him away and his bottle away, which is all he has left since she left him: and so many others have left him, and so many hours have gone: and the fire in his body is fading and either the children have gone – for the chill in the air is autumn or evening or . . .

. . . somehow beyond the sun and behind the horizon where long girls fly with their pale legs floating and red planes wheel into birds and Paradise sometimes still seems to hang somewhere over the green gates, burning and dreaming . . . infinitely kind and infinitely far: where all thought thins into air and the air is a clear high singing, or *he* is . . .

. . . either the children have gone or else for today they will not be coming:

and evening is near and kind and his face like the high pale star which is steadying over the poplars floats and shines and his body is now long gone and the grey dimmed regions are slowly dispersing and darkening, blurring, slipping away beyond sleep: and the star still floats quite alone on the slow dark swell of the evening, the great wheels infinitely slowly slowing, taking the lonely and all that is lost into darkness, taking the solitary visions of love and the feathers of Paradise also, taking the years of believing in something to mitigate pain and also quite casually taking the tears and the pain into infinite dark:

and the solitary star stays still in the loveless and colourless dark, and his song flies out where his son never went, not of love, exactly, but living.

Memories

[*Handwritten note*: Death of each separate story. Blending, fading away. (If the one thing that matters falls, blind missiles edging towards us . . .) Words for the world I loved: the end that I fear is silence . . . Let it not come today. May the sheets of memory hold us.]

There are no trees for miles: but here there are trees left standing, and the silent stems reach up for the light. There are miles upon silent miles where the trees have gone, and the cold light leaks into chaos.

Here there was once a house: in the rubble and under cover of darkness lie chairs without backs and beds without legs and books with bare shattered spines: something there flutters and blinks a pale lid at the stars like the lost last page of a letter, something here turns a white leaden eye on the light like a drunken mirror, something there floats and drags like a torn woman's scarf. There are silent miles upon miles.

Here there are trees left standing with tall cool stems. The cold light strips them and coats them with regular ice: no buds and no leaves, though the stems are still slender and young. They stand in ice.

There are seas. They run in the dark for ever. There are no boats and no movements down in the moon-thinned depths of the water. Here in the great still centre there are no waves and the cold light breathes in immense slow swells and falls. The beaches are long and grey with black shadows.

Who is there here who remembers that once there were also bodies. Once in the lost white sunlight their shoulderblades flashed like wings and the brown limbs of shivering children ran for the sea: they thought they would run for ever. Flying and falling. The beaches are grey, with black tremulous shadows of grasses or are they the shadows of memories, running and trembling for ever. And the bodies, yes, they had voices, but no-one asked them. Dying, in other words, nobody asked them to die.

Who is there here who remembers. Here there were once machines and the dark and the light are strangled together in steel. Here there was glass in great glittering sheets, now shattered: light falls on a forest of terrible grounded stars. Here they made missiles, a message of death for the neighbours. They could not read what the sky wrote out for themselves. Once there were faces at windows and eyes in the faces looked out or skywards, watching the small clear sun (though the sun was shrinking and slowing) and small red planes: and the languorous trail of vapour behind them, hanging and spreading in long white plumes into white afternoon and white faces still at the windows watching, behind the warm glass into evening: the sun was shrinking, now gone. And the faces, their whiteness increasing as darkness reached them, the thing which was coming come pressing against the great vulnerable panes, now gone. And the panes are now stars but are big blind stars with the dead grey dust sifting round them, only reflecting.

This was a park, now nothing. Who is there here who remembers that here there were swings, and the seats and the chains were the colours of somebody's lost toy soldiers, scarlet and bright grass-green and the soldiers long lost in the rusting green of the grass by the rusting autumnal railings, the railings now buckled and bent and the soldiers gone (for the final war didn't need them), their beautiful poppy-stalk colours long gone from the seats and the chains of the swings and who knows that this litter of dull grey splinters and dust was a swing and a glorious carmined and leafy thing for small children flying: now gone.

And their mothers sitting on jackets watching the four o'clock curl of smoke from their cheap cigarettes curving round in a slow known question, too peaceful to answer, watching their children screaming and flying and feeling the slow damp rising and calling them in: they said they would wait for ever, oh who is there now who remembers the way they complained they would have to sit there for ever, half-laughing and calling their children away at the height of their arcs into evening, the swing flying into the promise of heaven, just turning chill: then dizzily fell where the mothers' voices were calling, now gone and the swings and the children now gone and if they could ever return they would find there was nobody waiting and nothing.

Yet this was a park and this was a seat where a happy old drunk was tearing his liver to blazes, now burned, now torn. And even his bottle (where once his heart swam in the fiery dark till it drowned and his face floated up very sober and young and alone to elide with the tipsy moon) is now gone: dreaming when death bit down. And his heart is gone, and who is there here who remembers. Somebody says there are no more stories, none.

The children are gone, and surely whatever it was that removed his heart in the bottle and twisted and shattered and mangled and melted the glass into litter and ice in the starlight could not be the children, and who is there here who remembers how once he suspected the children of breaking and stealing. The children, now broken, now stolen.

This is a city, though who is there here who can tell. For miles there is nothing left standing: light falls upon miles and miles of litter and ice and ice and litter and chaos, miles of grey litter and silent miles of dust and such sightless dullness that even the gross beached ice-floes of dusty glass lack teeth to glitter: no lips and no heart, though who is there here who remembers what these things were. No speech, and no stories. The last great story was death: someone failed to tell it, or else no-one wanted to hear.

Yet the city was full of apartments and towers with faces at windows and flowers, red flowers, bright red in a grass-green box: there were orange beacons and black-and-white crossings where children were waiting to cross, *come on* someone said, *you can't wait for ever*, but who is there here who remembers the things someone said (now gone) or the echoes which hung for an hour in the hot blue klaxoning haze of the street (now gone), and the desolate questions re-echo for ever: *who is there here who remembers   the children   you can't wait for ever   now gone   now gone*.

Here there was once a lift and a couple bending there kissing as everything flew and the sky sank stilly towards them, then suddenly vertigo, violence, gone: and the lift-shaft is bent in a terrible echoing question, the answer and everyone trying to answer gone and the kisses blown drily and silently over the litter, the memories of kisses blown drily and silently dying for miles of what once was a city and now is an echoing desert of litter and ice and chaos and loss . . . though those who have lost are not here to remember: no-one to kiss or to tell.

Yet these were bright screens beaming greetings, WAKE UP AND GOOD MORNING, GOOD PEOPLE, WORK HARD UNTIL NIGHT, now gored by great blundering girders of steel and the fragments scattered like snow, not smiling or speaking, good night, good night: for the last dazzled greeting was death, and over the memories that once there were communal greetings lie grey screens of dust, seeing nothing. And once there were also solitary visions and dreams which could fly on their own until morning (too lonely and dreaming too long, still dreaming when death bit down: didn't see that all stories would end, and did nothing to stop that ending.)

And the towers and the windows are fallen, the faces and tears on the faces and kisses on rapt flying faces are fallen, the hands which held hands or held bottles or

252

bright red flowers or the catches of bleak high windows are fallen, the hands of the clock which were set to keep time for ever, the gold-fledged Company clock, have been cruelly wrenched from their sockets, or was it the office-boy trapped in the crumpling lavatory, thin bones wrenched from their sockets, falling and screaming: and grave men who sat on committees (and voted for death, but not theirs) are tipped into communal chaos, unburied, their genitals dangling from daggers of dirty glass ten miles away, and now long gone rotten, and rot long gone into dust, and the dust blows over the pain: and all those agonized armies of dying are stilled now, quiet now, done.

This was a street: this a house, and this was a park and a city. This was a crescent of dreamers. This was a world.

Up above there are stars and a moon, still slowing, still shining. Their still light falls upon chaos, once breathing and kissing and flying.

The stars and the moon shine still but no men in their fabulous silver planes or their dreams ever reach them, oh who is there here who remembers how men in a silver capsule of terror and cunning and deep dreaming love for the light once flew. For the flight never reached its objective: dead on the ground in the morning, starless, flightless, done.

And the still cold light of the stars and the moon in their sightless turn reach no-one. Who is there here who remembers?

No-one. No-one. Gone.

Dedication

To the people who helped me survive, with gratitude and love: my parents, and other friends who are family in Aberystwyth, Brighton, Fen Ditton, London, Oxford, St Andrews, writing from Washington or walking in the snow of the wild West Midlands: and to friends I don't know in the distant cities, standing in bus-stations, shadows, long queues, or glimpsed behind glass as the curtains open and close.

OUTSTANDING WOMEN'S FICTION IN GRANADA PAPERBACKS

Barbara Pym

Quartet in Autumn	£1.25	☐
The Sweet Dove Died	£1.50	☐
Less Than Angels	£1.50	☐
Some Tame Gazelle	£1.50	☐
A Few Green Leaves	£1.50	☐
No Fond Return Of Love	£1.50	☐
Jane and Prudence	£1.50	☐

Diane Johnson

Lying Low	£1.95	☐
The Shadow Knows	£1.50	☐
Burning	£1.95	☐
Loving Hands At Home	£1.95	☐

Jackie Gillott

War Baby	£1.50	☐
Salvage	£1.50	☐
A True Romance	£1.50	☐
Crying Out Loud	£1.50	☐

Elizabeth Smart

By Grand Central Station I Sat Down and Wept	85p	☐
The Assumptions of the Rogues and Rascals	95p	☐

GF1281

All these books are available at your local bookshop or newsagent, and can be ordered direct from the publisher or from Dial-A-Book Service.

To order direct from the publisher just tick the titles you want and fill in the form below:

Name _____

Address _____

_____

Send to:
Granada Cash Sales
PO Box 11, Falmouth, Cornwall TR10 9EN

Please enclose remittance to the value of the cover price plus:

UK 45p for the first book, 20p for the second book plus 14p per copy for each additional book ordered to a maximum charge of £1.63.

BFPO and Eire 45p for the first book, 20p for the second book plus 14p per copy for the next 7 books, thereafter 8p per book.

Overseas 75p for the first book and 21p for each additional book.

To order from Dial-A-Book Service, 24 hours a day, 7 days a week:

Telephone 01 836 2641 – give name, address, credit card number and title required. The books will be sent to you by post.

DIAL-A-BOOK

Granada Publishing reserve the right to show new retail prices on covers, which may differ from those previously advertised in the text or elsewhere.